Dorian softened his tone. 'A lady doesn't build ships. Therefore Miss Sutton isn't a lady. Indeed, she can't be a lady by the very definition of what Society says a lady is. Do you see my point?'

A furrow of twin lines formed between her eyes, the look not unattractive. It stirred him to want to do something about it, to erase the consternation. He wasn't used to such chivalrous feelings.

'I understand your meaning quite well and I respectfully disagree.' Elise's chin went up a fraction in defiance.

'You will have to choose,' Dorian insisted. 'My being here or not is the least of your worries if you're thinking about your reputation. Building your yacht is enough to sink you in most circles. No pun intended.'

Instinctively, he moved close to her, his hands going to her forearms in a gentle grip to make his point, to make her see reason.

She swallowed nervously, the pulse at the base of her throat leaping in reaction to his nearness. 'Again, I disagree,' she said with quiet steel. 'I think this yacht will be the making of me.'

'If it is, it will be the making of a lady most improper.' Dorian [illegible] ng in the t [illegible] his mou [illegible]

From the fabulous

Bronwyn Scott

comes a wickedly naughty
and sensational new duet

Ladies of Impropriety

Breaking Society's Rules

Practised gambler Mercedes Lockhart takes on the
big boys—and the irresistible Captain Barrington—
in England's billiards clubs
in
A LADY RISKS ALL
July 2013

Elise Sutton is a lady in a man's world
when she finds herself fighting for her family's
company at London's Blackwell Docks—
but that doesn't mean she can't show the
roguish privateer Dorian Rowland who's boss
in
A LADY DARES
August 2013

Two scandalously sexy stories.
Two alluringly provocative ladies who dare to
flout the rules of the *ton*—and enjoy it!

Also, don't miss out on the seductive Lucia Booth,
proprietor of Mrs Booth's Discreet Gentleman's Club
and former spy in A LADY SEDUCES, July 2013
in Mills & Boon® Historical *Undone!*

A LADY DARES

Bronwyn Scott

First published in Great Britain 2013
by Mills & Boon, an imprint of Harlequin (UK) Limited.
Harlequin (UK) Limited, Eton House, 18-24 Paradise Road,
Richmond, Surrey TW9 1SR

ISBN: 978 0 263 89842 2

Harlequin (UK) policy is to use papers that are natural, renewable and recyclable products and made from wood grown in sustainable forests. The logging and manufacturing process conform to the legal environmental regulations of the country of origin.

Printed and bound in Spain
by Blackprint CPI, Barcelona

Bronwyn Scott is a communications instructor at Pierce College in the United States, and is the proud mother of three wonderful children (one boy and two girls). When she's not teaching or writing she enjoys playing the piano, travelling—especially to Florence, Italy—and studying history and foreign languages.

Readers can stay in touch on Bronwyn's website, www.bronwynnscott.com, or at her blog, www.bronwynswriting.blogspot.com—she loves to hear from readers.

Previous novels from Bronwyn Scott:

PICKPOCKET COUNTESS
NOTORIOUS RAKE, INNOCENT LADY
THE VISCOUNT CLAIMS HIS BRIDE
THE EARL'S FORBIDDEN WARD
UNTAMED ROGUE, SCANDALOUS MISTRESS
A THOROUGHLY COMPROMISED LADY
SECRET LIFE OF A SCANDALOUS DEBUTANTE
UNBEFITTING A LADY†
HOW TO DISGRACE A LADY*
HOW TO RUIN A REPUTATION*
HOW TO SIN SUCCESSFULLY*
A LADY RISKS ALL**

And in Mills & Boon® Historical *Undone!* eBooks:

LIBERTINE LORD, PICKPOCKET MISS
PLEASURED BY THE ENGLISH SPY
WICKED EARL, WANTON WIDOW
ARABIAN NIGHTS WITH A RAKE
AN ILLICIT INDISCRETION
HOW TO LIVE INDECENTLY*

†*Castonbury Park* Regency mini-series
**Rakes Beyond Redemption* trilogy
***Ladies of Impropriety*

And in M&B:

PRINCE CHARMING IN DISGUISE
(part of *Royal Weddings Through the Ages*)

AUTHOR NOTE

Yachting is nearly as English as horse racing! The Royal Thames Yacht Club has a rich history. For locations of race courses and information regarding 1838 club officers I drew from the records contained in Captain A.R. Ward's *The Chronicles of the Royal Thames Yacht Club*. 1838 was also an exciting year for yachting, as serious racers began transitioning from river racing to open water racing on the Solent.

I should add a final note about locations used in the story: the Sutton Shipyards at the Blackwell Docks and the restaurant foray to the Italian trattoria. To determine the locations I consulted the excellent book *London: A Life in Maps* by Peter Whitfield. This is one of my favourite books and I consult it over and over. The Blackwell Docks had become the West India Docks by 1838, but were often still referred to as the Old Blackwell Docks, so I did take a bit of licence there. However, Soho was indeed a thriving immigrant neighbourhood that took advantage of the 'new' fad to dine out. And the tavern, The Gun, where Elise first meets Dorian is real! You can still visit it today, and maybe if you're lucky you'll meet your own sexy 'almost' pirate too, just like Elise.

Stop by my blog at www.bronwynswriting.blogspot.com to see what else is coming!

Enjoy!

DEDICATION

For Amber and Scott in commemoration of our great day sailing Commencement Bay. And for the Lindsleys who took me on my first and only sailboat ride.

Chapter One

Blackwell Docks, Sutton Shipyard, London—mid-March 1839

She was screwed! Absolutely royally screwed in the literal sense of the word; the word in question being 'royally', of course. Elise Sutton crumpled the letter in her hand and stared blindly at the office wall. Like the other investors, the royal family had finally withdrawn their patronage. And like the other investors, they'd politely waited a 'decent' interval to tell her. They were very sorry to hear of her father's death, but the result was the same. The Sutton Yacht Company was on the brink of bankruptcy, brought to its knees by the sudden and tragic death of its founder, Sir Richard Sutton, six months earlier.

In truth, the idea the company had survived its owner by six months was something of an illusion. It had likely died with her father, only no one had bothered to tell her that. Apparently, courtesy demanded she be allowed to rise at dawn every morning and spend the next sixteen hours a day poring over account books, cataloguing inventory and lobbying investors who had no intentions of staying. She'd worn herself out all for naught and what passed for courtesy let her do it.

Well, courtesy be damned! It wasn't a very ladylike thought, but according to the *ton*, she hadn't been a lady for quite some time. By their exalted standards, ladies didn't work side by side with their fathers in the family business. Ladies didn't design yachts, didn't spend their days adding up columns of numbers and most certainly didn't set aside mourning half a year early to try to save sinking businesses. Ladies meekly accepted the inevitable with hands folded in their laps and backs held rigid.

If that's what ladies did, she most definitely wasn't one. She'd spent the last seven years working with her father. The yacht company was as much hers as it had been his. It was part of her and she would not let it go, not without a fight.

At the moment she had admittedly few tools to fight with. The investors had gone, unconvinced the company could produce a worthy product without her father at the helm. The craftsmen and master builder had gone next. The presence of females had long been anathema in the nautical world and no reassurance on her part could induce them to stay. Even her mother was gone. Playing the devastated widow to the hilt, Olivia Sutton had retreated to the country after the funeral and simply disappeared.

Elise had told enquiring souls that her mother was taking her father's death very poorly. Secretly, Elise thought her mother was managing quite well, too well for her personal tastes. In the months since the funeral, her mother's letters from the country had become increasingly upbeat. There were quiet card parties and dinners to attend and everyone was so kind, now there was no longer an often absent husband to consider.

Her mother had loved Richard Sutton's

title; *Sir* Richard Sutton had been knighted two years prior for services to the Royal Thames Yacht Club, but Olivia Sutton hadn't loved the work that had driven and absorbed him, taking him away from her. The marriage had been a convenient arrangement for years. Olivia had been more than happy to leave her daughter and son to manage the business of coping with solicitors, creditors and the other sundry visitors who hovered over a death like vultures.

The pencil in Elise's hand snapped, the fifth one today. The sound drew her brother's attention from the window overlooking the shipyard. 'Is it as bad as all that?'

Elise pushed the pieces into the little pile on the corner of her desk with the remains of their fellow brethren. 'It's worse.' She rose and joined William at the window. The normally bustling shipyard below them was silent and empty, a sight she was still having a hard time adjusting to. 'I've sold anything of value associated with the business.'

There hadn't been that much to sell, but that was only partially true. The shipyard itself was a valuable piece of property for its location on the Thames. She wasn't sure she could face the prospect of giving up the business entirely. This had been her life. What would she do every day if she didn't design yachts? Where would she go if she didn't come here? Giving up the yard would be akin to giving up a piece of her soul. In society's eyes she'd already done that once when she'd chosen to follow her father and not the pathway trod by other gently reared girls with means.

William sighed, pushing a hand through his blond hair, the gesture so much like their father it made her heart ache. At nineteen, William was a taller, lankier version of him, a living memory of the man they'd lost. 'How much are we short?'

'Twelve thousand pounds.' Just saying the words hurt. No one had that kind of money except noblemen. Elise thought of the crumpled letter. She'd been counting on that. Royal patronage would have sustained them.

William whistled. 'That's not exactly pocket change.'

'You could always marry an heiress.' Elise elbowed him and tried for levity. William didn't love the business as she did, but he'd loved Father and he'd been her supporter these past months, taking time away from his beloved studies to visit.

'I could leave my studies.' William said seriously. He was starting his third term at Oxford and thriving in the academic atmosphere. They'd been over this before. She wouldn't hear of it.

'No, Father wanted his son educated,' Elise argued firmly. 'Besides, it wouldn't be enough.' She didn't want to be cruel, she appreciated her brother's offer, but the money would hardly make a difference. Since it didn't, it seemed unfair for William to make a useless sacrifice even if it was a noble offer.

'What about the investors—perhaps they would advance funds?' William suggested. The last time he'd been home, there'd still been a few remaining who had not yet discreetly weaned themselves from the company, still hoping there might be a way yet to continue with the latest project.

Elise shook her head. 'They've all pulled out. No one wants to invest in a company that can't produce a product.' They'd more than pulled out. It was largely the investors' faults she was in such a pickle. Her father had not been debt ridden, but neither had he been wallowing in assets. The investors had withdrawn their support *and* asked for their money returned, unconvinced the latest project they'd financed would see completion.

Said project lay below them in the quiet yard—the half-completed shell of her father's latest design for a racing yacht, planned with new innovations in mind, lay dormant. For the last several weeks, the investors were proven right. Supplies purchased with the investors' money from the outset lined the lonely perimeter, tarp covered and forgotten. 'A pity the investors didn't want to be paid in timber and pitch,' Elise muttered. 'I've got plenty of that.'

William's eyes settled on her, brown and thoughtful. 'All the supplies have been purchased?'

'Yes. Father buys—*bought*,' Elise corrected herself, 'everything up front, it makes production faster and we don't have to worry about running out at a crucial point.'

William nodded absently, his mind racing behind his eyes. 'How much would the yacht have brought?'

She smiled wryly. 'Enough. It would have been plenty.' It wouldn't have been just about the yacht. There would have been other orders, too. This yacht was meant to be a prototype. Rich men would have seen it and wanted one for themselves. But it was no use now counting hypothetical pounds.

'You could finish the boat,' William suggested.

Elise furrowed her brow and studied her brother carefully. Was that a joke? Had he been listening to anything she'd said? Her temper snapped. 'I can't finish the boat, William. I don't know the first thing about actually *using* hammer and nails. And in case you haven't noticed, there are no men down there, no master builder.'

She regretted the sarcasm immediately. William looked hurt. It wasn't fair to take her agitation out on him. He was suffering, too. He knew what people had said about him behind their hands at the funeral. 'There's the son, but he's too young to take over the company. If only he was a couple years older, then things might have come out all right.' That was usually followed up by the other unfriendly speculation. 'Too bad the daughter doesn't have a husband. A husband would know what to do.' Husbands solved everything in their little worlds.

'I'm sorry, William.' Elise laid a conciliatory hand on his sleeve. 'It's a nice theory. Even if I had the men, I couldn't finish that yacht. The innovations require the knowledge of a master builder. More than that, I'd need the best.' They would have managed without a master builder if her father had been there to oversee the project, as he so often had been, but no workers were going to take orders from a woman even if she had been instrumental in the boat's design.

She needed a master builder more than anything else to finish that boat. Beyond her father, she didn't have a clue who the best was when it came to ship design. Her own talent notwithstanding, she was female and thus excluded from that circle. It had not bothered her unduly in the past. She'd had her father and he'd given her every opportunity she'd desired to advance her skill even if it was often anonymously. She'd never thought further than that. Why should she have? Her father had been in his late forties, in excellent health and at the top of his game. She'd not appreciated by how slim a thread the privilege to indulge her passion had hung until it had been destroyed in one precarious accident.

'What if I could get you the best?' William persisted in earnest.

Finish the yacht? He was absolutely serious. It was crazy. The idea started to take hold along with the most dangerous of games, *what if*? *If* she had a master builder, workmen would come. *If* those men came, she could pay them with the proceeds from the sale of the yacht. It could be done. There was less than a month's worth of work to finish. It was March now, the yacht would be ready by the time society came to town for the Season. Elise's mind was whirring. Most of all, if they finished the boat the investors would come back. If that happened, the possibilities were as endless as her imagination.

'I'd say we were back in business,' Elise said slowly, reining her thoughts back to the present. Finishing the boat had suddenly become the gateway to the future, a future where the company was saved, where *she* was saved. But there was still this crucial step to accomplish. Everything hinged on the master builder. 'How soon can we meet?'

William flipped open his pocket watch and studied the face. 'I'd say right about now, but you'd better bring Father's pistol from the safe.'

'His pistol? Whatever for?' Warning bells went off in her head. What sort of master builder had to be met with a gun? The shipyard was relatively protected. The docks were surrounded by high walls with guards posted to discourage intruders. Inside the walls, a person was fairly secure. Outside those fortressed walls was a different story for the unwary, but not for her. The docks were her territory. She'd walked them with her father, much to her mother's complete and regular dismay.

If her brother wanted to be protective, she'd let him. Elise checked the gun to see that it was primed. 'Again, why do I need to bring the gun? I've never needed one before.'

William merely grinned at her objection. 'Well, this time, you might.'

Elise took the pistol more to humour him than out of any genuine belief that she'd actually need it.

She was, however, seriously rethinking that position half an hour later when their carriage pulled up in front of a tavern on Cold Harbour Lane ominously named The Gun. Like most streets in London's East End, this one was crowded and busy, full of the dock and industrial workers that generated so much of the city's wealth through the strength of their backs.

The crush and smell of the crowd did not daunt Elise, but what happened next nearly did. They'd barely stepped down from the carriage when the door of The Gun flew open in a violent motion. A man crashed into the street, his careening form barrelling straight into her. She might have fallen entirely if the carriage hadn't been at her back, a rather hard bulwark against the assault. It stopped her from falling, but certainly didn't cushion the blow. As it was, the force of the man's exit bore her against the carriage, his arms braced on either side of her to stop his own flight, his body pressed hard and indecently to hers, his blue eyes taking a moment to register he was quite obviously staring at her bosom as they both struggled to find their equilibrium. He found his first and let out a whoop that nearly shattered her eardrums for its closeness. 'What a day! You're the prettiest pillow I've yet to lay my head on.'

'You'll be laying nothing of the sort,' Elise replied coolly, bringing the pistol up and holding his eyes with an unflinching stare. It was a deep-blue gaze, dark midnight like the sea itself, and the press of his body was not entirely unpleasant. There was muscle and strength beneath his rough clothes and the hint of morning soap mingled with the faint whiff of whisky. All very manly scents when presented in the right proportions. Still, she could not stand there and ponder his masculine aesthetics. Propriety demanded his removal from her person. Immediately.

'Please step away.' Where was her brother? Hadn't he been right beside her?

'That's not who you want to shoot.' Was that laughter she heard in her brother's voice? If he wanted to be protective, he was a bit late.

'Maybe I should shoot *you* instead, William,' Elise said through gritted teeth, tossing him a sideways glance over the man's notably broad shoulder. She shoved at the blue-eyed stranger, who'd made no move to distance himself. Her hands met with the steely resistance of a muscled chest. 'Are you going to get off?'

'Probably at some point. Most women don't like a man who gets off too early, though, if you know what I mean.' He finally moved away, laughter crinkling his eyes as he studied her. She knew exactly what he meant and she would not give him the satisfaction of blushing over his crass remark. Years on the docks had immured her from taking offence at such colourful references. To be sure, such remarks weren't allowed in her father's shipyard when she was in earshot. Her father had been protective in that way, but the language and innuendo of the docks were hard to escape altogether.

'Elise—' William stepped in '—allow me to make the introductions. This is Dorian Rowland,' he said with a flourish as if the name alone explained it all.

She eyed the man speculatively, taking in the tanned skin, the long tawny hair loosely held back by a strip of leather and streaked from the sun of faraway climes—England never had enough sun to achieve such a look. She was momentarily envious of such artless beauty until the import of her brother's words sunk in. *This* was the man who was supposed to save her business?

The door to the tavern opened again, ejecting three tough-looking men with clubs. Her stranger shot a look over his shoulder. 'Could we finish introductions in your carriage?'

The three men were momentarily dazzled by the sunlight as they searched the area for something. *Someone*, she realised too late. Their eyes lit on her stranger. 'There he is! You're not getting away from us! Halsey wants his money.'

'Come on, Elise, let's go.' William hustled them into the carriage, giving a shout to the driver before the door was shut behind him and they were off, navigating the traffic with as much speed as possible.

'Who are those men?' Elise hazarded a glance out the window, recoiling when a rock hit the carriage as they pulled away. They were going to ruin the paint, yet another expense she could ill afford.

'Suffice it to say, they don't like me very much.' Dorian Rowland, whoever he was, smiled as if he hadn't a care in the world. Then again, it wasn't his carriage being chipped.

She threw an accusing glare at her newly acquired companion. William had clearly made a mistake. 'Well, that makes four of us.'

He laughed, a loud, clear sound that filled the carriage. 'Don't worry, Princess, I'll grow on you.'

Chapter Two

In Dorian Rowland's opinion, the ruckus outside the carriage was entirely unnecessary. Some people were simply unreasonable. Yes, he was late with his payment but he was good for it and Halsey knew it. Another cargo, which he'd been *trying* to negotiate when he'd been so rudely and violently interrupted by Halsey's bullies, would have seen it right within the week.

The carriage hit a mud-filled rut in the street and sent a spray of water up, dousing his pursuers. Dorian could hear their curses outside as they gave up the chase. It served them right. They'd got what they so richly deserved and so had he. *He* was sitting in a plush town coach across from a finely dressed lady and her brother.

He definitely didn't know the woman. He remembered pretty women and he'd have remembered her: all that inky black hair, alert green eyes and a bosom to die for. As for the young man, Dorian didn't quite recall him, although there was something of the familiar about him. He was apparently supposed to know him from somewhere. He racked his brain for the last decent party he'd been to. In these cases of questionable identity, he'd found it worked out well to play along, especially when he sensed he was on the brink of an exciting new opportunity. Halsey could wait.

'So you're the best?' The princess was talking, words forming from those kissable pink lips of hers. What a lovely mouth she had, far too lovely for that tone of voice. The way she said it made it sound like an accusation. The princess struck him as a bit high in the instep.

Dorian grinned and slathered his response in innuendo. He might have even shifted his posture ever so slightly to better display the 'goods', not that he'd admit to such feeble vanity. 'Depends on what you want, Princess.'

Her pretty mouth set in a firm line and he knew a moment's regret. Perhaps he'd pushed things a bit too far.

'Stop the carriage, William,' she said sharply to the young man before turning back to him with a cold politeness that suggested she could rise above the situation.

'I am sorry…Mr Rowland, is it? It seems my brother has made a mistake. I'm glad we could assist your escape from imminent danger, but now it is time to part ways. I'll have our driver put you down at the next corner.'

The brother—what was his name again? She'd just said it. William? Wilson?—intervened patiently. 'Elise, wait. I tell you he is the best. If you would just listen to me.' Ah, so she was definitely *not* in the market for a little blanket hornpipe, because her brother would have absolutely *no* knowledge of his skills in that regard. His wind didn't blow that way.

'Give him a chance to explain himself, please.' The brother waved a hand towards him, tossing him a beseeching look. *Feel free to intervene at any time.* Dorian opened his mouth to assist, but too late.

'He has explained himself,' the haughty

princess fired back. 'Just look at him! He's unkempt, he was in a public house in the middle of the day and he was brawling. That's just in the last fifteen minutes. Who knows what else he's been doing?'

It was on the tip of his tongue to say 'the captain's mistress'. But then he thought better of it. A becoming colour was riding her cheeks. The princess had been provoked enough already.

'You would entrust our future to *that*? I don't even want to know how it is that you know him, William.' Too bad. He was counting on her making William explain the connection. Now, he'd just have to keep guessing. But that last comment set him on edge. Pretty princess or not, no one could talk about him as if he weren't in the room, or worse, as if he were an object in the room.

'I hate to interrupt this lovely example of sibling quarrels, but please note, I'm still here.' Dorian stretched out his long legs and crossed them at the ankles. 'I think it would be best if you tell me what you really want and then I'll tell you if I'll do it. I find business is usually much simpler that way.'

The carriage turned on to the docks and

stopped before a barred gate. His haughty princess shot him a glare as she leaned out to give a password to the guard. 'You might as well see what I have in mind.'

First pistols, now passwords. This was growing more interesting by the moment. What was a young woman doing down on the docks, throwing around entrance codes like she belonged here? For that matter, what was she doing roaming Cold Harbour Lane in search of *him*? She wasn't his usual type, that type being a bolder, brassier woman, a less-well-dressed sort. Not that she wasn't bold. She had come armed, after all. Hmm. A girl with a gun. Maybe she *was* his type. By the time she led him into the shipyard his curiosity, in all its healthy male parts, was fully engaged.

'There it is,' she announced with a proud wave of her hand, indicating the hull of a racer. 'That's the yacht I need finished.'

She needed a finished yacht? It just so happened he needed one, too. That meant the shipyard was her place. Very impressive. Dorian began a slow tour around the yard, attempting to assimilate the various pieces of information. He made note of the supplies lining the perimeter: the casks of pitch, the piles of timber, the buckets of nails. He peeked under heavy tarps. Everything was new and well organised. These were not supplies that had lain in the weather so long they were rotten or rusted.

He took in, too, the silence and the absence of men. Whatever had transpired had brought work to a halt, an interesting concept of its own given the scarcity of jobs. Plenty of men were out of work these days. It made one stop and wonder.

'There's no one here. Why is that?' He stopped in front of Miss Elise Sutton, his tone far more serious than it had been in the carriage. This was no longer a laughing matter. 'I think it's time you tell me what you really need and why.'

That got her attention. She stepped back instinctively, but her eyes were as unflinching as they had been outside the tavern. Lord, she was magnificent. 'My father passed away recently and left this boat. I want to finish it and sell it.' It was a succinct tale, but Dorian took nothing at face value. In his world it was best not to if one wanted to live long enough to collect payment.

'Let me guess—the work crew left because there was no one to run the company?' Dorian surmised immediately. Things were becoming clearer: a brother too young to assume responsibility and a woman with too much on her hands. He was starting to remember the lad, too. Sutton. William Sutton. That elusive first name of his was more familiar when paired with the last. There'd been a house party near Oxford last autumn. Perhaps they'd met there during one of his own brief forays into the fringes of society?

'Yes, but I assure you I am more than capable, I—'

Dorian held up a hand and shook his head. 'Enough, Miss Sutton. I am sure you are very capable, but men won't work for you. However, they'll work for me for the simple fact that I am male, although they'll be glad enough to take *your* money. I trust you've thought about how to pay them?' He'd bet his last piece of gold she wanted to sell the yacht because she needed money.

'From the proceeds of the sale,' she said shortly, irritated by his insights.

'I might know some men who'd be willing to work for a future profit.' Dorian shrugged, but his mind was racing. He'd need five men who knew what they were doing and another dozen skilled in carpentry. The promise of delayed payment meant he might have to look harder and in less-savoury places for seventeen adequate workers.

'Would you care to see the plans before you take this any further?' Elise offered coldly. 'This is not just any yacht. It's been designed with several new innovations in mind. It will be important that you understand them.'

Dorian smiled. There wasn't a ship he couldn't build, couldn't sail and couldn't steal, for that matter. 'I can build your yacht, Princess. You can innovate all you like. The bigger question is—why should I?'

Elise put her hands on her hips and a wry smile on her lips. 'Because you need money. The bullies at the tavern intimated as much. Who is it you owe? A Mr Halsey?'

Dorian stifled a laugh. 'Black Jack Halsey hasn't been called "mister" his entire life, Princess. He's been called a lot of other things, but not that.'

'I'll pay you one hundred pounds from the sale to finish the yacht on time.'

'Five hundred,' Dorian countered. A man

had to live and pay his debts. If he could make a little extra that was fine, too. It wasn't his fault part of his last cargo had been confiscated for non-payment of port fees. He'd told Halsey they'd not pass inspection and he'd been right.

'Five hundred! That's highway robbery,' Elise retorted, outraged by his exorbitant fee.

'Have much experience with highway robbery, do you?' Dorian chuckled.

Elise chose to ignore his question and stood her ground. 'I'm asking for one month's worth of work, Mr Rowland. You can't earn that much in three years of honest labour.'

'*Honest* being the key word there, Miss Sutton.' He'd make more than that on his next cargo, but he wouldn't attest to those goods all being legal.

'All right, two hundred.' The sharp point of her chin went up a fraction.

'Let me remind you, *you* came looking for me.'

'Two-fifty.'

'Three hundred and I get three meals a day and that shed over there.' He jabbed his thumb at a wide lean-to on the perimeter of the yard.

Her eyes narrowed. 'What do you want with the shed?'

'*That* is none of your business.'

'I won't tolerate anything illegal on these premises.'

'Of course not.'

'Or illicit.'

'Now, you're parsing words, Miss Sutton. Do you want me to build your ship or not?' No doubt they could disagree on the nature of 'illicit' all day.

'We still haven't established why I should let *you*,' she challenged.

'Because I've built boats for the pashas and the Gibraltar smugglers that rival anything your Royal Thames Yacht Club can put on the water. Have you ever heard of the *Queen Maeve*?' He was gratified by the flicker of recognition in her eyes. So the princess wasn't just desperate for money. She knew something about boats, too. 'Fastest racer on the Mediterranean and I built her.'

Built her and lost her, much to his regret. She'd been his dream, but in the end he'd had to let her go. There would be other boats, other dreams. That's what he told himself anyway, although there hadn't been that many opportunities since coming back to England. Not until now. This boat could be his ticket back to Gibraltar, back to the life he'd built there. But that life was based on having a fast ship.

Dorian ran his hand over the smooth, sanded side of the hull where it was finished. The yacht had good lines. The familiar magic started to hum in his veins; the itch to pick up tools and shape something into sleekness thrummed in his hands. Best not let the princess see that longing. It was better they assume she was the only desperate party here.

'You built the *Queen Maeve*?' she queried in sceptical disbelief.

'And others, but she was my favourite.' An understatement.

'I told you, Elise, Rowland is the best,' her brother said, entering the conversation for the first time, apparently happy enough to let his sister handle negotiations. Dorian wished he could remember the young man more clearly.

Miss Sutton studied him. She was weighing hope against desperation. Dorian could see it in her eyes. Could she afford to let him go? She had to know already she could not. Who else would take her deal? She knew the answer to that as well as he did. She'd had a look at reality. Still, caution carried some weight with her. 'You've spent a lot of time in the Mediterranean, an area known more or less for its lawlessness on the seas.'

'Less these days,' Dorian muttered under his breath. If Britain hadn't been so steadfast in taming the seas, he might still be there, but tamed seas were bad for business, his business at least. Tamed seas forced a man to be more creative in his ventures.

She huffed and raised an eyebrow in censure over the interruption. 'I must ask, are you a pirate, Mr Rowland?'

'If I can build your yacht, does it matter?' He winked. 'That's a rhetorical question, Miss Sutton—we both know I'm your last best chance. I'll start tomorrow.' He didn't give her a chance to respond. He strode across the yard to the shed, calling over his shoulder as he opened the door to the lean-to, 'If you need me, I'll be in my office.'

Chapter Three

He was the last thing she needed! And if *he* needed *her*, which would be the more likely case, *she'd* be in her office, a fact Elise demonstrated by loudly stomping up the stairs and slamming the office door, an effect which was ruined by her brother immediately opening the door and quietly shutting behind him when he entered.

'Did you see how he just came in here and tried to take over?' Elise steamed, pacing the square dimensions of the office with rapid steps. 'He's the builder, not the owner. Five hundred pounds, my foot. This is my yard and he'd better remember that.'

'He'll build the yacht, Elise, you'd better remember *that*.'

The firmness of her brother's tone stopped her steps. William had never spoken to her harshly. 'What do you mean?' Elise faced him slowly. He lounged against the wall, casual and elegant, a subtle reminder that he wasn't the adolescent boy she was used to after all these years. The mantle of manhood was starting to settle about him in the sternness of his features. Why hadn't she seen it before?

'I mean, I will be away at university. Mother is gone. There's no one to help you if you lose Rowland. Pay him what he wants, get the boat finished and let's be done with this.'

Elise struggled to keep her mouth from falling open. 'Let's be done with this? What does that mean?' She suspected she knew, but that was not at all what she wanted to hear.

'It means let's clear the debt and start a new life.'

Oh, that was better. She breathed a sigh of relief. 'A new line, yes, of course. I have a lot of ideas about yacht lines and how we can branch out into sailboats. I think racing will fully shift from rivers to open sea in the next few years. We might even think of relocating to Cowes to be closer to the Solent.' She was babbling excitedly now, reaching for a tube containing rolls of her drawings, but a shake of William's head stopped her.

'No, Elise, I don't mean to redefine the company. I mean we should close the book on the company once the debts are paid. There will be a little left over for you until you marry and you can always stay with me. I hope to find a living somewhere or take an associate's post at Oxford.'

It took a moment for William's words to sink in. 'Close the company?' She sat down behind the desk, stunned. Had her brother been thinking this all along?

'Well, what did you think we'd do after the yacht was finished?' William pressed.

'I thought we'd build more boats. You'll see, William. After people view this yacht, there will be other orders. This yacht will re-launch us. It will show everyone we can turn out the same superior product we've always turned out. The investors will come back.' It made so much sense to her. Surely William could see the logic in that?

'How many master builders do you think I know?' William gave a soft laugh.

'I'm not sure how you knew this one.' Elise put in tartly. 'Care to explain?'

William dismissed the question with a wave of his hand. 'It was just a house party put on by the parents of a friend of mine. A few of us went to help balance out numbers and Rowland was there. One night, we started talking and discovered we both had a common interest in yachting.'

Elise wrinkled her brow. 'He hardly strikes me as the Oxford house-party type.' Whatever Dorian Rowland was, she didn't imagine he was the scholarly sort. Tan, blond and hard-bodied, he definitely didn't spend his days poring over books in libraries.

William was growing impatient with her prying. 'Look, I don't know what he was doing there. He said he'd made a delivery, brought something up from London. How I know him is not the point. The point is, I was lucky enough to know this one. He'll finish your boat, but he won't stay. You'll be right back where you started.'

'I'll pay him more,' Elise blurted out, looking for an easy solution. But inside her heart she knew her brother was right: Dorian Rowland wouldn't stay. He'd made it clear he was a man who did what pleased him, when it pleased him. Her proposition suited him for the moment. That was the only reason he'd taken her offer.

'Money won't always be enough for a man like him,' William said with a maturity that surprised her. 'I've bought you time, Elise, to wrap up business and clear the bills, nothing more. Besides, you need to get on with your life, get out to parties and meet people.' By meet people, he meant meet men who would be potential husbands. Elise frowned in disapproval. She'd seen those men and been disappointed *with* them and *by* them.

When she didn't respond he paused awkwardly, his tone softening. 'Not every man is Robert Graves,' William said quietly.

Elise wasn't quite ready to relent. 'Well, thank goodness for that.' Robert Graves, the biggest, worst mistake she'd ever made. She'd thought William might have been young enough to not remember him, or at least to not understand the depths of her mistake.

'Charles Bradford has expressed an interest in you,' William cajoled. Charles was the son of one of her father's former investors. 'He's a very proper fellow.'

'Sometimes too proper,' Elise said briskly. She began looking needlessly through some papers on the desk, wanting to bring this conversation to a close. She wasn't interested in a suitor. She was interested in building a yacht and getting the company back on its feet.

William coughed awkwardly, taking her rather broad hint, once more the younger brother she knew. He made a stammering exit. 'Errm…um…I have some errands to run. I'll see you at home, don't stay too late.'

Elise sank down in the chair behind the desk and blew out a breath. *Welcome to the world of men, you can begin by following our orders and forgetting to think for yourself*, Elise thought uncharitably. In the last months she'd become heartily tired of men.

She was starting to understand all the ways in which her father had shielded her and she'd been unaware. Oh, how she missed him! She thought the missing would get easier with time, not harder. But everywhere she looked, everywhere she went, she was reminded of his absence. Even here, the one place where she'd felt truly at home.

When she'd been with her father at the shipyards no one had questioned her opinions on yacht design; no one had contradicted her numbers in the ledger. People did what she told them to do. Right up until his death, she'd believed they'd done those things because she'd earned their respect with her hard work and intelligence. Then they'd deserted one by one: the workmen, the investors. The message could not be any more concise. *We listened to you because we wanted to please your father so he'd build us fast boats and pay our salaries. Listening to you was just part of the game.* Elise put her head in her hands. It was a cruel blow.

Today had been more of the same, just to make the point in case she'd missed it the first time around. Dorian Rowland had walked in and assumed an attitude of control as if he had a right to this place in his rough shirt and trousers. Her brother had stealthily issued an edict—she was to give up yacht design after this boat and resign her life to one of three unappealing options: marriage, keeping house for her brother or living with her mother. She was to be passed from man to man, father to brother, brother to husband. She'd had fun playing at design, but now it was time to put away her childish things.

She wouldn't do it. Elise squeezed her eyes tight, pressing back tears. Closing the company would be like forgetting her father, as if his life hadn't mattered. This place was his legacy and she would not discard it so easily. There were more selfish reasons, too. She *needed* this. She never felt as alive as when she was designing a model and watching it come to life from her ideas. What would she be without that? The answer frightened her too much to thoroughly contemplate it for long. Well, there was nothing for it; if she wasn't going to contemplate it, she'd simply have to conquer it.

Alone at last! Dorian flashed a lantern up in the direction of the dark office window as he shut the heavy gate to the yard behind him and breathed a relieved sigh. Elise Sutton had finally gone home for the evening and he'd returned successfully from his little foray on to the docks. After the day he'd had, he couldn't ask for much more.

Dorian set down the heavy bag he carried and rubbed his shoulder. When it had become apparent Miss Sutton planned on staying either because she didn't want to go home in a snit or because she didn't want to leave him alone in *her* shipyard, he'd decided to go out and take care of his business in the hopes it would convince her he'd gone home or wherever it was she imagined he went when the sun went down. Whether the princess knew it or not, this was his home now—that nice little shed in the corner of the lot.

He'd gone back to his now-former room, paid the landlady his paltry rent with the few remaining coins he had and gathered up his clothes and tools and made arrangements for his trunk to be delivered in the morning. It was far too heavy and too conspicuous to haul through the streets. No matter, it didn't contain anything he considered absolutely essential. Those items were already packed away in a black-cloth sack. Still, between a single trunk and one black satchel, it was humbling to think they made up the sum of his worldly goods in England, but it had made packing easy.

It also made getting away easy. The last thing he wanted was to be noticed by Halsey's thugs. On the way back, he'd stopped at a few taverns, looking for likely workers. In this case, 'likely' meant whoever would be willing to show up and work for future pay. He just had to get them here. Once they saw the yacht, the project would speak for itself.

Dorian raised the lantern higher to cast the light on the boat. It was showing itself to be an absolute beauty. Longer and leaner than most yachts, it would be fast in the water. He recognised the influence of the American Joshua Humphreys in the design.

He hung the lantern on a nearby peg and reached into his sack for a drawing knife with its two handles and slender blade. The tool felt good in his hands as he slid it against the hull, scraping roughness away from the surface of the wood. There wasn't much to catch—the finished portion of the hull was smooth already—but it felt good to work. Dorian let the rhythm of the drawing motion absorb him. The only thing better was standing at the wheel of a boat feeling the water buck beneath him like a woman finding her pleasure—perhaps a particular black-haired woman with green eyes.

When he'd awakened this morning, he'd never dreamed he'd be building a ship by evening. The arrangement might be a good one. He could hide out from Halsey until he made back his money or until Halsey forgot he owed him. In the meanwhile, he could work a new angle. There was plenty of potential here in the shipyard. Dorian ran a hand over the surface he'd finished scraping. He could make plans for this boat. If the finished yacht was as promising as the shell, he might just find a way to talk Miss Sutton out of selling. It might mean cosying up to the ice princess, but he'd never been above a little sweet talk to get what he wanted. With a boat of his own, he'd be back in business and the possibilities would be limitless.

The possibilities *should* have been limitless, Maxwell Hart mused dispassionately as he listened to young Charles Bradford report his latest news concerning the Sutton shipyard. Elise Sutton had become a thorn in his side instead of bowing to the dictates of the inevitable. Her father was dead, her brother not prepared or interested in taking over the business, investors withdrawn and no obvious funds to continue on her own. All the pieces were in place for her to abdicate quietly, *gracefully*, to those with the means to run the shipyard. Instead, she had not relinquished the property, had not sought out a buyer for the plans to her father's last coveted design. In short, she had done *nothing* as expected. Now there was this latest development.

'There were lights at the shipyard tonight,' young Charles Bradford told the small group of four assembled.

'Do you think it could be vagrants?' Harlan Fox suggested from his chair, looking around for validation. Fox had pockets that went deeper than his intelligence. Those pockets were his primary recommendation for inclusion in this little group of ambitious yachtsmen. 'It's been several months, after all. It's about time for the vultures to settle, eh?'

Maxwell shook his head. 'No, *she's* been going to the office regularly. *She* probably worked late.' He spat the pronouns with distaste. The best thing to do with thorns was to pluck them.

Charles Bradford interrupted uncharacteristically. 'I beg your pardon, sir. It couldn't have been Miss Sutton. She left around five o'clock and she was the last to leave. There were two other men, her brother and a man I didn't recognise. But they'd both gone by then.'

Damien Tyne, the fourth gentleman present, said, 'Any of them could have come back.'

'It wasn't likely to have been her or the brother,' Charles pressed. 'There was no carriage. Whoever returned came back on foot.'

'I still vote for vagrants,' Fox insisted.

But Damien Tyne leaned forwards, curiosity piqued. When Damien was intrigued, Maxwell had learned to pay attention. He and Tyne had made a tidy profit off those instincts and they were unerringly good. 'What are you thinking, Tyne?'

Miss Sutton needed to be prodded in the right direction and in short order. He wanted that shipyard. It held a prime spot on the Thames and he'd coveted it for years. It would be the perfect place to move his own more obscure yacht-building operation and his warehouses. A good location would garner him the notice which to date had eluded him from his current locale in Wapping.

Obtaining the shipyard would just be the start. Hart also wanted to get his hands on the plans to Sutton's last yacht just as badly for the future of his more private, less legitimate side of business with Tyne. Tyne could have the yacht. He wanted the plans. The key to any business venture was the ability to reproduce success.

'I'm thinking,' Damien drawled, his dark eyebrows looking particularly satanic in the coffee house's uneven lighting, 'our Miss Sutton is not going quietly. Nothing she's done in the last months has suggested she is closing up the business as we'd hoped.'

'She has to, there's no money, no workers,' Charles protested. Young and smitten with Miss Sutton, he was also a bit obtuse, a literal fellow who saw only the obvious. 'I should know. My father was a former investor. We were at the funeral.'

Damien smiled patiently at the young cub. 'We know that, but does she? Maybe there's something she knows that we don't, which seems likely.' He nodded towards Maxwell. 'She's held on to the two things that matter most right now: the property and the last yacht. It seems to me that she means to try something before the end.'

'Impossible. The yacht isn't finished,' Charles argued sceptically. 'There's nothing *to* try.'

'Unless she has a builder,' Maxwell put in bitterly. That would drag things out. He had no doubt Miss Sutton would fail in the end, but prolonging that end didn't help his cause. The group had wanted to be in position by the time yachting season opened in May. Back in October when the opportunity had first presented itself, the objective to take over the shipyard had seemed perfectly reasonable. Now, with a month to go, it seemed far more unlikely.

Maxwell pushed a hand through his hair and sighed. 'We have to be certain. Charles, of all of us here, you are closest to the family. Perhaps it's time to pay a friendly visit to see how the daughter of your father's friend is coping with her grief?' He winked at the young man. Everyone in the group knew Elise Sutton had set aside mourning weeks ago, but the subtle sarcasm had flown right over Charles.

Maxwell hoped Charles's decent good looks and refined manners would encourage Miss Sutton to disclose her plans. Even beyond that, he hoped Charles would be able to give Miss Sutton a gentle nudge in the right direction through whatever means of persuasion possible.

Maxwell preferred to accomplish his goals

subtly and without any overt force. He was happy to play nice until it was time not to, and that time was rapidly approaching. He and Tyne had money, time and pride wrapped up in this venture the others knew nothing about. He meant to see it succeed. Failure meant he'd lose a lot more than his shirt.

Chapter Four

His shirt was off! It was the first thing Elise noticed when she arrived at the yard late in the morning. For the first time since her father's death, she'd actually slept late. And look what happened. Her master builder was running around without his shirt on. Her mother would have shrieked it wasn't ladylike to notice, but how could she not? The sight was just so riveting.

Elise knew she was staring, but she could hardly look away. His chest was nothing like the average Englishman's. Gone was the pasty skin and skeletal lankiness, replaced by a smooth, *tanned* expanse of torso. It was quite possibly the most perfect chest she'd ever seen. Not that she was a connoisseur of men's chests, but working around the shipyard, she'd caught accidental glimpses on rare occasions.

She might have been able to pull her gaze away if that had been all, but it wasn't simply his chest. There were arms and shoulders to consider, perfectly moulded with muscle, to say nothing of his lean hips where his culottes hung tantalisingly low on his waist, revealing the secret aspects of male musculature and hinting at even more. All this masculinity had been pressed against her yesterday. It was somewhat shocking to see it on such bold display without the buffer of clothing to mute the reality. She was still gaping when he sauntered over, an adze dangling negligently from one hand, that impertinent grin of his on his face.

'Good day, Miss Sutton. Is everything to your liking?' He motioned towards the yard, the veneer of the gesture narrowly saving the comment from being outright indecent. She knew very well he'd caught her staring, and 'liking' hadn't only referred to the yard. Elise looked around for the first time, trying hard to ignore the distraction beside her.

There were workers! There was the noise

of industry. Not nearly as much as the yard was used to, but it was better than the silence that had marked the past months. 'Where did you find them?'

Rowland shrugged, thrusting the adze through the rope belt holding up his culottes. 'Here and there. It hardly matters as long as they know their job.'

In other words, don't ask, Elise thought. She shouldn't look a gift horse in the mouth. Men were here, willing to work on her boat and willing to take future payment. That should be enough. It was more than she'd had yesterday.

'As you can see, all is well in hand. Is there anything else I can help you with, Miss Sutton?' Rowland said briskly, impatience evidencing itself in the shift on his stance.

Elise bristled at his tone. He wanted her gone. 'Are you dismissing me from *my* shipyard?' His audacity knew no bounds.

Rowland lowered his voice and jerked his head to indicate the workers beyond them. 'They're starting to look, Miss Sutton. They're wondering what a woman is doing here. You're distracting them.'

Elise was incredulous. '*I* am distracting

them? I'm not the one strutting around the yard half-dressed. You might as well be naked the way those trousers are hanging off your hips.'

'You noticed? I'm flattered.' Rowland, damn him, grinned and crossed his arms over his chest. 'And here I was thinking you didn't like me.'

'I *don't* like you,' Elise said in a loud whisper. People were starting to look, but she would not take responsibility for that. She wasn't the one dressed like...like *him*. No wonder society demanded a man wear so many layers over his shirt. No one would get anything done otherwise; they'd be too busy staring.

Rowland laughed. 'Yes, you do, you just don't know what to do about it.' The man was insufferable.

'I want to see what progress you've made.' Elise tried to put the conversation back on a more professional level. It was just her luck her brother had found the best-looking shipbuilder in London. She'd come down here with the express purpose of overseeing the project. She wouldn't leave until she'd done that, half-naked master builder or not.

Rowland had other ideas. He took her arm, drawing her complete attention to the strong tanned hand that cupped her elbow and steered her out of the yard. 'If you want to watch,' he drawled with a grin that made watching sound like a decadent fetish, 'I suggest you adjourn to the office. You, Miss Sutton, are bad for business.'

Elise shot Rowland a hard look. She'd had enough of these games. 'I am their business.' The slightest shake of his head caused her to reassess.

'These men answer to me, Princess. They'll build your boat because I tell them to.'

Elise entrenched, ready for battle. She'd let such reasoning go yesterday. But it would not work twice. 'Is that your mantra? I should accept your decrees simply because you're building my yacht? Do you think that puts paid to any questions I have? This is my shipyard and everything that happens in it is definitely my concern.'

'Upstairs, now,' Dorian growled. It was all the warning she had before a firm hand gripped her arm and propelled her up the stairs to the office. The door slammed behind them. Dorian Rowland's blue eyes blazed with a temper she'd not suspected. His grip on her arm tightened. 'How long do you think these men will work if they think they're working for you? You are the owner's daughter and nothing more as far as they're concerned.'

'You lied to them!' She saw all too clearly what he'd done. He'd set himself up as the boss, the chief. The man with all the power.

He raised a blond eyebrow in exaggerated query. 'You are not the owner's daughter? Did I misunderstand yesterday?'

'No, but—' She didn't get to finish.

'So you are the owner's daughter. Good, then I've told no lies,' he said as if this were the worst sin he had to worry about.

'I'm more than someone's curious daughter. Did you tell them *that*? Without me there'd be no project.' Elise wrenched her arm free and stepped away. She needed space where her logic wouldn't be distracted by more masculine charms.

'Allow me to be blunt. *With you*, there will be no project if you don't let me do this my way. I am trying to help you. You have nothing without me.'

He advanced and Elise fought a losing battle to retreat. Her back hit the wall. He leaned forwards, one arm bracing himself on the wall over her head. He seemed bigger at close range, not menacingly so, but overwhelmingly potent. Even the smell of him, fresh lumber and salty sweat, was all man—all *nearly naked* man. It was hard to forget that one thing with his bare chest mere inches from her. She'd like to forget it, though. Handsome men had proven to be her weakness in the past.

Elise tried to look anywhere but at him. She could see every intimate detail of his skin: the fine dusting of blond hair, the thin white scar beneath his right breast. Lord, it was hard to concentrate! Even her breathing seemed more erratic.

'Have I made you nervous, Miss Sutton?' He smiled. 'I can't help but notice the inordinate amount of time you've spent staring at my chest.'

Did she imagine it or did he puff that chest of his out intentionally just then?

Elise opened her mouth to respond and then shut it. Had she really just seen his breast jump? Flex? Whatever one wanted to call it. 'Stop that!'

'Stop what?' Pop! There it went again. He was doing it on purpose.

'That thing you're doing with your chest!'

'Oh, this? Flexing my muscles?' He straightened up and treated her to a bawdy show of alternately flexing each side of his chest.

'Yes, *that*.'

He laughed. 'Do you know what your problem is, Princess? You don't know how to have any fun.'

Elise crossed her arms over her chest to make a barrier of sorts between them. How dare he think she was a stick in the mud just because she wore all of her clothes to the office? She knew how to have fun. 'And I suppose you do?'

Another smile split his face. 'Absolutely.'

Elise felt her breath catch. His eyes lingered indecently on her mouth. She was acutely aware of his nearness, that he still bracketed her with his arm leaning against the wall. She licked her lips self-consciously. 'I'll have you know I've had *plenty* of fun.'

'Really?' he drawled, doubt evident. 'Well, maybe you have. I suppose I could be wrong. Let's see, hmmm. Have you kissed a man?'

'I most certainly have,' Elise said indignantly, although why it should matter what he thought was something of a mystery. There'd been a few safe kisses in gardens after dancing, but that had been before society had made her choose between it and the shipyard. It had been before Robert Graves, with whom she'd done far more than kiss.

'Unh-unh.' Dorian wagged a finger. 'Let me finish. Parlour games don't count. Have you kissed a man just for fun in the middle of the afternoon in a public place where you might be caught at any moment?' He was definitely flirting now, the images conjured by his words causing a slow heat to unfurl low in her belly.

She fought it, trying to sound more affronted than aroused. No good could come from letting him see how he affected her with his teasing. 'What, exactly, are you suggesting?' No *gentleman* would imply her virtue was in question.

A slow, wicked smile curved on his lips, his voice low and intimate in the small gap of space between them. 'I'm suggesting you try it. With me.' His mouth took hers then, without waiting for a reply, the press of his lips gently insisting that she give way to his greater experience. His tongue flicked over the seam of her lips and she opened to him, to the heady pleasure rising inside her at the leisurely decadence he invoked: mouth on mouth, tongue to tongue, body to body, cloth to skin. This was a naughty exploration indeed. Of their own volition her hands went to his shoulders, kneading the exposed muscles. He was right; she'd never been kissed, not like this. Those other kisses seemed childish by comparison, nothing more than play, pretend. But this was real, this man was real. And the consequences would be real, too. She'd been down that road before.

That was enough to wake her senses. Elise pulled away. She would not repeat the mistakes of the past; this had to end now. She had scandal enough to worry about without being caught kissing her master builder. 'Mr Rowland!' She hoped her exclamation carried enough chagrin for more words to be unnecessary.

'How about we dispense with the "Mr Rowland" bit?' He made no move to back up and release her. 'You can call me Dorian and I'll call you Princess.'

'My name is Elise,' she snapped, realising she'd been manoeuvred too late.

'Well, Elise it shall be, then, if you insist.' He shoved off the wall. 'Now you can say you've had fun.' He winked. 'If you'll excuse me, I must be back to work if you want your yacht done by the deadline. Have a nice rest of the afternoon, *Elise*.'

She could not stay in that office a moment longer. It took all her patience to wait until *Dorian* was safely engrossed in his work before leaving. She would not give him the satisfaction of knowing he'd succeeded in driving her off her own property.

How dared he? Elise strode through the crowded streets surrounding the docks, burning off her excess energy and anger, if that's what it was. He'd kissed her in broad daylight and for no apparent reason other than the fun of it. One thought overrode even that: he'd been audacious, but *she'd* liked it! Hadn't she learned her lesson with Robert? Handsome men were not to be trusted. They knew they could barter on their looks to take what they wanted unless a woman was careful. Elise was so wrapped in her thoughts, she nearly ran into Charles Bradford before she noticed him.

'Miss Sutton. I was just on my way to see you.' Charles righted her after their near-collision, tucking her hand through his arm. 'Whatever are you doing out here in the street? It's no place for a decent lady.'

'Lunch,' Elise improvised, pulling her skirts to one side to avoid a barrel being rolled to a nearby store.

'Out here?' Charles had to shout to be heard above the street din. 'Might I suggest a quieter venue? My carriage is just the next street over. Perhaps I could escort you?'

There was no gracious way to refuse and perhaps it would be better to be with someone instead of fuming alone over her latest interaction with Dorian Rowland. In no time at all, Elise found herself ensconced in Charles Bradford's open barouche. Of course, it was open. Being alone with a man in a closed carriage was unheard of for an unmarried woman and Charles was first and foremost a gentleman. He'd known he was coming to see her and had planned accordingly. Unlike certain other males of her recent acquaintance, came the unbidden comparison. She doubted Dorian Rowland planned accordingly for anything or even planned at all. He just did or said the first thing that came to mind.

'I must confess to being surprised to find you here,' Charles began as the barouche started to move. 'I stopped at your house first and your butler told me where you were. I didn't think there'd be anything more to do at the shipyard. If there's still business to take care of, you should have contacted me. My father and I would have handled it for you.' There was reproach in the comment.

The Bradfords had offered as much earlier when the tragedy had first happened, but she'd insisted on overseeing it all on her own. She knew what Charles meant. There wasn't that much to do if she was closing the yard. 'You might be surprised at what a girl finds to amuse herself with,' Elise answered vaguely, her thoughts going straight to shirtless men and afternoon kisses. Charles might be all that was proper in a young man with his well-cut clothes, fashionable hair and polished manners, but he wouldn't understand her latest endeavour or the need behind it. If he had understood, he and his father would never have pulled out.

It occurred to her that this might be a prime

opportunity to pull them back in. What if they did know what she was doing? They might re-invest and there would be money again. She wouldn't have to wait until the yacht was finished. That thought only lasted a moment. Charles was looking at her with his calm, brown eyes and she almost blurted it out. But caution held her back. It had only been a day and Dorian Rowland had amply demonstrated he was uncertainty personified. What if he suddenly quit? What if he lacked the skill to finish the yacht? She'd do better to wait and see if her project could be completed before she told a soul. It wouldn't do to be seen as a failure just now. If she was to fail, she wanted to do it in secret.

Charles found them an acceptable tea shop where they could have sandwiches and a quiet table. He was solicitous, asking after her well-being, her brother's plans to return to Oxford and her mother's time in the country. The more solicitous he was, the more the contrast grew. He was nothing like Dorian Rowland. To start with, he wore all of his clothes and he was unlikely to steal a kiss in a public place. Charles was safe. Charles was comfortable. But she couldn't help but wonder—would Charles's chest be as muscled beneath his linen shirt? It certainly wouldn't be as tanned. She blushed a little at the thought. It was most untoward of her to be picturing gentlemen without their clothes on. She could blame that, too, on Dorian.

'Miss Sutton? Are you all right?'

'Oh, yes. Why do you ask?' Elise dragged her thoughts back to the conversation.

'I asked you a question.' Charles smiled indulgently. 'What are you planning to do with the shipyard? My father would be able to help you arrange a sale. I'm sure you'd rather be off to join your mother.'

Actually, that was the last place she wanted to be. How to answer without lying? She opted for part of the truth. 'I'm thinking about keeping the yard, after all,' Elise offered quietly, waiting for his shocked response.

To his credit, Charles kept his shock to a minimum. He didn't disagree with her, but merely voiced his concern. 'Miss Sutton, your fortitude is commendable. But you have no one to run the place. Surely you can't be thinking of doing it on your own?' She knew what he was thinking. To do so was to invite social ostracism for the last time. She'd already skated so near the edge on other occasions. With her father gone, there'd be little pity left for her.

'I have someone.'

'Who?' Charles reached for his tea cup.

'A Mr Dorian Rowland,' Elise said with a confidence she didn't feel.

The tea cup halted in mid-air, never quite making it to his mouth. 'Dorian Rowland? The Scourge of Gibraltar?' The tea cup clattered into its saucer with an undignified clunk. 'My dear Miss Sutton, you must be rid of him immediately.'

She'd hired someone called the Scourge of Gibraltar?

Elise was glad she wasn't holding a tea cup, too, or it might have followed suit. 'Why?' she managed to utter.

The horror in Charles Bradford's eyes was so exaggerated it was almost comical and it would have been, too, if it wasn't aimed at the one man she'd pinned all her hopes on.

'Don't you know, Miss Sutton? He isn't received.'

Chapter Five

'I was not under the impression craftsmen were in the habit of being received at all,' Elise answered coolly, some irrational part of her leaping to Dorian's defence. Perhaps it was simply that she wanted to defend the shipyard and her own judgement, or her brother's judgement for that matter. He'd been the one to recommend Dorian.

Charles smiled indulgently. 'Oh, he's not a craftsman, not by birth anyway.'

'I'm afraid you'll have to explain that.' Elise mustered all the bravado she could. With a label like the *Scourge of Gibraltar* she could guess the reasons without the specifics, though details would be nice.

Charles set his jaw, looking fiercer than

she'd ever seen him, a look at odds with his usually calm demeanour. 'Of course you don't know and understandably so. It's hardly a topic of discussion worthy of a lady. I will say only this: he's not fit company for you.'

The fervency in Charles's eyes should have warmed her even if his sentiments did not. She ought to overlook his condescension in light of its motives: he was putting her honour first. He was thinking of her, concerned about who she associated with, even if the tone with which that care was voiced sounded a bit high in the instep. Her father had been a self-made peer, knighted for his efforts, and Charles's own father was a baronet, neither family far removed from the efforts of work that had attained such positions. Yet she could not warm to Charles's efforts with more than polite kindness. Her own body and mind were still engaged in recalling a less-decent gentleman with blunt manners and a blind eye for scandal.

'I appreciate your concern, although it's hardly fair to tell me he's unsuitable and then not tell me why.' As if she needed reasons other than the ones Dorian had already provided this very afternoon with his unorthodox kissing episode. Out of reflex and remembrance, Elise's eyes dropped ever so briefly to Charles's lips. She couldn't imagine Charles behaving so outrageously. The thought was not well done of her. There could be no true comparison between the two. Charles was all a gentleman should be and Dorian Rowland simply was not. Charles would be eminently more preferable. Wouldn't he? He was precisely the sort of man her brother wanted her to find: attractive, steady and financially secure. But even with all these credentials, Elise couldn't help but feel Charles would still come out lacking.

Charles seemed to hold an internal debate with himself, his features suddenly relaxing, decision made. He leaned across the table in confidentiality. 'He is Lord Ashdon's son, second son,' he offered in hushed tones as if that explained it all.

It certainly explained some, like how William might have encountered him at an Oxford house party. Even after William's explanation, she'd been hard pressed to believe William had stumbled across a master shipbuilder in the course of his usual social routine. But the one word her brain kept coming back to was *scandal*. It was the very last thing she needed. Her father's death had been sensational, but not scandalous. Dorian Rowland, however, was both. If society had seen him today, one of their own, half-naked and toting tools around the shipyard, shouting orders, it would be outraged. Then again, it already was. If Charles could be believed, Dorian's transgressions preceded this latest. This venture into the shipyard was just one of many escapades for him. But she would be the one who suffered.

It was slowly coming to her that Dorian Rowland simply didn't care who he perpetrated this fraud on. He could have told her who he was and he hadn't. He'd let her believe he was a craftsman. And why not? He wasn't received. He had nothing to lose, whereas she had everything to risk.

Her place in society was tenuous. She was the daughter of a dead man who possessed a non-hereditary title. Society had to acknowledge her father. It didn't have to acknowledge her, especially if she put herself beyond the pale. She had only her virtue and reputation to speak for her if she wished to remain in society's milieu. To be honest, her reputation wasn't the best to start with and this latest effort to keep the shipyard open wouldn't help, with or without Dorian Rowland's presence.

Oblivious to the tumult of her thoughts, Charles leaned across the table ready to impart another confidence 'Enough of such unpleasant things. I confess I had other reasons for seeing you. I wanted to ask if you might consider going for a drive some afternoon? I know you're in mourning, but a drive wouldn't be amiss.'

Hardly. Elise thought of her mother's version of mourning in the countryside. A drive was nothing beside her mother's card parties and dinners at the squire's, and Elise had made no secret that she'd set many of the trappings of mourning aside. All right, all of them. She did wear half-mourning, but that was the only concession she continued to make and even that transition had been rushed by society's standards. She returned Charles's smile, but the offer raised little excitement. 'I'd like that.' She really should try harder to like him, to see him as more than a comfortable friend.

They finished lunch in companionable conversation, the subject of Dorian Rowland discarded until Charles dropped her off at the town house. He saw her to the door, his hand light at her elbow. 'It was good to see you, Elise. I'm sorry if the news about Rowland disturbed you. Now that you know, I trust you'll manage the situation appropriately.'

Somehow, Elise thought as the door shut behind her, she didn't think 'managing appropriately' included afternoons pressed up against the office wall kissing her foreman with all the abandon of a wanton.

Dorian had abandoned all pretence of being in a good mood since the previous afternoon. The encounter with Elise had left him aroused with no hope of immediate satisfaction save that which he'd had to provide for himself. At the sight of a haphazard nailing job, he ripped the hammer out of one worker's hand with a snarl. 'Take it out and do it right.' The others gave him a wide berth.

He didn't blame them. Kissing Elise had put him out of sorts even though he'd got what he wanted. He shouldn't have done it. Technically, he knew better but that had never stopped him before. He took what he liked and he'd liked her, a princess with her temper up, her professional reserve down. She'd been furious with him and it had done fabulous things to her, turning the green of her eyes to the shade of moss and staining her cheeks to a becoming pink. In his arms, she'd become a woman of fire, burning slow and hot, desperate to prove herself.

That made him chuckle. She'd not wanted him to think she was entirely inexperienced. Most decent girls were just the opposite, wanting to prove their virtue. Even so, there was no question Elise Sutton *was* a lady in spite of her adventurous streak. Men like him didn't mess with ladies. Ladies came with expectations while a man like him came with none.

'Lover girl's here,' one of the men called out, a surly fellow named Adam. He was not the sort Dorian preferred to hire, but choices had been few and he'd been eager to get the project under way.

'Shut up and show some respect,' Dorian growled. He looked up from his work on the hull to see Elise crossing the yard. The princess in her was intact this morning, helped along no doubt by a careful choice of dress. He knew very well that clothes were a woman's armour. Elise was turned out to perfection in a lavender morning dress of figured silk, complemented by the soft grey of her shawl and the matching lace trim of her Victoria bonnet. The ensemble was very demure, very respectful, although not quite up to the standard for a daughter's mourning. He wondered briefly if she'd forgone mourning altogether. Yet the subdued qualities of the outfit did not diminish her. Perhaps that was due to her walk, Dorian mused, watching the sway of her hips and not necessarily her clothes.

She crossed the yard with a purpose, hardly deigning to give any attention to the eyes attracted by her movement. Her superior attitude was for the best. Dorian felt a twinge of guilt over the sort of men he'd hired. These were rough men unaccustomed to ladies. But also he'd not expected her to make herself a daily fixture in the shipyard.

'Clearly my message yesterday eluded you.' Dorian set down the wrung staff he was using to attach planking on the hull.

'Good morning to you, too.' Elise smiled cheerily and ignored the cool greeting. 'I've some things we need to discuss. Do you have a moment?'

The comment elicited a mean chuckle from Adam Bent. 'Are you going to take orders from the little woman? You're not so big now.'

There were other nervous laughs. He had to nip such conjecture in the bud. These men would never respect a man who appeared to be at a woman's beck and call. But he'd dealt with men like Bent before on his ships. With a quick movement, Dorian divested Bent of the racing knife in his hand and pressed it against his throat. 'It's sharp and it will hurt, in case you're wondering,' Dorian said with savage fierceness, leaving no doubt he was not bluffing.

Bent's eyes bulged in fear. Behind him, Dorian heard Elise gasp at the sudden violence. Around them, men stopped their work to stare. Good. Let them. Let them be very sure they knew who was in charge here and what he was willing to do to prove his claim. 'Say you're sorry,' Dorian pressed.

'Really, is that necessary?' Elise stepped forwards, picking a rotten time to intervene.

'It damn well is.' Dorian locked eyes with the frightened Bent. The man was a bully. He would cave. Bullies always did at the first sign of real terror and there was nothing as terrifying as a blade against one's throat. A racing knife, whose purpose was to trace a shape before cutting it out with its thin blade, could leave an especially wicked line. A small bead of red began to show.

'I'm sorry, boss,' Adam stammered.

'Say it won't happen again.'

'It won't happen again.'

Dorian released him with a shove. 'You're right it won't. Now, Miss Sutton, if you'll follow me up to the office?'

Perhaps the office wasn't the best of locations with the memories of yesterday still so recent and hot, but there was no other place to take her.

'Is this how you run your shipyards, Mr Rowland? At knifepoint?' She didn't wait for him to begin the conversation once the door was shut.

'When I must.' Dorian folded his arms. 'I told you yesterday your presence was a disturbance and yet you persist in making appearances.'

'I needed to see you,' she said evenly. Dorian admired her aplomb. There wasn't an ounce of apology in her eyes.

'You could have asked me to call on you at your home. This is no place for a woman.'

'I wasn't sure you'd put your shirt on,' she replied, her implication clear. 'I can't have you scandalising the butler.' She shot him a sideways glance that made him uneasy. 'Although, it's probably too late for that,' she said cryptically. 'I doubt a shirt will make much difference at this point.'

'Shirt on, shirt off, it's all the same to me, Princess,' Dorian drawled. She hadn't slapped him or any of the other things ladies did when they were too ashamed to admit their passions had been provoked and they enjoyed it. He would take it as progress.

'It *is* all the same to you, isn't it?' She gave him a wry, intelligent smile. 'You're not received. What do you care? You could run around naked if you wanted. Oh, wait, you do.'

So that was the bee in her pretty bonnet this morning. She'd found out who he was. He did wonder how she'd come by that information. It wasn't something a lady would know. 'There are a few homes where I'm welcome,' he offered in his defence.

'Enough to have met my brother.'

'Ah, yes, the house party outside Oxford. It was nothing, just an invite from a friend of a friend I hadn't seen in a while,' he admitted. Meeting William had been a fluke really. Decent society had shut their doors ages ago on him once conjecture of his Mediterranean activities reached them. 'Does it matter? I assure you being received has nothing to do with my ability to build your ship.'

She huffed at the response. 'You seem to think your ability to build my ship excuses all nature of things. I disagree. I think you should have told me you were Lord Rowland, son of the Duke of Ashdon.'

He smiled and leaned his hip against the desk, half-sitting on its edge. 'But then you wouldn't have hired me and we both would have missed out.' His eyes drifted purposely to her mouth, letting her guess on what they would have missed out.

'You've brought scandal to my business simply by being here. If anyone finds out, I'm finished.'

Dorian's smile faded. 'Only if you care about such things.' This was dangerous ground. Had she come here to let him go? The thought sat poorly with him. It had only been two days, but he'd invested effort in this proposition of hers, beating the docks for any worker he could find. He fiddled with her paperweight, a pretty amber piece with an insect inside, giving her a chance to think. 'And do you, Miss Sutton? Do you care?'

He had her there. The look on her face suggested she wasn't sure how to answer. He answered for her, pushing off the desk and pacing the floor like an Oxford professor delivering a lecture. 'That's the thing about scandal, Miss Sutton. It only has teeth if everyone playing agrees to give it power. Frankly, I don't see how you *can* care and pursue this line of work you've put before yourself. Surely you see the dichotomy, too?' He rather worried that she didn't, though. She was the sort whose boldness came from a combination of *naïveté* and ideals, a deadly mixture once society got a hold of them. Somebody was going to have to tell her the truth. This venture of hers simply wasn't going to work. It *couldn't.*

Dorian softened his tone. 'Are you familiar with syllogisms, Miss Sutton? A lady doesn't build ships. Miss Sutton builds ships. Therefore, Miss Sutton isn't a lady. Indeed, she *can't* be a lady by the very definition of what society says a lady is. Do you see my point?'

Her dark brows were knitted together, a furrow of twin lines forming between her eyes, the look not unattractive. It stirred him to want to do something about it, to erase the consternation. He wasn't used to such chivalrous feelings.

'I understand your meaning quite well and I respectfully disagree.' Her chin went up a fraction in defiance.

'You *will* have to choose,' Dorian insisted. 'My being here or not is the least of your worries if you're thinking about your reputation. Building your blasted yacht is enough to sink you in most circles. No pun intended.' Instinctively, he moved close to her, his hands going to her forearms in a gentle grip to make his point, to make her see reason.

She swallowed nervously, the pulse at the base of her throat leaping in reaction to his nearness. 'Again I disagree,' she said with quiet steel. 'I think this yacht will be the making of me.'

'If it is, it will be the making of a lady most

improper.' Dorian gave a soft chuckle, breathing in the tangy lemongrass scent of her just before his mouth caught hers.

Chapter Six

'Rowland's back.' Maxwell made a grimace before taking a swallow of his brandy. He and Damien Tyne had the corner of the coffee house to themselves in the late afternoon. He preferred it that way. The conversation he wanted to have with Tyne might possibly become too dark for the others.

Tyne raised slender dark brows in interest. 'Really? I wonder if his father knows? Gibraltar must have finally got too hot for him. Still, it's gutsy of him to come back here where he's got a number of enemies waiting for him, you and me included. Don't tell me you wouldn't mind a shot at him after what he did?'

Maxwell gave a thin smile. 'We will get our chance. It will be an opportunity to kill two birds with one stone.' He dangled the thought before Damien like bait.

'And how is that? We're rather busy with the Sutton project at the moment. It doesn't seem like the right time to go after Rowland.'

Maxwell's thin smile turned into a grin as he dropped the news. 'He's working for our Miss Sutton. She told Charles herself over lunch.'

'And he scampered back here like a good boy and told you.' Tyne leaned back in his chair, fingers drumming on the table top beside him. Maxwell could almost see the thoughts running through Tyne's mind.

'You were right,' Maxwell offered, wanting to be included in those usually lucrative thoughts. The fastest way to get Tyne to open up was to compliment him. Tyne was a smart man and a bit of an egomaniac. Tyne liked others to recognise his intelligence. 'Miss Sutton does mean to give it one last gasp. She's hired Rowland to do something.'

'But we have no idea what that is?' Tyne asked.

'She wouldn't tell Charles.'

Tyne snorted. 'She probably didn't get the chance. Charles would have been too busy lecturing her about Rowland's unsuitability. I do hope he told her to fire the reprobate.'

'Charles served his purpose today,' Maxwell reprimanded lightly. Tyne thought Charles was a silly young pup. 'He's our best connection to the inner workings of Miss Sutton's life at the moment without spending money on people to watch her. Charles is happy to do it for free.'

'He's infatuated with her,' Tyne grumbled.

Maxwell idly stroked the short stem of his snifter. 'Yes. If he'd marry her it would be all the better for us, get her out of the business for good. For the record, Charles did tell her to let Rowland go, but I doubt she'll listen to his advice. She hasn't listened to anyone so far.' Certainly not the investors who'd come to her after the funeral and encouraged her to sell. She could have made this much easier on all of them, herself included.

Tyne's eyes glinted. 'Maybe it's time to make her listen.'

Maxwell leaned forwards with keen interest. He and Tyne had been partners in questionable commerce practices before, but those notorious practices were conducted far from home where their countrymen were less likely to notice what they were up to. Going after someone in London would be different. They'd have to exercise extraordinary caution—something Tyne was not always good at. 'What exactly do you have in mind?'

'I think a nocturnal visit to the shipyard is in order so we can figure out precisely what she's doing behind those walls. It doesn't take a genius to speculate about what she might be doing, but we can't take an appropriate course of action until we know for sure. I know just the men to do it.'

Maxwell nodded his approval. 'I like the way you think. In the meanwhile, I'll tell Charles to continue his courtship.'

'Miss Sutton, there's a gentleman to see you.'

Elise looked up from her reading, more than surprised to see Evans, the butler, in the doorway of the sitting room. It was after seven and she'd given the staff permission to retire for the evening. 'I'm not expecting anyone.' The house was quiet tonight. She'd seen William off earlier in the day and dinner had been a lonely affair, one of many, she supposed. Mourning and the absence of a decent chaperon made attending any social functions out of the question.

'He has a card, Miss Sutton, and he says he has business to discuss.'

Not Charles, then. That had been her first thought. But Charles would never have called on her so late at night, knowing her brother was gone, or have come to discuss something as dirty as business. Unless, of course, he wanted to remind her of the impropriety of a lady living alone. Elise took the card from the silver salver. The paper was a heavy white affair of cardstock with simple black letters in crisp block print. It was of good quality. The name on the card wasn't. Lord Dorian Rowland. Just seeing the name was enough to make her stomach flutter for any number of reasons: a reminder that she'd hired a man who outranked her socially to *work* for her, a reminder that same man kissed liked the very devil whenever the fancy struck him and reduced her insides to jelly.

'Did he say what he wanted specifically?' Elise fought the urge to check her appearance in the little mirror on the wall. She'd obeyed his order not to go to the shipyard today and apparently he'd obeyed hers. Evans didn't look too offended. She could assume Dorian had come with his shirt on.

'No, miss, just business.'

'Then I suppose I shall have to see him.' Elise tried to sound cool. She rose and paced a few steps, trying to gather her thoughts, but to no avail. They continued to run amok. Why had he come? Was something wrong at the shipyard? Had there been an accident? Had something happened to the boat? Surely if something was seriously wrong he wouldn't have come in person and waited patiently in the hall. He would have stayed to oversee the situation and sent a note, or he'd have come barging up the steps, shouting for her. Elise smoothed her skirts in an effort to quiet her nerves.

Footsteps sounded in the corridor. Evans announced the guest. Dorian stepped into the room. Her hands stilled in the folds of her skirts at the sight of him. Dorian had put on far more than a shirt to make this call. Dark breeches were tucked into high black boots; a claret-coloured coat was tailored to show off broad shoulders and the gold-patterned waist-coat and pristine linen beneath. She could almost believe the man standing before her was a lord. Almost.

There were other tells that gave him away. His thick sun-gold hair might be neatly pulled back and tied, but it was still too long for convention. His blue eyes were still too bold when they met hers. A gentleman would never look at a lady in a way that made her mouth go dry.

'Lord Rowland, to what do I owe the pleasure?'

'Dorian, please,' he insisted. 'I've come as I promised to give you an update and because I have questions about the plans.' He held up the long roll of paper in his hand. 'I hope my visit isn't inconvenient? You don't have plans this evening?'

'You know I don't.'

'London's loss, I think.' Dorian smiled and their eyes held in the moment. She felt her face heat. She really shouldn't let him get to her like this. Nothing could come of it and this was absolutely the wrong time to become involved with someone when so much else depended on her attentions.

'Where shall we unroll these?' Dorian looked around the room and gave the plans a little wave, calling her attentions back to the intent of his visit.

'Oh, yes, the plans. There's no place to lay them out in here. Why don't we try the library?' At the last moment she remembered Evans still standing by the door. 'Evans, have a tea tray sent up, please.' She hoped she didn't appear as flustered as she felt. It occurred to her as they headed towards the library that she'd never entertained anyone alone and certainly not a man. Her mother or father had always been with her. The servants were here, of course, but it wasn't the same.

In the library, they busied themselves spreading out the plans on the long reading table and anchoring the corners with paper-weights and books to keep the edges from rolling up. Dorian stirred up the fire while she lit lamps. The tea tray came and they found a place for it at the end of the table. The little tasks helped her regain composure. She designed yachts and ran a business, for heaven's sake. It was silly to be daunted by a simple task and one handsome man.

When everything was finally settled to their satisfaction, Dorian pointed to the area in question. 'Here's the problem—I think the centre of the hull is too narrow. It will increase the chance of capsizing. Do you know what your father was thinking when he established these dimensions?'

'These aren't solely my father's plans. We designed this boat together,' Elise said slowly. Even now, no one quite grasped her level of involvement in the shipyard. 'This is my boat, too. I simply don't know how to build it, but in theory it should work.'

Dorian swore softly under his breath and she braced herself for the worst. But it didn't come. He didn't harangue her for the idea that she thought she could build a boat. '*In theory it should work?* Do you have a model? Did you do any kind of trial?'

'No. It will work. I modelled this after Joshua Humphreys's work, only we've used his design with more intensity. This boat is longer, lower and leaner.' She could see he was unconvinced. 'We've installed extra buoyancy bags on the port and starboard sides to compensate for any drastic heeling.' She warmed to her subject now, making her argument with passion as she pointed to the various adaptations they'd made. 'So you see there was no need to test it. Humphreys's design works. We've just modified it.'

Dorian was starting to thaw. 'We'll have to be careful through here and here.' His finger drew invisible circles on the plans. 'But it could work, I guess. It's just that I've never seen it done. Once we get the frame timbered, it will be too late for any alterations. It's almost too late now.'

A little thrill ran through her at the prospect of the fully timbered hull. 'How long?'

'Two days. Then there will be the rigging to discuss.' He gave her a wry grin. 'I don't suppose you designed the rigging, too?'

'Perhaps you'd like to discuss rigging over tea?' Elise smiled, feeling relieved. There'd been a moment when she'd thought he might quit the job.

With tea and biscuits on plates, they settled into the big chairs in front of the fire to discuss the merits of sloop versus ketch and cutter-rigging styles. It was an animated discussion and, for a while, Elise forgot she was entertaining alone, forgot what a scoundrel Dorian was. It felt good to talk about boats and sailing with someone who knew something about it. It had seemed ages since she'd had this sort of discussion. She and her father used to talk boats all the time. They'd talked about yachts the day he'd gone out on the test run. It was the last conversation they'd had.

Dorian broke off in mid-sentence. 'What is it? It looks like a shadow has just crossed your face. Have I offended your sensibilities with my position on ketch rigging?' he joked.

'No.' Elise looked down at her hands, embarrassed over having been caught with her mind wandering. 'This talk of boats reminds me of my father. We had conversations like this all the time. In fact, we'd talked about new ways to increase windage the day he went out.'

'I'm sorry.' Dorian's tan hand covered hers where it lay in her lap. He gave it a warm squeeze. 'You must miss him.'

Elise nodded, not daring to trust her voice. She'd not expected such a tender gesture from the king of insouciance himself. It threatened to undo her. She managed a smile and then a few words to turn the conversation away from herself. 'What about your family? Do they enjoy boats and yachting as much as you?'

Dorian gave a harsh laugh. 'Hardly. My father is a horse man and my brother, too.

My father is always quick to remind me that horse racing—the sport of kings, mind you—didn't have such plebian beginnings as yachting. He is also quick to point out that the black sheep of the royal family, Cumberland, was the one who went slumming in the first place.' There was a naughty glimmer of mischief in Dorian's blue eyes. 'To which I say, "My hero".'

She could well believe it. Dorian and the previous Duke of Cumberland likely held many traits in common. The latter had been known in his lifetime as a 'loose fish', a scandalous womaniser who had taken his mistress riding in Hyde Park, and the former was no doubt following down a similar path.

'Your family is not close,' Elise ventured, feeling a little sorry for him even if he didn't feel sorry for himself. He was alone, too. 'Does your father know you're…?' What were the words she was looking for—'working on the docks', 'running questionable cargos for the dockside underworld', 'overseeing a shipyard shirtless', 'threatening workers with knives to their throats'?

He seemed to divine her dilemma and saved her the indelicacy. 'Maybe. He's the

Duke of Ashdon, he knows everything he has a desire to know. I stopped caring about what he thought a long time ago.'

Elise could hear the hint of resentment behind the words. She should probably leave it at that, but curiosity propelled her forwards. 'When you became the Scourge of Gibraltar?'

'Something like that.'

'Will you tell me?' The late hour, the fire, the warmth of the tea were all conspiring to create intimacies, pushing her to take chances with the blond stranger who'd fallen into her life a few days ago.

Dorian gave a slight shake of his head, a scold, a warning. 'No, I will not. You're better off not knowing.'

'And the *Queen Maeve*? Will you tell me about your ship one day? She was a legend even up here for those of us who appreciate such things.' Stories of his ship had circulated throughout polite society: how fast it was, how fearless the captain, how the *Queen* had outrun French pirates by manoeuvring them up on to a reef and sheering off in the nick of time to save herself from the same fate.

Elise wondered if she mentioned that tale would it provoke him to reminisce? But she'd left it too late. He rose and set down his tea cup, a prelude to farewell. She felt deflated. She'd pushed too far, pried too much and now he was leaving. Never mind that leaving was the right thing to do. It was late and they were alone. He had no business being here.

Elise rose and helped him roll up the plans. 'I hope my descriptions have been of assistance?' she asked, stacking the books they'd used as corner weights. 'Perhaps it would be best if I came down to the shipyard. I could be there if more questions arose.' She hadn't the foggiest idea what she'd do with herself if she didn't go into work.

'No, it would not be best. We don't need any more incidents like the one earlier. I will keep you informed of every little detail.' Dorian paused. 'I enjoyed our evening, Elise. It is not often I encounter a woman of your rare intelligence. I can show myself out, you needn't go to the bother.' He gave her a short little bow. 'Until next time.'

Elise waited until she heard the front door shut and the sound of Evans shooting the bolt before she left the library and headed upstairs to bed. She undressed on her own and sat down to brush out her hair, replaying the events of the night in her head. The evening should have been a success. Dorian had reported to her. He'd asked her opinion. He'd come dressed the part. He had argued with her, but respectfully so and had acceded to her wishes. He hadn't blinked an eye when she'd told him the plans were hers.

What more could she have asked for? She doubted any other master builder would have been as gracious. His manners had been impeccable. He hadn't importuned her with his provocative remarks.

Elise halted the brush in mid-stroke. That was when she realised it: he hadn't kissed her. He had simply bowed and walked out the door, taking his secrets with him. She wasn't sure she liked this version of Dorian Rowland any better than she liked the other, which surprised her very much because she should have.

Chapter Seven

A walk was precisely what he needed to clear his head. Dorian pulled at his cravat, tugging it free with a sigh of relief. He'd played the gentleman tonight in high form, clothes, manners and all. It was a role he hadn't assumed for some time, but it was as stifling as ever, limiting what he could and could not say or do. But that was society's way—demanding manners until it made castrati of its men and vacuous dolls of its women. He understood entirely why Elise Sutton resisted. The road propriety laid out for her was unappealing, demanding she marry or fade into the background as a respectable spinster, living with her mother or brother.

Her resistance wasn't completely flagrant.

She wasn't protesting in the streets or walking around in men's clothing or something equally as rebellious. She was trying to resist within acceptable confines. Dorian saw plainly what she was playing for. She was hoping society would accept her running her father's business, that she wouldn't have to choose, that she could live in a world of greys instead of blacks and whites. He wasn't convinced such a world would make her happy. Greys could be just as frustrating as the black-and-white boundaries that marked who was 'in' and who was 'out'. He knew, he'd tried it. Black and white suited him better and he suspected it would suit Elise better, too, if she could be made to see it. *Not* that it was his job to help her along that path. He gave himself a stern reminder that he was in this for the boat, nothing more.

Dorian crossed the road, looking carefully into the dark side streets before he did. Even Mayfair had its thugs after hours. He would catch a hackney soon for the rest of the journey back to the shipyard. Only a foolish man would tempt fate by walking through the docks at this time of night. He'd been foolish enough already tonight, sitting with Elise and letting the conversation wander afield from the business he'd come to discuss. They'd ended up in front of the fire and the next thing he knew she was asking questions about his family, about *him*: the two things he never discussed with anyone. Yet he'd discussed them, however briefly, with her.

At least he'd left before anything untoward had happened. That was one thing he'd done right, although it had been hard. Elise had looked positively beautiful, the firelight picking out the chestnut hues from the dark depths of her hair, the delicate sweep of her jaw in profile, the slender length of her neck shown to subtle perfection by a loose chignon at her nape. It would have been the work of moments to have her dark hair free and her lips plump from kisses. She'd proven on more than one occasion to be a willing participant in those kisses.

But tonight would have been about more than kissing. Fireplaces and cold evenings worked all nature of magic and the following mornings brought all nature of regrets. It wouldn't have stopped at kissing. His thrumming body attested to it still, after several bracing minutes in the cold night air. He'd heard the loneliness in her voice as she'd spoken of her father and he'd heard the loneliness in his own bitter response. Even if she didn't recognise it for what it was, he did. It was a deuce terrible feeling to know he'd been home for two months and no overture had been made to acknowledge his return.

Dorian hailed a hackney trolling the streets where a party was in progress, looking for a late-night fare. If he waited much longer, his options would dwindle to nothing. He jumped in, giving directions to the Blackwell Docks, and sat back.

The ride was accomplished in short order, a much shorter order than during the day. Without traffic filling the streets, the transition from West End to East End was far swifter. It wasn't until after he'd paid the driver and had stepped through the heavy gates that his senses went on alert.

Something was wrong. Dorian reached stealthily for the knife in his boot and stood still, letting his eyes adjust to the darkness. There was the sound of muffled motion to his right, the sound too heavy to be mistaken for a rat or stray cat. Besides, this shipyard was impeccable. There'd been no earlier signs of animal life.

He swung towards the sound and called out in a strong voice, 'Show yourself! You are trespassing on private property. Show yourself now or face charges from the law.'

They were on him then, stupidly both from the same side. Two burly forms with clubs of their own came at him out of the darkness, but he was ready for them and ready for a fight after the frustration of leaving Elise's with an uncomfortable hunger.

The first attacker swung his club. Dorian moved into him, grabbing his wrist and twisting hard, disarming him before bringing a knee up into his groin. The man fell heavily to the ground, groaning.

The second attacker was more cautious after seeing his comrade fall. He would need his knife for this one, Dorian reasoned, lifting the blade to catch the lantern light in hopes of scaring the second man into surrender. Knives had a special persuasive power all of their own and he had no real wish to carve the man up. The second attacker might be more cautious, but not necessarily more intelligent. He didn't take the surrender option. Instead, they circled each other while he waited for an opening.

'You're taking too long. Are you going to strike or not?' Dorian goaded him, flashing the blade in a fancy arc. Just the feint on his part was enough to send the other man back a step. Dorian feinted again, but provoked no aggressive response. At this rate they'd be here all night. The man's left side was unprotected. The third time, Dorian lunged and drew blood. The man dropped his club out of reflex to clutch his wounded arm.

Dorian was on him, blade to his throat. 'Who sent you? What do you want?' Even in the dim light, he could see the man was pale.

'Don't tell him!' the man's companion wheezed out between groans.

'If he doesn't tell me, I'll try you next,' Dorian growled. 'We'll see how well you do up against a blade.'

'I don't know exactly,' Dorian's man prevaricated. 'A cove with money. He said all we had to do was look around and report what we saw. We didn't come here to hurt anyone.'

Dorian pressed the blade harder. 'You came with clubs.'

'For our own protection.'

Dorian didn't believe that for a moment. 'What were you supposed to look for?' Had Halsey tracked him down already? The blade bit into the skin, drawing a tiny bead of blood, just enough to convince the man he meant business if he didn't get his answers.

'The b-b-boat,' the man managed.

Dorian eased the pressure as a token of goodwill and a sign that the man was now supposed to supply more details. He did. 'We were supposed to come and see if she was building a boat.'

That was not the answer he was looking for, but there was no time to fully dissect what it meant right now. Dorian pressed again, his efforts redoubled. 'I'll ask one more time, who sent you?' It obviously wasn't Halsey, which meant he had absolutely no clue. It also meant he couldn't kill them. Halsey couldn't very well go to the law without incriminating himself. But whoever had sent these chaps would come looking for them if they didn't return and he might bring the watch with him. Unless Dorian got to the watch first.

Dorian backed his man to a post and reached for the twine, tying him thoroughly before turning his attention to the other man with the rest of the twine, trussing him up like a stuck pig. 'If you won't tell me, perhaps you'll tell the watch.' Dorian shoved his knife back in his boot with a grin. 'I've used about twelve different knots on those ropes, so I expect you to be here when I get back.'

That made them nervous. He thought it might. 'Um, maybe we should tell him, Bert,' said the one tied to the post.

'Don't use my name!' the other one hissed.

Dorian stopped at the gate and pulled his knife back out. 'I think your name is the least of your worries right now.' He fingered the blade. 'I can be reasonable. If you tell me who sent you, I won't call the watch.' Dorian shifted his eyes from man to man. 'But we'll do it my way. I don't want any lies. So I'll come to each of you and ask you to whisper a name in my ear and a description. That name had better be the same from both of you or I'll get the watch, no second chances. I can't imagine the man who sent you would be all that thrilled to come and bail you out. He might just ignore you and leave you to rot in order to save his own hide,' Dorian reminded them.

He strode over to the man at the post. 'You

first.' The name the man whispered caught Dorian entirely off guard. He knew this name. It was not a good name to know. It made men like Halsey look like saints. '*He* definitely would have left you to rot.' Dorian masked his surprise and moved on to the other. 'All right, Bert, it's up to you. Give me a name that matches your friend's over there and you are free to go.' Dorian almost hoped Bert would give another name. It would be worth the hassle to call the watch and stay up all night sorting this out if the culprit was anyone other.

But Bert whispered two disappointing words, 'Damien Tyne', and Dorian's heart sank. The encounter mopped up quickly after that. He untied them and marched them at knifepoint to the gates, Bert being heavily assisted by his comrade, and he locked the gates behind them. Not that locked gates would stop Damien Tyne.

Dorian went into his shed and stripped out of his clothing, carefully packing it away in his trunk. He was going to need those clothes more often than he thought. Tomorrow he'd have to pay another call on Elise Sutton. She had to know what had transpired here tonight. Dorian lay down on the cot, hands folded above his head. He didn't expect to sleep, not right away. Tonight would be a long one and tomorrow even longer.

Damien Tyne had made a fortune in the Mediterranean with several unethical business ventures. He was ruthless and thorough, not exactly the enemy anyone wanted to have. The question was: whose enemy was he? Had he sent those men tonight because he'd learned Dorian was back? There was definitely enough bad blood between them from their Gibraltar days to warrant such an action, or had Damien sent those men because of Elise?

Dorian suspected it was the latter. The man had said they'd been sent to see if *she* was building a boat. That didn't make him feel better. He'd far rather have Damien Tyne after him than Elise. If Tyne was after him, he'd have answers. He'd understand perfectly what the situation was. If Tyne was after Elise, he was starting at ground zero.

What business did a reprobate like Tyne have with Elise, or, more probably, with Sir Richard Sutton? Why would Tyne care if Elise was attempting to build a yacht? Dorian could come up with some plausible suppositions, but even so they seemed extreme for Elise's world, which brought Dorian back to the same conclusion that had been lurking in his mind since Bert had confirmed the name: Elise was in danger.

Dorian shifted on the cot, stretching his back. This conclusion suggested several things: his presence at the shipyard doubled her peril. Tyne would be overjoyed if he thought he could get the two of them in a single effort. Second, that he wasn't the only the one with secrets. Beautiful Elise Sutton wasn't as open a book as he'd been led to believe.

It was just his luck. He should have known better. When something looked too good to be true, it usually was, Elise Sutton notwithstanding. Most men would walk away and see to their own safety. But he'd never counted himself among their number. Dorian smiled in the darkness. Tomorrow he'd ferret out Elise's secrets, right after he got a dog or maybe two. Miss Sutton was in danger and she'd just dragged him into it along with her. Of course, that made her all the more interesting, too.

'I do say, Miss Sutton, you are a most interesting font of knowledge.' Charles stood back a step to let her precede him through the door of her town house. They'd just returned from a drive in the park, taking advantage of a rare fine day in early spring.

'I'm not as interesting as all that.' Elise laughed off the compliment. 'I think you're being polite.' They'd been talking of wind and sails. Rather, she'd been talking and Charles had been listening. It had been disappointing to discover that even though Charles's father had been one of her father's investors, the interest in boating stopped there. Charles like the social aspect of the yachting season, but didn't care much for the engineering. In fact, he'd known nothing at all about the differences in ketch or cutter riggings.

'You make it easy to listen,' Charles offered gallantly with a smile.

'Will you stay for tea?' Elise asked, removing her bonnet, only to be met with a discreet cough from Evans, who waited to take her things. 'Is something wrong, Evans?' She couldn't imagine what it could be. Evans never interrupted. But even the littlest things could be a crisis in his eyes. Perhaps Mary the cook had burnt the scones, or there weren't enough tea cakes. It would be her own fault.

She'd been encouraging Mary to scale back her food preparation now that there was only one person in the house to feed. Well, two, counting the meals sent down to Dorian.

'Miss Sutton, you have a caller waiting,' Evans said neutrally.

'More specifically, *I* am waiting.' Low, masculine tones drew Elise's eyes to the doorway of the drawing room. Dorian stood there, leaning negligently against the door frame, but his eyes belied his informality. There was tension behind them and displeasure. 'I've been waiting over an hour.'

He was scolding *her*! He'd barged in unannounced and made himself comfortable in her home and then accused her of being unavailable to him. His audacity knew no limits. Elise drew herself up and squared her shoulders. 'Then you should make an appointment.'

'I wasn't aware I needed one.'

Charles was looking decidedly uncomfortable at the interchange. 'Lord Rowland, I had heard you were back. Welcome home.' But there was no welcome in Charles's voice. She heard the coldness, the implication that Lord Rowland was not appropriate company for her. She heard the scold, too, over her disobedience. He'd asked her to dismiss Rowland and she hadn't. 'Miss Sutton, might I have a word with you in private before I go? Lord Rowland, if you'll excuse us?'

Charles's face was red with emotion when they stepped into the small music room off the main hall. 'Will you allow me to stay? Or perhaps you will allow me to escort him from the premises? You cannot be alone with the bounder!'

Poor Charles, she doubted he'd have any success removing Dorian even if she wanted him to. She'd seen Dorian take on a bully much larger than Charles. Such an action would only serve to embarrass Charles. 'I appreciate the offer, but I assure you it is unnecessary. Lord Rowland has news of the shipyard, nothing more.'

Charles's faced turned even redder. 'There is another issue, Miss Sutton—*Elise*, if I may? We've been friends for a long time. I feel it is my duty to bring this to your attention. Your conduct is not all it should be. It hurts me to say it and I know this is a difficult time for you. Your family has abandoned you, but you cannot abandon convention. You cannot continue to live alone in this house and you certainly cannot entertain men without a chaperon!'

He warmed to his subject, his ardour for the topic not in doubt. 'Elise, you should not have invited even me in for tea. But to have one man invited in and to have another man waiting for you, it is most unseemly. If anyone were to find out, it could be disastrous. We are fortunate town is still deserted and the Season isn't under way yet.' He paused to gather his breath after his last rush of words. 'Let me send someone to you. My aunt, perhaps?' He looked at her expectantly. 'I know you are alone. But you don't need to be.'

'Thank you, Charles. I will think about it.' She hoped she sounded sincere. She had no wish to hurt his feelings. He was doing what he thought best. But frankly, she was mortified by his outburst. Was he really as prissy as all that? She had not noticed that vein had run so deep before. Of course she'd never stepped so far out of line before, either. There'd been no need for him to preach. Really, that was the only word for it. There was being concerned about propriety and then there was *concerned.* Charles was of the latter and she had no tolerance for that. She was a grown woman of twenty-three. She was more than capable of looking after herself.

He gave her a stiff bow, hat in hand, his demeanour slightly colder than when he'd arrived. 'Good day, Miss Sutton.'

'Are you happy now?' Elise faced Dorian once the door was shut on Charles's departing back. 'You've managed to anger one of my dear friends and make me look quite the strumpet.' Whatever *détente* they'd experienced last night over tea and a fire had been nothing more than a mirage. Except for the clothes, there was very little of that gentleman about Dorian today.

'He'd like to be more than a friend,' Dorian scoffed. 'Is that the sort you prefer? No wonder you'd never been kissed. I can't imagine he knows the first thing of how to go about it.'

'My preferences are none of your business.' Elise felt her face heating up as she swept past him into the drawing room. She was not having this conversation where the servants could hear whatever outlandish remark might come out of his mouth.

'You might think differently about what is my business or not after you hear what I have to say.' Dorian eased the doors to a half-shut position, allowing them some privacy.

'I do not like the look on your face or the tone of your voice,' Elise replied.

'I assure you, you will like even less what I have come to say.' Dorian gestured to the sofa and settled into the matching chair across from her. 'Now that we're comfortable, why don't you tell me how you've come to know Damien Tyne?'

Chapter Eight

'I don't know him at all,' Elise didn't even hesitate to answer. The name was nothing to her.

'Did your father?'

Elise shook her head. 'No. I kept all the orders and accounts. If we'd had any business with him, I would have known.'

Dorian looked doubtful and she felt the need to protest her point. 'I would have known,' Elise insisted, wanting to wipe that sceptical look off his oh-so-sure face.

'Unless your father had private dealings with him.'

'Is "private" your way of suggesting "secret"?' Elise bristled at the connotations wrapped in Dorian's implication that all was not as it seemed. 'My father was not that sort of man.'

Dorian remained unfazed by her challenge. 'I'm not insinuating he was. But Tyne is exactly the sort. Most of his dealings are not public.' He leaned back in the chair, assuming a pose of relaxed confidence, so certain he had the upper hand, so certain he knew more than she did about her own business's dealings, and the assumption galled. 'Let's assume for the moment that you are correct and you or your father had no knowledge of Tyne. Explain, then, why he sent two men to your shipyard last night.'

'What?' Elise's earlier fears that something had happened surged to the fore. 'The boat? Is it all right?' She didn't know what she'd do if the boat was ruined. There was no question of starting over. Until this moment she'd not fully realised how much she was counting on that yacht. It had come to hold all her dreams, her future, her *everything*.

'The yacht is fine.' Dorian gave a wry smile. 'I'm fine, too, thanks for the asking.'

'Of course you are.' Elise covered her impolite manners hastily. It wasn't well done of her to think of the boat first. She'd just been so shocked. 'Otherwise, you wouldn't be sitting here.' She was rambling now, still trying to digest the implications of *armed* men coming to her shipyard. Dorian's comment clearly indicated it hadn't been a social call or even a business call. 'If you'd been hurt, I'd have been outraged,' she protested.

Dorian laughed. 'Your concern is touching and almost believable. Maybe next time you should flutter your eyelashes and look a bit pale when you say that. Fortunately, I was more than a match enough for the two of them, no need to worry.'

'Perhaps that's why I wasn't,' Elise replied smartly. Whatever sympathy she'd been mustering on Dorian's behalf fled at the teasing. The man who'd pressed a knife to an employee's throat for a simple infraction was more than able to handle two night-time thugs. She could also easily imagine that such men were not as foreign to him as they were to her. It had not escaped her, in all the shock of Dorian's revelations, that he was worried because *he* knew this Damien Tyne.

Elise folded her hands in her lap and looked Dorian squarely in the eye. 'Let us reverse our roles for a moment. I cannot answer your question, but it seems you can answer mine. Why don't *you* tell *me* how you know Damien Tyne?'

She noted the tight line of Dorian's mouth as he answered, 'He's a man you don't want to know.'

'Some say that about you,' Elise challenged, recalling Charles's reaction when she'd told him. 'I'm afraid I'll need to know more than that before I can decide what is to be done.' She was tired of men deciding who she should or shouldn't know. For a moment, she thought Dorian would refuse, but he had none of Charles's qualms.

'He's a gun runner. I came across him in the Mediterranean.'

Elise schooled her features to give nothing away. She'd been prepared for unpleasant news and Dorian was trying to shock her. Still, this was *quite* unpleasant. 'How do you know this?'

Dorian shrugged noncommittally. 'I was in a position to know, that is all. Tyne is a man with no code, no loyalties, and now he's come looking for you.'

'Or for you.' She would not let shock overrule her sensibilities and reason. 'I had no such trouble until you came along. Forgive me for saying it, Mr Rowland, but this Damien Tyne seems more like your sort.'

Such words would get a rise out of any man she'd ever known. But he merely sat there, an infuriating grin on his face as he nodded, carrying on some secret discussion in his mind she was not privy to.

'I liked it better when you called me Dorian,' he drawled. His blue eyes held hers in a most disconcerting fashion reminiscent of spontaneous kisses and the promise of illicit pleasures. 'For your information, Tyne *is* more my sort, but he definitely came looking for you. The men last night said explicitly they'd been sent to see what was going on at the shipyard.' He paused, his tone softer when he spoke again. 'If it makes you feel better, I'd hoped it might have been me, too.'

That caught her off guard. It reminded her briefly of the man she'd glimpsed last night in front of the fire, who had for a short period of time seemed almost like a gentleman. Best not to be swayed by the clothes, she scolded herself. Beneath these layers lay the man who swaggered around in low-slung culottes. Still, Elise couldn't help but be touched that this man she barely knew had wanted to take her place.

His hand reached out across the short distance between them and covered hers where they lay in her lap, his eyes serious. 'I might suggest you start thinking about the identity of the rat who would have tipped Tyne off about the boat.'

'I've told no one,' Elise answered truthfully. She'd held her tongue on the one opportunity she'd been tempted to tell Charles.

'Then who did you tell about me? Anyone besides Charles?'

'No.' There'd been no one else to tell. It was a rather sad realisation. With her brother gone back to university, there'd been no one else to discuss her days with. The house was as empty as her social calendar, not that her acquaintances would have approved of such conversation. The only one of her friends who might, Mercedes Lockhart, was miles away in Brighton and newly married.

'Well, there you go. Charles is your rat.' Dorian released her hand and sat back with smug satisfaction at a mystery so easily solved. 'It's not a huge leap of logic to assume you've hired a foreman because there's actual work to do.'

No, it wasn't. She couldn't argue with that and Charles's father had been an investor. He'd known there was a yacht left uncompleted. Even the obtuse Charles could put two and two together. 'I can't imagine Charles would be acquainted with a man like Tyne.' Elise rose and walked to the window, looking down into the street.

'And yet, I'm here. I'm sure there are those who'd argue it isn't likely for a gently bred young lady like yourself to know a man like me. If you could know me, what's to stop Charles from knowing a man like Tyne?'

Elise turned from the window. 'I find it doubtful. Charles is so very proper, as he demonstrated today, so very conscious of his social standing. It makes little sense that he would run to a man such as the one you've described and give him that information. And for what reason? Charles doesn't want to hurt me.' They hadn't even begun to address motives for Tyne's sudden interest in the shipyard.

Dorian gave one of his disbelieving shrugs.

'Perhaps it's more of a question of who does Charles know who might know someone such as Tyne?'

Elise blew out a breath. His cynicism made her head swim. She just wanted to build her boat and here he was spinning conspiracies. 'All we know for certain is that two unsavoury individuals sent by another unsavoury individual came to the shipyard last night and suddenly you have Charles selling secrets to gun runners.'

'If a duke's son can work for the daughter of a knight, anything is possible. The yachting world has always made for strange bedfellows. Just ask the Royal Thames Yacht Club—they were nothing more than a group of citizens with boats until Cumberland came along.'

She couldn't entirely discredit him. Just like horse racing, yacht racing had its own culture and underbelly. Races were contested all the time over foul play, sliced rigging and dashed hulls. What would she do if Dorian was right and this was just the tip of some sordid effort to claim her father's boat? The boat itself had been meant to be revolutionary. What if Tyne had heard about it and wanted the boat for himself for whatever reason? She had to stop those thoughts. Now she was sounding like Dorian. The emptiness of her world must be hitting her hard today.

Elise sighed. 'It must be very exhausting living in your world full of informants and dangers lurking around every corner.'

'I prefer to think of it as exciting.' He was up and moving, crossing the room towards her, his eyes hot and sincere all at once as if he could read the myriad emotions surging through her: the anger, the frustration, the loneliness and the fear that for once she might not be equal to the task, that all it would take would be more than she had.

Elise liked to think it wasn't clear who moved first, but in her honest moments she was certain it was her. There was such a small distance between her and Dorian, it had been the merest of motions to turn into his arms, to find her head resting on the strong expanse of his chest, breathing in the clean soapy scent of him, no masking colognes for this one. His arms had welcomed her, folded around her, held her close. When was the last time some-one had held her thus?

'All I wanted to do was build my father's boat,' she whispered, fighting back the sob that threatened in her throat.

His voice was muffled against her hair. 'And we will.'

Dorian felt an utter fraud in those moments. He would protect her from Tyne, but who would protect her from him? He'd taken this position knowing if he could manage this boat for himself he would. Yet here she was, in his arms, looking to him for protection, for answers. How desperate she must be! She was not the type to seek those things from another, a sure sign of how draining these past months had been on her mental resources. He had stepped into the breach at a most convenient time for his own enterprises, but now that he was here, there were other emotions at work.

He'd seen the forces arrayed so covertly against her: Tyne and his underworld, Charles and his virtuous pomposity, attempting to bring her back into the bland fold of society. The Charles Bradfords of the world were plentiful and they would make her choose between themselves and the boat. That stirred something else in him—jealousy? Surely not. Protectiveness? Perhaps, although it seemed irrational on short acquaintance. But he'd travelled this path of hers, too, once upon a time. He'd faced similar choices long ago, albeit for different, less-noble reasons.

He smiled over her shoulder into space. When he'd jumped into her carriage, he'd been looking for an escape. He'd not thought to find a kindred spirit—not that she'd believe any such thing. She thought him a scoundrel. The idea they had anything in common would be ludicrous to her. But he knew better.

Dorian's arms tightened about her. He didn't want to give this vibrant, intelligent woman over to the cold fish of the aristocracy that would have no use for her skills. Ah, he was being covetous. Being protective was one thing; a decent man was always protective of those in his purvey even if that man was something of a pirate. Being covetous was another, more worrisome, thing altogether. Covetous implied a level of wanting. Dorian tested the statement in his mind. Did he want Elise Sutton beyond a short physical liaison? If so, how had that occurred? At what point had he begun to think with something other than his libido? For his own welfare, the answers to those questions deserved exploration in the near future.

All he knew for certain right now was that he did not want to give her to the likes of Charles Bradford, who would never be man enough for her. Would she know that? For all her own strength, did she know what she needed? He couldn't free her, only she could do that, but he *could* open the door and see what happened, starting tonight. Out of the window, dusk was falling on a crisp, clear night.

'Come on, let's go.'

She looked up, green eyes quizzical. 'Go where?'

He smiled, unwilling to give up his secret. 'Just out. You'll see. You need to get out of the house and away from your troubles.'

'Should I change?'

'Put on something warm and grab a cloak. I want to get a few things from your kitchen.

You still owe me a meal for today.' Dorian released her with a wink. 'Trust me.'

She laughed at that. 'Do you think that's wise?'

Dorian grinned. It felt good to make her smile. 'Maybe not wise, but it's bound to be fun.'

Chapter Nine

'We're not going to the shipyards?' Elise pulled her cloak tighter around her shoulders and stared about the dark pier, a quiet reminder that she'd gone out into the night with a man she barely knew and with no idea of their destination.

'I told you, no work.' Dorian waved down a wherry man. 'The Vauxhall Stairs,' he called.

'Vauxhall?' Elise questioned, taking his hand and stepping aboard. 'It's March.'

'So?' Dorian grinned.

'So? You do know Vauxhall is closed. It's not open until June.' She hated to ruin his plans, but he'd been gone—perhaps he'd forgotten.

'I know.' He gave her a lazy smile, his hand

warm at her back as he guided her to the railing of the wherry for the short trip across the Thames. He leaned close, making her acutely aware of his proximity. 'It makes it more fun. We shall have the place to ourselves and no one shall be the wiser.'

It took Elise a moment to digest his meaning. 'We're going to break into Vauxhall?'

The wherry bumped against the wharf, signalling their arrival. Dorian leapt on to the pier, slinging a haversack over his shoulder. 'In answer to your question, simply yes.'

This would be the perfect time to turn back, her conscience prodded. *Before* it was too late. This was the height of insanity. He had her lying to her butler about her whereabouts and breaking into pleasure gardens.

'Well? Are you coming, Elise?' He turned towards her, hand outstretched, blue eyes dancing with mischief. 'Don't tell me you've got cold feet now? If you're worried about being seen, I've provided you with the perfect outing. No one will even know we're here.'

'This is outrageous!' she scolded. He really meant to do it, really meant to break into the closed pleasure gardens.

'Outrageous? Well, you should know.

You're the woman who is building a boat.' Dorian laughed and she was helpless to resist. His enthusiasm was infectious. Her feet moved of their own accord, her hand slipping into his with astonishing ease, even knowing this was poorly done of her. He had taken advantage of her on more than one occasion. She should have dismissed him from the start. But he was still here, still tempting her towards yet another indiscretion, this one larger than the first.

Earlier, she could have taken comfort that she had no other choice. She couldn't dismiss him. Who would finish her boat if not him? But that logic's usefulness was long past now. Sneaking into Vauxhall had absolutely nothing to do with finishing her boat and she could take no refuge in the idea that she was forced to endure his company. Tonight she'd turned to him quite voluntarily for reasons she'd care not to explore too closely.

At the entrance, she knew a moment's reprieve. The gates were locked against them, strong sturdy iron bars. Dorian's lark would end here. But Dorian merely turned aside and followed the high hedgerow that hid the garden wall. 'Ah, here it is.' He stopped and parted the greenery, revealing a door in the wall. Dorian held up a slim tool from his pocket and waggled his eyebrows playfully before inserting it into the keyhole. 'Watch this, my dear.' Within moments he had the door open. He motioned her through with a gallant gesture. 'After you, my lady.'

Dorian shut the door behind them and reached for a lantern to light. 'This is technically a crime.' Elise tried one last time for sense.

'It's only a crime if we get caught.' Dorian struck a match and the lantern flared to life, casting its light on the deserted garden paths. She'd been here before with her parents on a few occasions. Then, the place had been thronged with people. Tonight, the gardens were less festive, but far more intimate without the noise of the crowds. Or it might be the company. Elise expected anywhere would be more intimate with Dorian. He could turn the most mundane of settings into something remarkable, as demonstrated by what had occurred in her offices on two occasions.

'Shall we take in the sights?' Dorian was all exaggerated gallantry, offering her his free arm, the other one burdened with his sack and the lantern. 'May I draw your attention to the statue of Handel?' He held the lantern high, illuminating the sculpture of Handel in his bathrobe and slippers. Elise laughed and let him talk while he guided her through the Grand South Walk. There were no other signs of life except for the squirrels in the bushes and she started to relax. Perhaps Dorian was right and scandal only became a crime if one was caught. This evening could be a moment out of time, something no one else ever had to know about.

'I must apologise, we have no fireworks tonight or gaslight display.' Dorian toured her past the rows of supper boxes to the open tables in front of the orchestra. 'But perhaps I can interest you in a little picnic?' He set down the sack and began unpacking.

'This is what you were doing while I got my cloak?' Elise watched in amazement as he produced a square of white linen and spread it on the table before settling the lantern in the centre.

'There, we'll have candlelight for ambience.' He grinned impishly and continued pulling out items: a loaf of bread, a wheel of cheese, slices of ham. 'Not nearly as thin as

Vauxhall's famed ham, but your Mary cuts it well.' There were plates and glasses, knives and napkins and, miracle of miracles, a bottle of wine. The bag seemed seriously depleted once the feast was laid out.

'This is incredible,' Elise breathed, taking a seat. She couldn't believe she was doing this; sitting down to a picnic in deserted Vauxhall with this rather extraordinary, if not eccentric, man. It begged the question. 'Why are you doing this?'

Dorian pulled the cork from the bottle and poured her a glass. 'Why not?' He raised his own glass, blue eyes mesmerising. 'You're an intriguing woman, Elise Sutton, and I like intriguing things.'

'Those are bold words.' Never had a man spoken so frankly to her.

'As bold as the woman herself,' Dorian said in low tones. 'To you, Elise, and your latest undertaking.' He drank to her, the words sending a delightful shiver down her spine. He made her sound so sophisticated in her unconventionality. She'd not thought of herself that way.

Elise reached for a slice of bread and cheese. 'I don't see my yacht as an act of audacity. It is simply an extension of who I am. Boats are what I do. You make too much of it.'

'Perhaps you make too little of it,' Dorian replied. 'It's not every woman who knows as much about yachts as you do. May I ask what sparked your interest in the first place?'

Elise smiled. 'I've been drawing designs forever.' She'd meant to keep the answer concise, but Dorian nodded and cocked his head in interest, his eyes resting on her, intent in her story. Before she knew it, one story became two and soon she was telling him how she'd gone to work with her father when she was a little girl, how she'd sit at the drafting desk by the window and draw, how her father would put her on his shoulders and walk about the yard with her, telling her the names of all the parts of a ship. How, later, she'd begun keeping his books to free up more time for him to conduct business, how he'd started consulting her on the builds and then the drawings. She told him how her mother had scolded that this was no pastime for a young girl, but that hadn't stopped her or her father. It had become the pattern of their days. Now he was gone and she knew nothing else.

'Perhaps that's why I'm so determined to

see this ship finished. I don't know what else I'd do. Even now, having been banned from the shipyard...' she looked up and gave him a pointed stare '...I don't know how to fill my days.'

'Having you there is difficult. These are not your father's men. Surely you understand this?' Dorian answered. 'But they were all I could find, given the circumstances.'

Elise nodded. She did understand, she just didn't like it, especially now with the threat of an interloper stalking the shipyard. She wanted to be there. Elise looked about the table. The wine was drunk, the food eaten. She'd talked far longer than she'd planned, exposed more of herself than she'd meant to. 'I'm sorry, I didn't mean to talk through the whole meal.'

'I didn't mind,' Dorian drawled. 'You're interesting.'

Charles had said the same thing that afternoon. It was what gentlemen said to ladies, to be polite. But Dorian made it sound as if he meant it and the thought warmed her unexpectedly. She shouldn't care what this rogue of a lord's son thought of her or her family. His opinion carried no weight, he was a social outcast by his own admission. Yet, here at their purloined supper table, the words meant the world.

Dorian might have been right. He might be starting to grow on her after all, a thought that both thrilled and dismayed her. He was merely passing through her life. One day in the very near future, as soon as he had his money, he would move on, taking his smile and his seductive brand of flirtation with him. But for the present, it did make a girl think about the possibilities that existed until then.

Dorian gathered up their plates and glasses, stuffing them back into his sack. 'Come walk with me, there are still some unexplored areas. We haven't taken in the Rural Downs yet.' He guided them towards a path that led away from the Grove. 'We should see Milton's statue at least before we go.'

'What about you? How did you get interested in ships if your family was disposed towards horses?' Elise asked, hoping he'd be more forthcoming than he had been.

'As I told you, at first I just wanted to be different. I was looking for a way to spite my father and yachting seemed perfect. After a while, though, I was genuinely interested.' He paused. 'A boat is freedom. I could go anywhere and everywhere. I could see parts of the world others only dreamed of.'

'And so you did. Is that why you went to the Mediterranean?' The Mediterranean sounded positively exotic to her, so far away although she knew British interests extended far beyond the south of Europe.

She could *feel* his smile in the darkness. 'Ah, Elise, the Mediterranean is a fascinating place with Europe on one side, Africa on the other and Istanbul somewhere in the middle, a gateway to the Far East and China and all that lies beyond. There are potentates and pirates, beaches and deserts and mysteries beyond imagining.'

She was in his thrall, hanging on each picture his words painted. 'Tell me more. Tell me about the sea.' They'd arrived at Milton's statue, a lead rendition of the author, but she was far more interested in the man beside her.

'It's warm, Elise. A man can bathe in it off the coast of Spain. Can you imagine such a thing? Swimming naked in the ocean with dolphins for playmates?' His eyes danced. He was deliberately being naughty. One did not talk of such things in polite company.

'Have you really swum with dolphins?' She suspected he was teasing her. She didn't dare ask about the naked part. She was certain he had.

'Yes, once in Gibraltar. I will never forget it. They're friendly creatures.'

'I envy you your adventures,' Elise said softly. The intimacy of the evening and the sweet blur of the wine were starting to conspire. They'd been down this path before. If she was smart, she'd suggest they leave before any damage was done, damage she'd regret once the wine and loneliness wore off.

'You could have adventures, too. You could feel the Mediterranean wash across your feet; you could bury your toes in the sand of its beaches.' His voice caressed her as assuredly as the hand at her neck. 'Do you ever think of it? Of sailing away in one of your creations?'

'A fantasy only,' Elise confessed. The practicalities eluded her. A woman alone was at risk even if she could sail a yacht on her own. But she could hardly think of that with Dorian so near, so charming, so seductive. She should not let him touch her. Any touch at all seemed to ignite her.

'You need a partner,' Dorian murmured,

his mouth at her ear, his teeth nipping gently at her lobe.

A wicked thought came to her. She needed him, this pirate in gentleman's clothing who talked of far-off places and laughed at propriety, who didn't care a whit for any of the things that occupied the hours of Charles's days, who could wield a knife and take on intruders. He would be the perfect partner. She would be safe with him.

That was definitely the moonlight and wine talking! Vauxhall's vaunted reputation for indiscretions among its many arbours was not unearned. There was magic here aplenty if she was ready to cast aside the hard-learned lessons of her dalliance with Robert Graves and the vow she'd made to never *need* a man. However, she'd been clear with herself that needing was not the same as wanting. Wanting was voluntary, needing was a necessity. All right, just as long as she understood her own rules, she could *want* Dorian Rowland.

'You smell like the lemons in the south of Italy,' Dorian whispered between the kisses he placed along the column of her throat. She should stop him, but all she did instead was arch her neck, inviting his lips, his caresses.

His hands cupped her face, his mouth taking hers in long drinking kisses that nearly made her weep. She *was* weeping—deep at her core she was hot and damp, desire gathering firm and insistent at the private juncture between her legs, demanding to be assuaged.

She knew precisely what she felt and she knew what she wanted—one night, just one night, out of time. Dorian would be the perfect lover. He wouldn't raise her expectations with false promises to be dashed later because this time there would be none. This time there would be only pleasure. She was older, wiser, and this time when she played with desire she knew exactly what she was doing.

Dorian knew, too. His hands were at her skirts, drawing them up, finding the slit in her undergarments that gave him access to the weeping centre of her, the wet heat that would not be quenched. She gasped in desperate frustration, urging him to hurry. Dorian's hand was on her even as his mouth claimed hers once more, his every touch riveting her body's attention. His fingers searched unerringly, intimately, for the little nub hidden in her folds. He rubbed gently, tantalisingly, drawing his thumb across the tiny, sensitive surface again and again until she thought she'd scream from the delight of it. Very soon everything would be resolved, her body knew it as she arched against his hand, her cries a mingling of sobs.

'Let go, Elise. Let go for me.' Dorian's voice was ragged at her ear, his own breathing coming in pants as he stroked her, his own body rigid against hers. It was all the coaxing she needed. Elise arched one last time and shattered, her world an expanding kaleidoscope of sensations, her body shaking, her knees quivering. She remained upright due only to the strength of Dorian's arms and the old oak at her back. Dorian's eyes glittered dark and dangerous in their desire, watching her explode.

'I think there is no more beautiful sight than a woman achieving her pleasure.' He leaned an arm against the oak, his hair falling in his face as he bracketed her with his body. He was hoarse, proof that the moment had not moved her alone.

'And a man? He is beautiful in pleasure, too?' It had not escaped her that he had yet to find his own release. His muscles were taut against the lines of his clothes, the tension of his own need obvious.

Dorian smiled wickedly, encouragingly. 'You should judge for yourself. After all, beauty is in the eye of the beholder.'

The moonlight had made her reckless. She reached for him, cupping him between his legs as he had her. He was hard against her touch, so very long, so very rigid, a potent force beneath his trousers. 'Or the hand, as the case may be.'

Chapter Ten

Dorian flicked open his trousers in a deft movement. 'Then by all means, my lady.' Her hand closed around him, firm and decisive, sliding to the root of him. Dorian sucked in his breath, letting her learn him. The firmness of her grasp was a sign of her confidence if not also her knowledge. There was wide-eyed appreciation in her gaze even as she recognised the power she held in those moments. She was newly come to such intimacies, but not without imagination.

She stroked up, finding the wet, tender tip of him, a smile lighting her face at the discovery. She stroked downwards and then up again, establishing a rhythm that fired his blood. Her hand was cool and welcome on his heated flesh. He would not last long at this rate, nor did he want to. The promise of exquisite relief waited just beyond the moment. Dorian reached back and dug his hands into the bark of the tree, pumping hard into her hand, uttering a harsh groan as release took him.

Elise was exultant. 'What are you smiling at?' Dorian teased.

'I'm smiling because I was right. A man *is* beautiful in his pleasure.'

'I don't think anyone has ever called me beautiful before,' Dorian drawled with a nonchalance he didn't feel. He kissed her then, drawing her close against him so she couldn't see his face, couldn't see how the comment affected him. He felt the first stirrings of new arousal. There was more he'd like to do with her, this bold princess of his, but not tonight, although his body was willing.

He was no stranger to seduction. He'd seduced women before: married women, widowed women, flirtatious débutantes, the touched and the untouched. He had few boundaries when it came to sex. What boundaries he did have, Elise was provoking. His earlier thoughts about coveting and protecting were threatening to resurface at a most vulnerable time—right after intimacy when he was open to susceptibilities. 'We need to get back,' he murmured against her hair.

The walk to the hidden door was quiet, but not awkward. They'd strolled slowly, his arm about her waist, keeping her close. He had no doubt her mind was as full as his was at present. Their spontaneous outing had been illuminating, although probably for different reasons. Dorian found it was easier, less troublesome to his conscience, to think about her thoughts than his. He was not convinced this was her first encounter with raw passion—perhaps with the depth of pleasure the encounter had wrung from her, but not the nature of the encounter itself. Still, first encounter or not, he could guess what was racing through her mind: what had she done? Was there shock or shame over her own audacity? Was she pleased at the discovery of such pleasure? Emboldened by it even? Or did she think herself the wanton for having enjoyed it? And she *had* enjoyed it, Dorian knew she had. Most of all, she was likely wondering what it meant. Anything? Nothing? Everything?

That was the place at which his thoughts intersected with hers and it was where he'd made his first mistake. By his own rules, he shouldn't have allowed it to happen—not yet, not without an agreement. Up until now, all of his seductions occurred *after* some explicit or implicit plan had been established, interest signalled and accepted by both parties.

With that signalling came an understanding. What would proceed would be a seduction in which he would gladly take the lead, but to which there would be an end. There would be nothing beyond. If and when both parties concurred on those negotiations, *then* such things as what had transpired tonight would take place, but not before.

Tonight had got the plan backwards. And he'd set himself up for it. He'd gone to her house to inform Elise of the break-in. He should have left it at that. He should not have allowed himself to be moved by the stoic sight of her bearing yet more bad news on those slender shoulders. He should not have been moved by the way she'd turned into him: *I just wanted to build my father's boat.* And he *never* should have said the words that had followed: *we will.* If Elise Sutton was walking beside him right now thinking they were in this together, that she could trust him, that he would stand beside her through whatever might come, it was his fault.

As if to confirm it, Elise spoke softly. 'When I first met you, I didn't like you very much.'

'And now?' They'd reached the hidden door and he held it open for her.

She smiled up at him as she passed. 'And now I like you a bit more. Are we becoming friends, Dorian Rowland?'

'Friends? No, never that.' Dorian chuckled. Whatever it was he wanted from Elise Sutton, he wanted far more than friendship. He waved down a late-night wherry man.

'Then what?' Elise asked once they were on board, watching the Westminster stairs come into view.

'Something else,' Dorian answered cryptically, wrapping his arms about her, hoping his touch would be answer enough until he could work out a better one. Although the answer, when he found it, might not please her. But tonight was not the time to tell her that women relied on him for sex, nothing more. Anything beyond momentary pleasure was not his to give. He'd not proven reliable in that regard in the past and he had no reason to believe it would be any different this time. He was coming to believe his father might be right. Singular devotion simply wasn't in him. And that's what Elise Sutton would expect from a man. It's what she had a *right* to expect.

He saw her safely home, part of him worried Tyne might try to personalise his attacks. It had occurred to him that Tyne would seek retaliation for the discomfort of his two henchmen and that Elise would be a natural target.

'Will the boat be all right?' she asked in the darkness of the carriage as it drew to a stop in front of the town house. Dorian chuckled. Her mind had moved on from the pleasures of the evening to what had brought them together in the first place. Or perhaps it was her way of restoring balance to what had become a deeply personal evening with an unlikely partner.

'I took on a guard dog today and alerted the watch, although I put more faith in the dog.' Dorian chuckled. 'He's a big brindle hound and *he* can't be bought.' Dorian was fairly certain Damien Tyne would see to the watch soon enough and there'd be little protection from that quarter once Tyne's machine was in motion.

Dorian opened the door and pulled down the steps. Playing the gentleman had come easy to him this evening. It was a bit of a surprise to see how easily it'd come back to him. 'Goodnight, Elise.'

'Goodnight, Dorian. Thank you for the evening.' She smiled politely at him as if she'd not pleasured him just an hour before, or screamed her own pleasure to the skies a quarter of an hour before that. When she wanted, Elise Sutton could be a cool customer. But he knew better. She wasn't cool in the least. An arousal started at just the thought of all her heat, all her passion hidden behind the calm exterior with which she met the world.

'The hull is nearly timbered, then we'll caulk,' Dorian said in hopes of subduing his arousal before it became troublesome. 'I will contact you when it's finished. Shouldn't be more than a few days.'

Disappointment clouded her eyes. Disappointment over not seeing him tomorrow or disappointment in not being invited to the shipyard? With Elise it could be either or both. 'You will contact me if there's trouble before that?'

'Yes, most certainly.' He gave her a short bow. 'Goodnight.'

Disappointment? Relief? Elise wasn't sure what she should feel. She tried to sort through those feelings while she got ready for bed. She'd dismissed her maid as soon as she could. Whatever those feelings were, she wanted to sift through them alone.

Her maid and Evans had waited up for her, concerned that she'd been working late. She felt terrible for the deception. They'd been worried and she'd been out having fun. Of course, they would have worried more if they'd known the truth. What she'd done to-night had been scandalous. Breaking into Vauxhall had been a minor scandal compared to what else had transpired.

Even alone in the dark of her room, she blushed at the memory. But not from shame. What had occurred between her and Dorian had been intimate and wondrous. She had never guessed such pleasure existed. Would it happen again? *Could* she let it happen again?

The right answer was no. She should not risk it. Dorian was clearly no stranger to such circumstances. But it would change the nature of their relationship. Perhaps it already had. He was building her ship. She was in charge. What if he sought to use seduction as a means to usurp her authority or to place himself in the role of an equal partner?

Elise bit her lip, thinking of all the mistakes she'd made over the evening. She had turned to him in the drawing room, seeking comfort from the disastrous news. She'd allowed him to be in charge of their adventure—an entirely *delinquent* adventure. In short, she'd allowed herself to be weak for a few hours only, but even those few hours could have been potentially damaging. He would finish the boat and he would leave. And she would what? Be alone? In the dark, Elise strengthened her resolve. She needed to begin as she meant to go on, by herself. Anything else was too risky and right now she had too much at stake for any more risks other than the ones she was already taking.

Besides, her practical self reminded her,

Dorian Rowland was a poor risk to take. He was fun and clever and he loved ships as she did. He'd had exciting adventures galore. In short, he represented a life she envied. But he was also dangerous; a social enigma with a clouded past that most likely involved exile from his family. What he had said about Damien Tyne had been most revealing. *I was in a position to know.*

It spoke volumes. Dorian Rowland had captained the *Queen Maeve*, was called the Scourge of Gibraltar and fraternised with gun runners. He might not have a golden earring dangling from his ear lobe or a tattoo on his cheek, but he was nothing more than a pirate himself, a most delicious and dangerous discovery indeed.

Chapter Eleven

'We've been discovered and so soon in the game. Your men were not as reliable as hoped,' Maxwell said bluntly, knowing full well that few men dared to speak to Damien Tyne with such arch boldness. In the privacy of his own study, he could say whatever he damned well pleased. It was part of the reason he'd insisted they meet here instead of the coffee house. The other reason was that one discovery was all he wanted to risk.

Tyne's single slip had changed the nature of the game. If he wanted his hands on that property and Sutton's last yacht by April, things would have to progress faster and more covertly than planned. For his part, Maxwell didn't want Rowland or anyone connecting him with Tyne while play was in motion. He wouldn't admit it to Tyne, but he was anxious. He couldn't afford for this gambit to get too messy. He was the legitimate face of their questionable business. He had to stay as clean as Tyne was dirty.

Across from him in the other chair, Tyne didn't appear the least perturbed by the latest developments. He gave his brandy an indolent swirl. 'It was unfortunate Rowland chose that moment to return.'

'What was *unfortunate*,' Maxwell said with emphasis, 'was that *two* men were overpowered by one. Two men, I might add, who specialise in violent living. They should have been more than enough for Rowland.'

Tyne shrugged. 'Our Miss Sutton is building a boat and Rowland is helping her. Don't belabour it. In the end we got what we went for.'

'Yes, and at a great price,' Maxwell groused, unable to be as glib.

Tyne leaned forwards, clearly undaunted by the scolding. Then again, he didn't have an identity to protect. Anyone who knew Damien Tyne knew exactly what he was. 'Maybe this can work to our benefit. Rowland will have told her. She knows it's me. That should scare her, perhaps enough for you to make an offer she'll listen to.'

'She rebuffed the investors when they first offered to buy her out.' Hart had been a quiet, invisible party to that negotiation. He'd been shocked when the lucrative offer had been turned down, even more shocked when the investors had offered it a second time after threatening to force a refund of their monies if she didn't sell. She'd refused and she'd paid their threat.

'She wasn't scared then. She was in the throes of mourning and wrapped up in sentimentality. Such emotions can make a person brave and stupid,' Tyne said silkily. 'Now, she's had months of realities. Now, she's alone, her funds are depleted and she knows with definite certainty there's no white knight riding to her rescue. She's far more desperate than she was earlier and she's about to be more so.' Tyne gave an evil smile that raised even the hairs on the back of Maxwell's neck.

'What have you done?' Maxwell asked cautiously. He was just as ruthless as Tyne, but far more subtle. Tyne didn't appreciate finesse.

'Don't worry, nothing much. There's a disgruntled worker at the shipyard who doesn't like our Mr Rowland. It seems Mr Rowland put a knife to his throat for looking at the lady wrong, which is interesting enough in itself. Seems Mr Rowland has developed a fascination for the Sutton girl.' Tyne sighed dramatically. 'The man would have left, but I'm paying him to stay. He will be useful not only for information, but for the odd bit of sabotage when the time comes. If I were you, I'd get my bid ready within the week.'

It had been a week since their outing to Vauxhall and Elise suspected she'd have gone round the bend before the morning was out if the note from Dorian hadn't arrived. She might still go crazy from the excitement the note had stirred in her. The boat was done! Well, not precisely *done*. The hull was timbered and caulked. There was still plenty to do, but this was an enormous step forwards.

Elise glanced at the mantel clock in the sitting room, the note clutched in her hand. Dorian would be here within the hour. There was just enough time to change. She rang for her maid and headed upstairs.

It was ridiculous to be so giddy over the prospect of Dorian's call and the subsequent journey out of the house, but she could understand it. In the past week she'd written countless letters, cleaned the attics and still had plenty of time left over for her thoughts. She'd thought about everything and anything in the interminable days since Vauxhall.

Never had she felt at such loose ends while she waited for news. By her efforts she'd become a prisoner in her own home. She was on her own for the first time in her life, had more freedom than ever and yet the very aloneness constrained her. Oh, heavens, just listen to her! She hated sounding like Charles. Worse, she hated *acting* like Charles. She could almost hear Dorian's mocking laugh in her head, chiding her for prudish notions. In fact, she'd been chiding herself over such behaviour this week. This was *not* who she was.

This week, she'd come to recognise that her father's death had left her in no man's land. She couldn't go out and socialise and yet she didn't want to stay home alone, hidden away. Young daughters weren't required to wear black, but she was too old to be considered in that category. Even her clothes were in fashion limbo, she thought, staring at the muted lavender and grey gowns. They weren't strictly appropriate for this phase of her mourning, but it was all the concession she was willing to make. Luckily, she looked fair enough in those shades. But she looked *better* in deep, rich jewel tones. With that erroneous thought, the ideas that had chased each other around her mind all week began to coalesce into one momentous decision.

'Perhaps this one, miss?' Her maid, Anna, held out a lavender gown trimmed in a thin black-velvet ribbon. Standing in front of her subdued gowns, everything changed. It wasn't just the dresses, although they'd certainly been the straw that broke the camel's back.

'No, Anna.' Elise drew herself up with squared shoulders. 'Bring me my other gowns. I am done with these. Have them packed up after I've gone today.' It had occurred to her during her dreary week that she owed the rules nothing. She'd already broken so many others. What had obedience to rigid strictures ever got her? Her best moments had come from breaking the rules: working with her father, designing racing yachts. If she meant to see her boat succeed, she could not let herself become marginalised.

Anna looked at her as if she'd grown two heads, or maybe four, and her skin had turned green. 'Miss?'

Elise stood her ground. 'Bring my other gowns. I want the green carriage ensemble with the black frogging on the jacket.'

The ensemble was wrinkled from storage and it took a bit of time to press it into decency but it was worth it. Elise smoothed the snug jacket over her hips. The outfit was perfect. People couldn't truly complain. There was a touch of black trim to lend respectability and the dark green was hardly garish or the classic lines ostentatious. Anna had recovered from shock and twisted her hair up neatly beneath a jaunty little hat that sat cocked on her head, more ornament than actual 'hat'.

Elise reached out a hand and took Anna's in appreciation of her efforts. 'Thank you. I'm not sure I can explain it, but I wasn't myself in those other dresses and there are things that need doing for which I most definitely need to be me.' There was a scratch at the door, a footman informing them of Lord Rowland's arrival.

Anna nodded. 'Truth is, we'll all be glad, miss. It's no good, you shutting yourself up in the house. It's not right, no matter what the rules are. Young ladies should be out in society.'

'I couldn't agree more. But there are bound to be people who will take issue with that sentiment,' Elise cautioned with one final look in the mirror. Her decision had been about more than putting on a dress. The dress was merely a public announcement. If people only speculated she'd set aside mourning by continuing about her business, her lack of mourning dress would take the guesswork out of it. Charles would have an apoplexy, and Dorian? Well, she would see what he'd do in just moments. Her heart was hammering as she took to the stairs.

She saw him first. He was in the hall looking at a painting, a minor work of Turner's, a nautical theme that had impressed her father. Today Dorian had chosen buff trousers and blue jacket along with high boots. His thick blond hair was once again pulled back at his neck into a luxurious tail.

He turned at the sound of her half-boots on the stairs, his blue eyes registering his surprise, the smile on his mouth suggesting he was enjoying it. 'If I'd known timbering the boat would get this sort of response, I'd have finished it earlier. What brought this on?'

Elise smiled and raised her head a notch higher. 'I have decided to be scandalous.'

Dorian's grin widened. 'You look enchanting.' He bowed over her hand. 'Scandal becomes you.'

'If you must know, it's probably your fault. I lay all blame at your feet.'

Dorian tucked her hand through the bend of his arm. 'I am glad to be of service, most glad.' An all-too-familiar tremble shot through her at his words, at his touch, at the mischief dancing in his eyes as he teased and flirted. It wasn't the man who raised such a flutter in her, she told herself resolutely, taking her seat in the carriage. It was the freedom he represented that explained her intense reaction to him. That was what she craved, not the man himself. Any interest in the man sprang from knowing he was not part of the rules. He was something else altogether.

* * *

Elise had nearly convinced herself of this line of logic by the time they reached the shipyard. She stepped down and let the familiar smells wash over her: scents of fresh timber, the strong smell of tar. Had she only been gone a week? It felt an eon and yet the sights and the smells were not strangers, not faded memories from another time. They were the scents of the present and of *home*. She belonged here. Elise shot Dorian a sideways glance. He'd have a fight on his hands if he tried to ban her again.

The men had known she was coming. Dorian had prepared them. Threatened them was more like it. Every one of them stood at taut attention like a staff receiving their lord, work clothes clean, eyes respectfully averted. Mostly. The man Dorian had drawn a knife against wasn't quite obedient. His eyes kept straying although his body held rigid.

'You told them,' she said in low tones after they'd passed the line of employees.

'Yes. I expect order on land or sea from my men,' Dorian said simply. 'No one is required to work here. They all had a chance to leave.'

His hand was firm at her back, guiding her towards the form of the yacht.

'There it is, Elise. Your hull.' There was no mistaking the pride in his tone as he presented it, or the seductive tone in his voice as his tongue ran over her name.

Her hull. The beginning manifestations of her dream come to life. Tears threatened, but she held them back. There'd been too many tears lately. There would not be tears now, she silently vowed.

'It's beautiful,' Elise managed. She bent under the prow, running a hand along the smooth side. 'It's just as I envisioned it.' Long, lean and low in the water, every ounce designed for efficiency, every angle destined to drink the wind and ride the waters. 'How much more time do you think?'

'Two weeks, assuming all goes well.' Dorian was watching her face and smiling softly as if he could read her mind—which would be a bit embarrassing because her first thought was that this meant two more weeks of Dorian.

What she said out loud was, 'The middle of April, in time for the Royal Yacht Club's opening trip.' She knew the club's calendar as well as she knew her own. Her father's life had revolved around the club and yachting season. The racing matches would begin soon afterwards. She'd been part of the boating trip since she was fourteen. She wasn't going to miss it this year.

Suddenly she brought her head up, her reveries interrupted by a smell, a smell inappropriate for the surroundings. At the same moment, a howl went up from the corner of the shipyard. Dorian's dog, the identity registered briefly with her as she shot a look at Dorian. 'Do you smell that?'

'Smoke.' Dorian's eyes were alert, quartering the yard. She followed his lead and scanned, looking for signs of that smoke or, worse, flame. Fire was anathema to shipyards. Whole forests of lumber could be lost and coal-based tar burnt nastily and thoroughly, spreading fire of its own when ignited. Elise didn't even want to think about what it did when it exploded. Her eyes went immediately to the barrels of tar lined along the perimeter.

'There!' She pointed to the beginnings of the flames a mere ten feet from the barrels. With all the other scents of the yard, the smoke had had plenty of time to gain momentum before they'd noticed it. 'Dorian, if it explodes...'

She—*they*—would lose everything. Dorian was off at a run, shedding his coat, before her sentence was finished. If the tar exploded, lives would be endangered along with the shipyard. 'Water!' he shouted orders. 'Form a bucket brigade!'

Fortunately, water was in good supply. Two huge barrels expressly for firefighting stood at the ready. But he could see flames travelling towards the tar as if guided there by a fuse. Dorian placed himself at the head of the line and threw the first bucket. If there was to be an explosion, he'd bear the brunt of it. He reached for a second bucket, positioning himself between the flames and the tar. 'Faster!' The water was slowing down the flames, but not dousing them. It wasn't until the third bucket that he realised who handed them to him. Elise. She should have been ushered to safety by now or had the good sense to seek safety on her own.

'Elise! Get out of here,' he shouted. 'There's no guarantee we can stop the flames.'

For an answer, she thrust a bucket into

his hands. 'We'll stop them. Now, come on.' Water sloshed on her green habit and her hair had come loose with the exertion of passing buckets heavy with water. She looked intent and wild, and really quite scandalous. That would please her. He'd tell her as much *after* he'd finished shouting at her.

Ten minutes later, the fire was out, the remains nothing more than a smoky smoulder. The damage was thankfully minimal; a perimeter fence had been scorched where the fire had started, ostensibly the product of kerosene-soaked rags left out in the open and a carelessly dropped match.

'How did this happen?' Elise stood beside him, surveying what used to be the pile of rags. Her jacket was off and the white blouse she wore underneath was spotted with soot. She'd worked hard next to him. Her efforts and bravery were admirable. 'One minute we were talking about the club's opening trip and the next the yard was on fire.'

Dorian bent to the ground, his hands digging through the ashy debris. The flames had run straight and true to their destination. He'd thought it the work of a fuse when he'd fought the fire. Now, as his hands ran across the tough, warm cording beneath the ash, he was certain. He held up the line. 'Here's your answer.' He lifted it and followed its trail, tightly hidden away against the fence. They were lucky they hadn't lost the fence. 'It's a fuse.'

Elise's face paled. 'Fuses aren't lit by accident.'

'No,' Dorian offered tersely. 'They are not.' He studied it for a moment. 'It's a miner's fuse, the kind used in Cornwall for opening rock walls,' he said quietly, letting her digest the implications. If it could open rock walls, it could easily have destroyed everything in the yard. *And everyone.* Dorian gauged its length. The fuse was relatively long. If someone had truly wanted to blow up anything, they'd have set a shorter fuse, one he couldn't have reached in time.

He took Elise's arm. 'Why don't we go up to the office and discuss this latest occurrence? We were lucky this time because someone wanted us to be.'

Chapter Twelve

The office had changed in the week of her absence. It bore an indelible sense of *him*. Papers and drawings lay on the work table. His tools were here, too, hanging from a belt on the coat tree. Resentment flared. This was her space. It was full of her father, of the time they'd shared together. The thought of another claiming the space sat poorly with her, even if that person was Dorian. *Especially* if that person was Dorian. How was she supposed to forget him if his presence lingered?

'I'm coming back to work, starting tomorrow,' Elise blurted out. She hadn't meant to begin the conversation that way, but memories and resentment had got the best of her in the aftershock of the fire. She would protect what was hers.

'I won't hear of it,' Dorian growled. 'You shouldn't have been here today. I was wrong to bring you here. It put you in danger.'

'You didn't know there'd be a fire.' Elise dismissed the comment impatiently. His logic was ridiculous.

'Not a fire specifically, but we knew trouble was brewing. Tyne wouldn't have risked a break-in and nothing more.' Dorian paced the length of the office, agitated. 'He was waiting and watching for the right moment.' The man had given them a week to grow confident.

'Fuses take premeditation.' Elise followed him with her eyes. He was like a great tawny cat, restless in a cage. His broad shoulders were taut beneath the ruined linen of his shirt. His body fairly vibrated with the angry energy of him. How could anything hurt her with this lion on guard?

Dorian nodded, pausing in his pacing long enough to swear. 'Damn that man. Tyne has someone watching from the inside, someone who would know when the hull was done. That someone would be ready to put a damper on the festivities and would have advance knowledge of that timeline, plenty of time to plan.'

Elise recalled the man with wandering eyes. 'The man who doesn't like you, perhaps? His gaze kept drifting.' Now that she thought of it, the man's gaze had kept going to the tar casks.

In response, Dorian opened the top drawer of her father's desk and pulled out the longest knife she'd ever seen. 'Stay here, I'll be back.'

'Dorian, no!' Elise put herself between him and the door. 'You can't go around threatening everyone with a knife.'

'It's not a knife, it's a machete and I'm not threatening "everyone", just him,' Dorian corrected, his eyes flashing with angry determination. 'Bent needs to learn he can't go around sabotaging shipyards in a language he understands.'

Elise wasn't sure if the 'he' in that sentence denoted the worker or the elusive, villainous Damien Tyne, but she was pretty sure the language in question was 'knife'. She stood her ground, arms crossed over her chest.

'This is my shipyard and I say this type of behaviour will not be tolerated. I'm not moving.'

'You will move, Elise, or I will move you.' Dorian put the blade between his teeth, looking utterly piratical, and took a step towards her. She didn't doubt he'd do it. She decided to move. The last thing she needed was to appear the fool and that was exactly what she'd look like trussed over his shoulder.

He gave her a short nod as he passed. 'Thank you. Now, stay put.'

Dorian wasn't gone long, but he was none the happier when he returned, his knife looking suspiciously clean. 'Our culprit has fled,' he groused, throwing the knife back in the drawer.

'We usually kept paper and ink in that drawer,' Elise said pointedly.

Dorian glared and continued, 'In doing so, he has declared his guilt, but I'm sure there's more he could have told us. Primarily, what purpose the fire was to serve. Fire is risky. If I hadn't acted quickly, much could have been lost and that would have defeated Tyne's purpose.'

'If he's after the boat, burning it makes little sense.' A bit of hope took her. 'This is good, then. The boat is safe. He won't harm it. The fire was nothing more than a warning, hence the long fuse.' There, logic had triumphed over the emotions of the moment to render a rational answer to their riddle of the fire.

Dorian allowed her a moment's peace before he pierced her with a hard blue stare. 'But you're not.' He closed the distance between them, reminding her of his complete maleness and strength with his nearness 'Have you thought of that? I'm safe for a while. If he wants the boat finished, he's got to keep me alive a few weeks longer at least. But you…' Dorian drew a long finger down the trail of her jaw and shook his head '…you are expendable, my love.'

The words brought a chill to her, but she shrugged them off. 'Kill me over a boat design? Over a yacht? A life for a boat? That's preposterous, Dorian. People don't trade lives over wood and sails. That's far too extreme.' But even as she said it, she doubted the strength of her conviction. She was remembering what Dorian had told her previously. Tyne was a gun runner, a man with no scruples.

'Of course they do, Princess. Sometimes

they do it for something even less tangible, something they can't hold in their hands: speed. The history of nautical advancement, after all, has been centered on the acquisition of speed.' Dorian gave a harsh chuckle. 'If you don't believe me, consider your yacht club's races. Grown men ramming other boats' hulls in a race to slow and disable, slicing sails all for the sake of speed. And that's just to win a paltry silver cup. Think what men will do when wars and kingships are on the line.'

'Thankfully, just a "paltry cup" is on the line then,' Elise replied tartly. 'I appreciate your insight, but I think the concern is exaggerated.' He needed to understand she would not be frightened easily.

Something flared in his eyes. 'Then appreciate this, Elise.' Dorian took her mouth in a bruising kiss, dancing her the short distance to the wall. Her back rammed up against its hard surface. This was harsh and punishing, nothing like the hot exploration of Vauxhall. Elise shoved at him, pushing with both her hands against his chest.

'Stop it, Dorian. You've made your point.'

'Have I?' Dorian stepped back, fury still etched on the planes of his face. 'I stopped.

Don't think for a moment Tyne will stop until he has what he wants, and he won't let up simply because you've asked. You're a clever woman, Elise. Don't let stubbornness blind you to the realities. This world you've stepped into is dangerous and you are new come to it.'

Elise summoned her confidence. She was a bit shaken; she wasn't foolish enough not to be. Still, she didn't want Dorian to see how exposed she felt. Danger was in motion, but she'd meet it as best she could without letting it rule her life. 'My father survived it and so shall I.'

Dorian's brows went up. 'Did he? As I recall, he's dead as a result of a freak boating accident.'

That was outside of enough. He was just being peevish now and those were cruel words. 'What are you insinuating?' Elise narrowed her eyes. It was just craziness, nothing more. He was angry with her; he didn't mean anything by it. But her brain sped up anyway, unearthing the thoughts she had tried so hard to stifle. Dorian couldn't possibly know how close to home the comment had struck, how many nights she'd lain awake, thinking the same thing. Only for her, it wasn't an angry shot in the dark.

'What do you think I'm suggesting?' His words were slow and measured, the anger going out of him. His face echoed the query, his brows drawn in question, his blue eyes sharp.

Elise shook her head. 'Nothing. It was merely your choice of words.' She was reading too much into a sharp rejoinder to an argument and words chosen in the heat of the moment.

'I disagree.' Dorian took up residence in a chair and settled in as if he didn't mean to budge. 'I think there's something you're not telling me.'

She said nothing. What she thought was almost too horrible to say out loud. But Dorian was far more stubborn and persistent than she'd given him credit for.

His voice was low and private, seductive almost. 'Tell me about that day, Elise. What happened? What do you know?'

'I know very little.' She studied her hands. The lack of detail regarding her father's death seemed like a great crime to her when it had occurred. Surely someone should know exactly what had happened. 'They were out in open waters. They'd wanted to try the new steam engine in rougher sailing than the Thames. The engine exploded. That's all. It was at sea, there was no one around.'

'They? Your father wasn't alone?' Dorian pressed.

'No, he was with a friend. The yacht was his and he'd wanted my father to test it.' She shook her head, anticipating Dorian's next question. 'There were no survivors. They were both lost. The only reason we know anything at all about the accident is because a nearby cargo ship saw the explosion and lowered a boat to investigate. A Captain Brandon was kind enough to pick up the bodies.'

'What else did he say?'

'There was nothing more to say. He said the yacht was in shambles, just pieces of wood really, by the time they arrived. It gave every indication of having exploded from the inside.'

'Steam engines blow up.' Dorian laced his fingers across the flat of his abdomen and stretched out his legs, giving the appearance of a man who had no intention of leaving his chair in the near future.

'Not my father's.' Elise bit her lip. She wished she hadn't spoken so hastily. She saw too late that that had been Dorian's plan. He'd meant to bait her with a statement she was loath to accept.

'It wasn't your father's boat.'

'My father would never have taken a boat out into open waters if he was not familiar with it,' Elise answered sharply. She drew a breath. 'I'm sorry. My mother says it's been hard for me to accept that a man with my father's skill would have been victim to an accident caused by his own ineptitude when he was an expert.'

Dorian did leave his chair then. He crossed the room to her and knelt before her, taking her hands. 'But you disagree?'

'Maybe it's just easier to disagree. Maybe thinking foul play was involved offers me the reasons I'm looking for to justify such a tragedy.' Elise sighed. 'There's been a lot of drama today.'

She said it as a way to excuse the conversation and move on, but Dorian seized the words as an opening. 'Exactly, Elise. There has been drama today—a fire. After a break-in. A break-in after an unlikely death. Perhaps your suspicions are not so far-fetched. Have you asked yourself the necessary questions? Who would have wanted to see your father removed? What could they have gained that would have required a death to achieve it? There's been a lot of drama in your life the last six months, all of it centered on letting go of this shipyard. Do you not feel it's more than coincidence?'

Elise pulled her hands free. She thought more clearly when he wasn't touching her. 'I think drama, as you put it, over the shipyard is a natural consequence of settling my father's affairs.'

'But we know Tyne is after the yacht at least. Why not the yard, too? I assure you he is definitely the sort to use extreme measures if there's enough on the line,' Dorian argued softly.

'Don't look at me like that,' Elise answered.

'Like what?' A little smile played on his lips.

Like I want to melt into your arms, lay

every trouble at your feet and forget every silly vow I've ever taken about swearing off the need for a man. 'Like you could solve my problems for me. I don't want that. I don't *need* that. I can solve my own problems.' Moments like this made her doubt it, though, made her want to find the easy road, and that was so very dangerous. Even if she did a need a man, Dorian wasn't precisely stable with his wandering ways and questionable lifestyle. He lived in her shed, for heaven's sake. But it was so easy to forget that in moments like this. He'd certainly been reliable today, acting swiftly enough to save the shipyard.

'We're getting away from the issue.' Dorian rose from his crouch. 'I understand how wild your thoughts must have seemed earlier. You had no idea who an enemy might have been. But now you do. You may not know the reasons, but you do know that Damien Tyne—a confirmed villain, I might add—has arranged a break-in and most likely was the mastermind behind the fire today. It is not beyond the scope of reason that he started this game with your father's death. That's something you could not have considered until recently.

It may be useful now with your new information to revisit your suspicions.'

'I don't know, Dorian. It seems useless to pursue it. There's nothing left of the boat. What remained has sunk to the bottom of the ocean. We'll never really know what happened.' She was right. Her thoughts and the conclusions they led to were too terrible to have mentioned. Thoughts became much more real when spoken aloud to someone.

'You're right. We'll never know,' Dorian echoed, his eyes on her. 'That's awfully convenient, isn't it?'

'Awfully.' It was positively horrific to think her father had been murdered—that was the only word for it if any of their suspicions bore merit—for a fast yacht and a shipyard.

Dorian reached for his coat on the coat tree, his voice quiet. The mood in the office was solemn, a far more sombre atmosphere than the more volatile one in which they'd arrived. 'I think we've had enough excitement for one day. I'll see you home.'

The gentleman was back, the mask of politeness and manners in place as surely as the return of his coat over those broad shoulders.

'I'm still coming back to work,' Elise said once they had settled in the carriage.

'All right,' he said quietly.

'All right?' Elise fired back, but there was little heat in it. 'I thought you were determined that I wouldn't?' After the disclosures this afternoon, she'd expected him to resist even more vehemently than before.

Dorian grinned, his first smile in an hour, and tucked his hands behind his head. 'I changed my mind, that's all. You should be pleased. You've got what you wanted.'

But he'd got what he wanted, too, and that's what had her suspicions on alert. He'd only capitulated because he'd seen a benefit in it. He laughed. 'What's the matter, Elise? Can't stand winning? Not everything has to be a fight.'

'But some things should be.'

'Before you go into battle, just remember I'm on your side.' Dorian winked. 'I don't get paid if that boat isn't finished.'

His humour was a startling reminder of yet another reality. That's all this was to him, of course. A job. She was part of the job, something she'd been apt to forget on occasion.

The word *we* had slipped into her vocabulary with alarming ease and stealthy regularity. When she thought of the yacht club's seasonal trip, she pictured them going together. When she thought of the upcoming races it was with Dorian at the helm of the new yacht, although they'd not spoken of it. These were especially dangerous fantasies and all because he'd kissed her and shown her pleasure beyond imagining. And, oh, how she wanted to feel that pleasure again! But that was setting herself up for disappointment because it could never be more than a fleeting satisfaction. She knew better and she had the experience to prove it.

The carriage rocked to a stop in front of her town house. Elise wished her thoughts would do the same. 'Do you still feel like being scandalous?' Dorian asked, handing her down.

She smiled. Her comment seemed hours ago in another lifetime devoid of mysterious fires and machete-wielding foremen. But her devotion to the claim hadn't diminished. If anything, circumstances had conspired to make her embrace that decision even more. 'Absolutely.'

'Then how about dinner with me tonight? I know a decent restaurant you'll enjoy. We should celebrate the yacht even if today wasn't perfect.' There he went again, acting more than the employee, more than the gentleman. This was the devastating rake who knew perfectly well the scandal he provoked by asking her to dine out and did it anyway.

She should say no. There might be more than a dinner on his mind. Their last dinner together had certainly led to more than dessert. 'You may call for me at seven.'

She was very aware she'd said yes for all the reasons she should have said no. He had her spinning; there was no doubt about it. He was a gentleman, a rogue, a pirate all rolled into one enticing package. She wondered which one would pick her up tonight?

Picking Elise up at seven was something of an illusion. *She'd* sent the carriage for him at half past six and now it would make the return journey to her town house. Usually, it irked him to be so reliant on a woman's hospitality.

It made him feel like a kept man. But tonight, Dorian was happy to let the illusion lay. He needed all the reasons he could come up with to keep her near him. Dorian flicked a speck of dust from his green jacket and settled back against the squabs.

Tyne would come after her. Elise's inability to believe it would not prevent it from happening. She was a rock through a town house window away from finding out he was right. He'd relented on her return to the shipyard because it served his purpose. He could continue to work on the yacht and keep an eye on her. Tyne would be hard pressed to get to her if she was at the office. Tyne would have to go through him first and, for now, Tyne was loath to do that.

Having her at the shipyard had *nothing* to do with actually wanting her there. She was bossy and dictatorial. She'd try to poke her nose into everything just when he had a system established. Dorian laughed out loud in the empty carriage. He could tell himself all he wanted that these precautions were for the sake of protecting the boat. This boat would be his way of getting back at Tyne for the

Queen Maeve. But that wasn't the whole truth. Elise Sutton had got under his skin in a most novel and intriguing way.

They'd quarrelled today after the fire and much that he'd meant to say had gone unsaid. The quarrel had sidetracked his intent. He hadn't scolded her for staying. In retrospect, it was for the best. He'd been furious she'd tried to fight the fire, to put herself in harm's deliberate way like that. He'd been furious because he'd been frightened for her, *by* her. She was fighting for her dream. She was strong in the face of adversity. He didn't want to like her, but he did. She didn't deserve any of the things that were happening and she didn't deserve him.

If he did care for her, what could come of it? She wasn't his usual sort of woman. If she knew the things he'd done, if she knew he wasn't much better than Tyne, she'd have nothing more to do with him. Her brother, William, hadn't known the half of it when he'd made his acquaintance. William thought he was the usual sort of rake, a gentleman who'd had an adventure or two. Young William would be furious, but Elise would feel betrayed.

She would be right to feel that way. He'd probably frightened away Charles, her very decent suitor who could have been brought up to scratch if she'd followed the rules. But Elise had opted for scandal instead of obscurity. His fault, too. He'd awakened her passions, her hopes, and when those crashed he'd be far away, in Gibraltar with a new ship beneath him, starting over.

That was the plan at least. There were holes in it, such as where he was going to come up with a new ship if he couldn't romance the yacht out from under her or convince her to give it to him. He'd convinced a pasha's daughter to give him the secret password to her father's arsenal once. He'd stolen the arms and resold them to the pasha's enemy. Surely he could coax a little yacht out of Elise Sutton. But there was the fact that he liked her. He hadn't much cared for the pasha's daughter. He was back to that again—liking was a damnable thing.

He was starting to have crazy thoughts—what would Elise think of Gibraltar? Recently, he'd started imagining her at his place in the hills overlooking the beach, taking her down the winding stairs to the beach at sunset, letting the water lap against their bare toes, making love in the sand. She could build her boats. Would that be enough for her? Enough to convince her to tie her fate to the Scourge of Gibraltar, a smuggler *extraordinaire* in his own right? Right now, it was simple enough to dream. There was no need to expose realities. They were together for a few short weeks; there was no need for details between them. But if he wanted more, he'd have to tell her all that he was.

At the town house, Elise made him wait, leaving him plenty of time to cool his heels in the drawing room studying the art. Her father had a decent nautical collection full of windswept seas and tilting boats in addition to the Turner in the hall. Skirts rustled at the door and he turned, his breath hitching at the sight of her.

Tonight, she'd chosen a gown of deep red with black velvet and jet beads for trim. It moved and shimmered with her in the light.

The ruby pendant at her throat glowed against the pale backdrop of her skin, her dark hair the perfect foil. Dorian took her hand and kissed it. 'You look like an Italian *signorina*, which suits my plans all the better.'

She looked up at him from beneath her lashes, a most coy gesture. 'It sounds as if you mean to seduce me.'

His groin tightened in reflex. Nights were much more exciting with her than their days: less sparring, more passion.

'Perhaps I do,' Dorian replied. 'We'll see how the evening goes. Have you ever had Italian food?'

Chapter Thirteen

Italian food. Yet another thing she'd never done, and most certainly, she'd never done it *this* way—dining out in Soho. Elise took Dorian's hand and stepped down from the carriage into the crowded *mélange* of the neighbourhood.

It was hard to believe they were still in the West End of London. The Soho area had a cosmopolitan feel to it that was entirely foreign to the stiff English uniformity of Mayfair's wealthy citizens. London's rich had forsaken Soho almost fifty years ago, leaving it to the immigrants who would make a home for themselves away from home. As they walked, the languages of Europe swirled around them. Elise laughed up at Dorian at one point, 'There's so much French being spoken here, I feel like we're in Paris!'

'We're to be Italian tonight, remember?' Dorian grinned. 'But perhaps we can be French the next time we come.'

The next time. Her heart gave an irrational trip of excitement. There was a wealth of promise and commitment in those words he tossed off so casually. Did he mean for there to be other nights like this one? And what did *that* mean? She knew what it didn't mean. He *wasn't* courting her. Dorian Rowland wasn't the courting type. Yet, he was investing time in her, time that went beyond an employee's obligation. It made her wonder what he wanted and what she'd give in return.

'Ah, here we are.' Dorian ushered her towards a little restaurant with three arched windows with a sign reading 'Giovanni's.' The immigrant population of Soho had taken good advantage of the growing penchant for dining out and opened eateries showcasing the foods of their native homes. Giovanni's was no exception: an Italian trattoria lodged between a French bistro and a German delicatessen.

Elise stepped inside and was immediately

wrapped in the enticing smells of tomato and basil, garlic and fresh baked bread. A dozen tables draped in white cloths with candles in red jars to mute the light filled the room, all of them occupied with patrons and enormous bowls of pasta. Elise closed her eyes and breathed deeply, taking a mental picture complete with scents. She felt adventurous and decadent in her red dress and she wanted to remember this moment, being here in this exotic neighbourhood with this exciting man beside her. Moments like this, experiences like this, had been rare in her life. Her world had been far smaller than she'd realised. 'It smells divine. What is it?'

'Spaghetti bolognese,' Dorian whispered at her ear. 'Giovanni makes it on Wednesdays and Sundays. It is his special dish.'

The kitchen door swung open and an enormous black-haired man swathed in a great white apron burst through, arms outstretched. There was only a moment's warning before he embraced Dorian, kissing him soundly on both cheeks. *'Buona sera, mi amico.'* More loudly, he called out, *'Che Capitano Dorian!'*

'It is good to see you, Giovanni.'

'You have brought a pretty *signorina*,'

Giovanni said in broken English, turning his attention her direction.

'Allow me to introduce Miss Elise Sutton. Her father has the yachtworks over at the Blackwell Docks.'

'It is my pleasure,' he effused. 'Come, take the table in the window, Capitano Dorian.' He led the way towards the one empty table in the little establishment.

'The best table, Giovanni?' Dorian teased. 'A beautiful woman is always good for business, *si*?'

'Ah, you wound me, *capitano*.' Giovanni put a hand over his heart. 'I would seat you at the best table always, even if you came alone.' He cast a quick look over his shoulder towards the kitchen. 'I'll send Luciano with a little bread and a little vino. But for me, I have to go back to work. There is always business, no?'

'Do not worry.' Dorian smiled in assurance. 'I will be here a while. There will be time to catch up later, my friend.'

'How do you know these people?' Elise asked once Giovanni had left.

'I know them from my adventures in Naples,' Dorian said evasively, conveniently saved from disclosing more by Luciano's timely arrival with fresh bread, olive oil and wine.

'Is this a *taurasi* of your uncle's?' Dorian sniffed the wine while Luciano beamed.

'Of course, *capitano.* Only the best for you.' Luciano poured two glasses after Dorian gave it his approval.

'A *taurasi* is a red wine native to Naples,' Dorian explained to her. 'Giovanni's brother has a vineyard there in the hills above the city. Every region has its wine. Tuscany has its *chianti*, but Naples has its *taurasi.*' Dorian lifted his glass to Luciano. 'Send my compliments to your uncle.'

Luciano inclined his head. 'I will. He will never forget how you saved them.' He looked at Elise. 'Do you know what he did for my uncle? There was a poor harvest one year and money was short. We had no way to get our wine to market to make back our money. No captain would take our casks with only a promise of future payment. But Capitano Dorian took the casks and he got the best price we've ever had. He saved us. My uncle would have lost everything. For that, his money is no good here. We will feed Capitano

Dorian for life as long as he is in England and not haring off on dangerous—'

'That's quite enough, Luciano.' Dorian held up a hand good-humouredly. 'Miss Sutton will get the wrong impression. I am sure you have other patrons to wait on.' He sent Luciano on his way, but Elise wouldn't let it go, especially not after that piece of insight. Assisting a vintner didn't seem like the usual activity for the Scourge of Gibraltar, but he'd been a long way from Gibraltar. Such a piece of information made her hungry for more.

'You're not getting off that easily.' Elise fixed him with a sharp look. 'I believe we were discussing how you know this family before Luciano arrived. What were you doing in Naples in the first place? Italy is a long way from Gibraltar.' It must be quite a story, she reasoned, to have earned a gratitude which spanned Europe. She was intrigued, too. She'd not known his interests, whatever they were, extended so far east.

Dorian shook his head. 'I doubt there's anything about those adventures you actually want to hear, Elise. Try the bread.' Dorian dipped a slice into the olive oil dribbled on a plate and held it up to her lips. 'Now, try the wine,' he coached.

Elise drank, acutely aware of Dorian's eyes on her as she swallowed. 'You will tell me nothing?' she said, meeting his gaze.

'Tonight is about the future, Elise.' A small, private smile flitted on his lips. He raised his glass. 'I would offer a toast. To the boat, Elise. May this be the first of many nights we toast its victories and milestones.'

Elise touched her glass to his, momentarily overcome with emotion. He was intoxicating like this—wine, candlelight and words that spoke the very thoughts of her own mind.

She drank to the toast and set her glass down. He'd adroitly shoved aside the personal in lieu of business, a reminder that perhaps he had bandied about his earlier words with carelessness. 'Since we have a better idea of when we'll be done, I can start contacting potential buyers. I have a list of my father's clients who may be interested. We can use the opening trip as a chance for them to join us on board.' In her mind, she was already planning that event. They would need cheese and wine and cold meats, maybe even champagne. Planning the event and writing the letters would take considerable time. She had her father's lists. But the idea of selling the yacht left an empty pit in her stomach. This was silliness. Selling the yacht was her plan, the *key* to her plan. She couldn't get sentimental now. Warm hands closed about hers, stilling her thoughts.

'Stop, Elise. Your mind is going a thousand miles an hour.' Dorian gave a soft laugh. 'It's a bit soon to think of selling the yacht. We should name it first.'

'Heavens, no! That will only make it worse.' Elise cringed. 'It's like naming a cow you have to slaughter for beef.'

'That's a very colourful way to look at it.' Dorian chuckled. Then he sobered and cocked his head to one side, studying her with those mesmerising blue eyes of his. 'Why sell it, Elise? Why not keep it? People can still purchase yachts built like it from you.'

He really could read minds. She took a sip of her wine to cover her agitation. 'Selling the yacht is part of the plan. You know it is. I need to sell the boat to raise money to make other boats and to get the word out that we are back in business.'

Dorian gave her an assessing nod. 'That may be. I think it's too soon to tell yet. There might be other options.' He slid the last of the delicious bread in her direction.

'What other options?' Elise sopped up the remaining olive oil with the slice, trying not to let her curiosity give away her interest. Could she save the boat? It would be an ideal solution and he made it sound easy. She'd learned to be wary of easy, though. There must be a catch.

Dorian shook his head. 'Not tonight, Elise. Tonight is about pleasure first and right now we have pasta to enjoy.' He gestured towards Luciano, who was bearing an enormous bowl of spaghetti with the bolognese sauce on top. Another man followed behind with a plate of Neapolitan meatballs.

'We'll never eat all of this.' Elise laughed, watching Luciano set down the bowl with effort.

'You'll never know until you try.' Dorian winked and dug in, undaunted by the size of the serving.

As they ate, he told her of Italy, the food loosening his memories and the wine his tongue, although Elise understood implicitly these stories were carefully vetted. Still, if it was all he would share of himself, she'd take it. He told her of foods and wines and cheeses, and lazy afternoons spent in hillside villas, of evenings roaming the seaside towns. 'More English will discover Italy in the near future, mark my words. But for now, it remains blissfully unanglicised.'

'*I* want to discover it,' Elise said. She meant it. The stories had transfixed her, as had the man telling them. She'd love to have listened to more, but the restaurant was emptying of patrons and still they lingered over the pasta.

Dorian nudged the last meatball in her direction. 'Yours.'

'I can't eat another bite.' Elise put a hand to her stomach.

'You'll have to eat dessert. Giovanni will be offended and his tiramisu is extraordinary. And you haven't tried the *vin santo* yet.'

Elise feigned a groan. 'I won't fit into any of my dresses.'

Dorian leaned across the table with a wicked smile. 'That's easily solved. We'll keep you out of them.'

Her blood boiled at such a thought—of Dorian slipping the gown from her shoulders, his hands on her bare skin as the silk slid to the floor. The wine, Dorian—perhaps both had made her a wanton. She wanted nothing more than what he described, she realised with shocking clarity.

'What? Nothing to say to that, *mio cuore*?' Dorian said in low tones.

'No.' She smiled. 'Absolutely nothing.'

Despite her protests, dessert was served. Luciano brought *vin santo*, a sweet wine.

'Are you trying to get me drunk?' Elise sipped from her tiny glass.

'I did promise to seduce you.'

'You said you'd think about it,' Elise teased.

'And I have. I've been thinking about it all night.' Dorian's eyes had darkened. She'd seen that look before. Her stomach did a little flip. As if on cue, Luciano appeared, violin in hand, and began to play a slow adagio, one of Vivaldi's.

Elise shot Dorian an accusatory glance. 'I feel immensely outgunned.'

Dorian shrugged. 'What can I say? The Italians are people of great passion. When they see a man with a beautiful woman, they naturally assume it is love. Will you dance with me, *mio cuore*? I wouldn't want to waste the music.'

He rose and held out his hand. She had

to take it. It would be the height of insult to deny the great captain in his own territory. She could only imagine what Giovanni would do. Slowly, Elise stood, half-fearful the wine had affected her legs but there was no need for such worry. Her legs held.

Dorian drew her to him. His hand was at her back, his other hand holding hers, her own hand resting at his shoulder, but this was to be no typical waltz. He held her far closer than she'd ever been held in any ballroom. Their thighs met, her breasts brushed the front of his jacket. Dorian began to move them. They swayed more than danced, turning in a small square instead of motions that took up an entire floor.

'Is this really a dance?' Elise murmured. But she had no complaints. It felt wonderful to be held in his arms, to be so close to another. She could smell the faint vanilla of his cologne, the cedar sachets that had protected his clothes in a chest. He was starting to smell familiar. She would forever associate these smells with Dorian Rowland. 'It seems more like an excuse to be together.'

Dorian's warm chuckle was near her ear. 'So it does. A pretty good excuse, wouldn't you agree? I like holding you, Elise.' There was no mistaking the low tones of want in his voice, or the hard thrust of his erection against her leg. She could have him, could have the pleasure again if she would accept the veiled invitation.

There needn't be any complications. Dorian wasn't the sort to deal in complications. He lived in the moment; he was offering her the same opportunity. After months of looking beyond the moment, it seemed like heaven. She'd promised herself not to make the same foolish mistakes she'd made over Robert. She was being true to that promise. What simmered between her and Dorian wasn't anything like it at all.

'Elise?' The sound of her name, low and seductive, sent a *frisson* of desire down her spine so strong she nearly trembled. 'Do you want me?'

She licked her lips. 'Yes.'

Chapter Fourteen

Elise settled herself in the carriage, her body thrumming with a delicious anticipation, her eyes on Dorian. The whole night had been leading to this. Perhaps they'd been leading to this since the first day when his body had pressed against hers in the street.

Every touch, every look, every illicit kiss, the wicked delight at Vauxhall, now served in retrospect as a prelude, arousing her curiosity until there was no other choice but to satisfy it about one question above all others: what would it be like to be with a man such as Dorian Rowland? A man who was not constrained by society or its expectations, a man who lived outside the rules? Now, miracle of all miracles, he was willing to answer that very question and she was going to let him.

Why not? There'd been no one beyond Robert Graves who'd grabbed her attentions in the nearly six years she'd been out. Her choices were limited to the staid likes of Charles Bradford and his ilk. If that were to be her lot, why not seize this chance to see what lay beyond such offerings? If there weren't any offers from the Charles Bradfords of the world, then her logic held doubly so. And, by heaven, she was going to enjoy her one night, no matter what society said. This brash, handsome man was about to be hers. For a little while at least. Dorian Rowland would never truly belong to anyone. He was too reckless, too wild, to be tamed and claimed. Perhaps she'd start with his cravat, pulling it slowly from his neck. At Vauxhall they'd been rushed by the overwhelming energy of their passion and more than partially clothed. Tonight there would be no hurry. Tonight there'd be no clothes. She was wet already, just thinking of it.

'You're staring.' Dorian's voice was husky, his eyes burning.

'I was thinking about undressing you,' she

confessed, her bold words only somewhat surprising her. She'd always been forthright in other aspects of her life—why not in this aspect, too? The unknown had not stopped her before from experimenting with copper fastenings below the waterline on a boat. Tonight should be no different. She was simply trading waterlines for belt lines.

'Ah, very good.' Dorian stretched his legs across the carriage and leaned back, utterly relaxed. 'We are of the same mind, then. I had you down to your chemise. How far did you get with me?'

'Your cravat.' It hardly sounded decadent now.

'We'll have to do better than that, unless of course you planned to tie me up with it before you undressed the rest of me.' The husky gravel of his voice acted like a friction on her body, caressing it from a distance. Her nipples hardened, her core wept. It would take the merest of touches, she was certain, and she would shatter as she had in the pleasure gardens.

'Would you like that, Elise? Would you like to have me at your service, naked and bound, existing only to pleasure you? Some women, bold women like you, enjoy such games. There is no shame in it. Others like games of possession where they can be the one who is controlled. Would you like to be my captive, Elise? Shall I come to you some time as your master and bend you to my will? I like games, Elise, and I would like playing them with you.'

She bit her lip to keep from crying out. Such games did appeal to the boldness within her. Her blood was hot from the images conjured by his words. Surely she would explode now. It was all she could do not to tear her clothes off in the carriage, waiting for the decency of her bedroom be damned. She didn't want to be decent, she wanted to be ravished.

Dorian was beside her in a fluid movement she almost missed, his hand gently cupping the curve of her jaw, a delicate kiss on her lips at odds with the rather indelicate discussion. 'Trust me, you don't want our first time to be a jolting carriage, no matter how fine the squabs. It won't be much longer now, *mio cuore*. We're nearly there. How shall I come to you?'

She knew what he meant. There was still the issue of logistics. Evans would have waited up and her maid, Anna, too. There was no question of Dorian marching up the stairs to her room or even stepping foot inside the house. She might have chosen to live scandalously, but that did not mean she could choose that for her staff. 'Use the garden gate in the back,' she whispered, trying to clear her mind of Dorian's decadent images long enough to formulate a plan. 'It will give me time to send away my maid. But how to get in?' She was having difficulty forming any rational thought.

'Don't worry, I shall be inventive.' Dorian chuckled.

'And shall I?' Elise asked. For all her bold willingness, she wasn't sure what her approach should be. They'd talked of undressing each other, but perhaps he'd prefer she already be naked, waiting for him.

The carriage drew to a halt. Dorian kissed her again, a private kiss full of promise. 'Do nothing but wait for me, *mio cuore*.'

The door opened and Dorian jumped out first, the gentleman once more as he handed her down. 'Elise,' he said quietly at her ear as she passed, a little reminder that he only looked like a gentleman. 'Don't worry. I know exactly what you want.'

Dorian eased open the garden gate. He'd told the coachman he wanted to walk and, after a decent interval to give the man enough time to make it back to the mews, Dorian had begun his own approach.

He did know what Elise wanted. She wanted the wedding night. She might be open to the more wicked games they could play, but she didn't want them tonight simply for that reason. They were so obviously games and while they were arousing and carried their genre of lusty satisfaction, they were not *romantic*. The fantasy she wanted was more oblique. The lines between fiction and reality could blur. She could pretend for a while all was genuine. And it might be.

Dorian searched the garden for something to use as an improvised ladder: trellises, vines, even a real ladder left by an errant gardener. He wasn't set on *having* to use an improvised ladder. He was happy enough to climb a real one. Improvised ladders were highly overrated in Gothic romances. A light flared in a window. Good. Her room was at the back of the house and, glory of all glories, it had a small Juliet balcony that arched out with enough room to accommodate a single person looking out into the garden. She'd forgotten to mention that bit of luck.

Such an omission of details was hardly surprising given her state when she'd left the carriage. She wasn't alone. He'd forgotten to ask such an elementary question. This wasn't the first woman's house he'd stolen into. But if she'd been aroused to the point of shattering—and she was, he could see it in her eyes when the carriage lamp had caught them, her pupils had been dilated wide—then he was as hard as timber.

Dorian's eyes lit on the shadowy outline of a wall trellis. He could climb it and pull himself up on the balcony. He crossed the garden and gripped the lower rungs, pausing before he made the ascent, the words *and it might be* haunting him. Elise wanted him, that much was true. He didn't doubt she knew her own mind on that issue. He *did* doubt if she understood the reasons for it. Tonight, she believed she wanted him to satisfy some physical curiosity. He could give her the night *and* the satisfaction, but heaven help her if she changed her mind in the morning. He understood, even if she did not, all else that had gone before had been extended foreplay, leading them to this consummation. *Consummation.* That, too, was a wedding-night word and one his body was all too eager to engage in. Well, he could certainly engage. He would make this good for her. Tonight he would be her bridegroom. The bottom line was, he wanted Elise Sutton and he'd deal with the morning when it came. With that in mind, Dorian began to climb.

The trellis held, although there was a questionable moment or two when he reached the top. There was a bit of irony in that; the higher one climbed, the weaker the trellises seemed to get. But he didn't want to contemplate such irony when he was hanging twenty feet above a rock-hard garden not completely thawed from winter. A fall would be unpleasant at this juncture, although it would undoubtedly dampen his libido.

Dorian reached over his head and grasped the iron railings of the balcony. With a strength born of years at sea hauling cargo and nets, he levered himself up until he could hoist himself over the railing. He took a moment to catch his breath before knocking softly on the French doors. He pushed the doors open and laughed at her quickly stifled gasp. She'd been startled. 'Who else were you expecting?'

'No one, of course. I just didn't expect...' Her words fell off and she made a little gesture with her hand to fill in the gap. Words were useless to describe the sight of Dorian Rowland standing in *her* bedroom, stripping out of his coat and making himself at home.

'You actually came.' Elise gave voice to the little fear that had niggled at her in the interim since she left the carriage. Would he change his mind? 'You climbed the trellis for me.' She was amazed he'd done it. That trellis was *old*. He could have broken his neck.

'How did you expect me to get up here?' Dorian moved towards her, taking her in his arms, his touch raising delightful prickles of sensation on her skin. 'Don't tell me there's an easier way. The rung at the top of the trellis is about to go.' Not all that different from him, if the bulge in his trousers was anything to judge by. It would be unseemly to mention she'd noticed such a thing, but it was comforting to know she wasn't in this alone.

'I will tell the gardener to have it fixed immediately.'

'The gardener can wait, but I can't, not any longer,' Dorian growled, sealing her mouth with his. In that kiss, he became the sum of her world. She could taste him, smell him, feel him. His hands were in her hair, searching for the pins that held her coiffure. He released her dark waves one by one until they cascaded over her shoulders, his fingers combing through them while he kissed her face, her throat, the place at the base of her neck where her pulse beat, a veritable drummer beating out the rhythm of her passion.

'I promised to undress you, Elise,' he murmured, moving to her back, hands swiftly undoing the tiny buttons marching down her spine. A button popped and he blew out a frustrated breath. 'This gown would drive a bridegroom insane, Elise.' He nipped at her ear, the last button finally free. His hands skimmed her shoulders, warm and confident as they pushed the material down until it slithered past her hips and to the floor.

'Turn around, Elise, let me look at you.' She turned and he took her hands, drawing her arms away from her body, a gesture that made her feel deliciously exposed. His breath hitched at the sight of her and she took pleasure in the effect. She was not without her own power here.

He turned them towards the long mirror in the corner of her room and positioned her in front of him, his voice low and naughty as his hands cupped her breasts through the linen of her chemise. 'Look at yourself, Elise. See how the lamplight outlines the curves of your breasts, see how they fill my hands, see how the dark press of your nipples strain against the fabric when I touch them?'

And she did see. The sight of the woman in the mirror in the early throes of passion was wanton and intoxicating, made even more powerful by the presence of the man behind her, coatless, his hair loose, his hands upon her, his eyes on the shadowy silhouette of her mons. 'You're a veritable Venus,' Dorian whispered huskily. 'Let me worship.'

He turned her and went to his knees, sculpting her with his hands on his way down, pressing a kiss to her navel through the linen of her chemise. Her own breath hitched as he neared her mons and then she exhaled with a tiny moan of disappointment when he passed over it. 'Later,' he vowed.

'Toes next. Now, my lady, you must sit for this next part.' He nudged her towards the bed and she went willingly. 'I'll need a moment to gather my supplies.' He rose and fetched the basin and ewer from her washstand, snatching up a small vial of lavender at the last moment.

'What are you doing?' She'd followed him with her eyes, watching every movement.

'Trust me. You'll like this and I haven't been wrong so far.' Dorian grinned. He knelt at her feet, taking her foot in his hand. 'Stockings next, I think.' He looked up at her, watching her breath catch as his hands disappeared beneath her pantalettes. He found the ribbons that held the stockings by touch, her skin warm against his hands. He rolled the silk down slowly, caressing the slim shape of her calf on first one leg, then the other until her feet were bare to him.

He pulled the stopper from the lavender vial, letting the scent fill the room as he poured a few drops into the basin. 'Breathe deeply, Elise.' He mirrored the action with a deep breath of his own. He bathed her feet, massaging and tugging at her toes by turn.

'A woman's foot is so much more graceful than a man's and usually much better kept. Did you know the Turkish physicians believe massaging the feet opens up our body's channels for experiencing pleasure?' He gave a gentle pull. 'Especially the big toe. What do you think, Elise?'

Think? He expected her to think at a time like this? She was breathless when she answered. 'I think they were right,' she managed. His eyes darkened. Her response pleased him. She was starting to understand; her arousal was his arousal and right now he was on fire, the slim shape of her foot sliding through his hands, slick with lavender water, was an intoxicating metaphor for what his body would do with hers shortly.

'They say sucking helps, too.' His voice was nothing more than a husky rasp. He took her toe into his mouth, stroking it with his tongue until she went rigid with her want.

'Dorian, please.'

'Not yet, I promised to undress you. We are not completely there. But this will help. Raise your arms.'

Dorian pulled the chemise up over her head. Never had undressing felt so licentious, so erotic, her breasts freed at last to his full gaze. He gently pushed her back on to the bed and slid the pantalettes over her hips, his own member making its presence known where he bumped her thigh, a reminder that she wasn't the only one in need of undressing. His trousers had to go. Her hands went to his waistband, but he stalled them, covering them with his own. 'Wait. Tonight, let me.'

She turned her head to follow him as he rose, offering the simple instruction, 'Stay just like that, Elise, I want to watch you watch me.'

How could she not watch him? She was helpless to do anything else. He was mesmerising, stripping himself with fluid grace. His cravat, his shirt fell to the floor followed by his boots and finally, oh, finally his trousers, which had housed that most tantalising bulge all evening, were off. She'd thought him glorious at Vauxhall, but it was nothing compared to him fully revealed.

Elise reached for him, instinctively wanting to touch, to cup. 'Come to me, Dorian.' And he did, levering himself over her, his mouth trailing kisses between her breasts to the wet juncture between her thighs. He kissed her there inside the private folds and she burnt. Vauxhall had not been a one-time fantasy. Tonight proved the pleasure could happen again. She arched against him in invitation.

'Open your legs for me, Elise, cradle me, *mio cuore*.'

His eyes burnt with coal-like intensity, holding her gaze as he slid between her thighs. The intimacy of their bodies threatened to overwhelm her. There was a wild, primal beauty in lying like this with a man, with *him*. He'd worshipped her tonight: with wine, with food, with dance, with his touch and his kiss. He'd coaxed her body to a fevered pitch as she had coaxed his and now those fevers were about to be joined in one conflagration.

Dorian took her mouth in a hard kiss just as he positioned himself at her entrance and thrust, a deep penetrating motion. She gasped into his mouth feeling the pleasure of a man sliding home. He picked up his rhythm, her hips matching him of their own accord, the pleasure returning like a flower opening to the sun.

Elise closed her legs around him, holding him close, unwilling to let him slip away until she claimed her release. His name became a hoarse litany on her lips until speech became an impossibility. Words were replaced by sounds and still they soared into that sun and finally, at long last, when all thought had become obliterated, she burst into the radiance of that sun aware only of Dorian beside her, joining her in the piercing brilliance of the moment.

Chapter Fifteen

Three simultaneous thoughts crowded Elise's waking moments the next morning. The first was that Dorian was gone. She didn't have to open her eyes and look around to know. She could *feel* the absence of him, which was a good thing because her second thought was that it hurt too much to do anything else like open her eyes. *So* he had been trying to get her drunk her last night. She'd been right and now she had proof. Her head ached, it hurt to open her eyes, her tongue felt thick and there was a dreadful taste in her mouth.

It was impossible to even imagine doing anything about those conditions since all solutions required sitting up—a monumental feat at present. The third thought was that it was unusually bright in her room. Against her better judgement, she did hazard one open eye to see the cause of it. Better judgement had been right. That was a bad idea. Even opening one eye hurt. But she had her answer: sunlight. Not that she was opposed to sunlight. Normally, she'd have been thrilled to wake up to a sunny morning in early spring. Goodness knew they were rare enough. But it was unfortunate the London weather gods had decided *this* morning had to be one of them. Unfortunate, too, that Dorian had left the doors to her little balcony open and now the sun streamed through. However, it did bring a smile to her lips to picture Dorian climbing down from her balcony.

The trellis rung! He'd mentioned it wasn't stable last night. A moment's worry crossed her mind. Elise tried to push it away. If he'd fallen, she would have heard him. Right? She wouldn't have heard a thing, not in her current state. She should go check and see if he was lying in her garden, if only she could move.

Elise risked another peep, this time at the white porcelain clock on her bedside table, and groaned. She was going to have to find a way to move. It was after ten o'clock. The morning was more than half over. She was late for the office and there was so much to do. By the time she got to the shipyards it would be noon.

Elise gave herself fifteen more minutes of recovery before ringing for Anna. She congratulated herself on being upright when Anna arrived, bearing a tray of hot chocolate and a morning pastry. Elise thought her stomach might be able to tolerate that much. She could use the need to get to the shipyard to circumvent the breakfast that would be laid out for her downstairs. The merest thought of eggs and ham was enough to turn her stomach just now.

Anna made cheery chatter as she bustled around the room, laying out clothes. The chatter did nothing for Elise's head. At one point, Anna stooped to pick up the red dress from the floor and shake it out. Elise tried not to look overly interested in the process.

'You should have called me, miss. I would have come back up to help you undress. And look, there's a button missing. I don't know how you got out of this by yourself with all the buttons down the back. We're probably lucky you didn't lose more than one.'

'It was late. I didn't want to wake you,' Elise mumbled into her cup of hot chocolate. She could feel her face blush, her mind a riot of memories as to how that dress had come off and what had followed afterwards. It was the one thing she'd avoided thinking about so far this morning. 'I want to wear the blue gown today.' Elise attempted to focus her mind on something else. She wasn't ready to contemplate the previous evening and she certainly wasn't going to do it under Anna's watchful eye.

Anna gave her a quizzical look. 'Are you all right, miss? You look a little heated.'

'My room got a bit warm last night.' That was an understatement. 'I opened the doors,' Elise offered hastily. Perhaps Anna would believe that also explained the absence of a nightgown. 'I've got to hurry now, though. I slept too late and I've got things to take care of down at the shipyard.'

If there was anything Anna disliked, it was a rushed *toilette*, and the mention of such a possibility did the trick, taking Anna's mind off any other awkward questions. Elise was feeling more herself by the time Anna finished. She looked slightly pale but, other than that, any telltale signs of her night of sin and dissipation were not in evidence.

Navigating the stairs and the short journey to the carriage proved it. Everyone greeted her as they did every morning. No one thought it odd that she eschewed breakfast, which she sometimes did, although not often. Her coachman helped her into the carriage and set off for the docks as usual.

It was something of a surprise to Elise that she didn't look different, nor did she feel different except for the headache and a bit of soreness between her legs. Such a momentous occasion should mark her in a more obvious way. But no one around her seemed to notice. For everyone else, it was another ordinary day. But it wasn't for her. Today was the first day after she'd slept with Dorian Rowland, the Scourge of Gibraltar. To her mind, this event posed a great divide: the time before and the time that would come. Nothing would ever be the same again.

Elise sank back against the squabs of the seat. What had she done? Her rationales last night had seemed solid enough, justifiable enough. This morning they seemed flimsy. Even if she lacked a logical understanding of the evening, she had enjoyed Dorian's seduction. Quite a lot. Perhaps that was what bothered her most. She *didn't* regret it. In fact, she thought she might even like it to happen again, and that was very naughty of her indeed. Of course, next time, they'd have to be more careful. They couldn't leave dresses around for Anna to find and she couldn't forget to put on a nightgown.

Elise stopped her thoughts right there. *Next time.* There wasn't supposed to be a next time and here she was planning it. She remembered very clearly one of her rationales was based on this being a one-time experience meant to satisfy curiosity. Only now there were other appetites begging to be fed. Next times were complicated. Next times implied a relationship which was absolutely not what she wanted with Dorian Rowland. *What* do *you want with him?* came the question.

I want him to build my boat, Elise answered staunchly in her mind. But her conscience wasn't appeased with a half-truth. *And?* it prompted.

And maybe I want to use him for sex. Then

she added hastily to her conscience, *There's nothing wrong with that. It's not as if anyone will know and it's not as if he'll mind.* There, that should satisfy.

How wicked she'd become in such a very short time. It was only yesterday she'd decided to embrace scandal and cast off her lavender gowns. Now, here she was recovering from a hangover and contemplating taking a lover on a more permanent basis. Of course, it was all Dorian's fault. No one knew how to be wicked better than him. All she'd done was change her gowns. Dorian had done the rest.

He was still doing it, too, Elise noticed once she was settled in the office. She'd glanced out the window and spotted him immediately in the yard, swaggering around in his culottes, chest bare, tools dangling from a belt slung at his hips, blond hair pulled back with a thong. She went hot at the sight of all that masculine beauty. There was a private, heady knowledge in knowing it had been hers last night, every intimate inch of it. Oh, yes, she was definitely using him for sex. It was a most liberating thought until her bloody conscience piped up again. *If you're using him for sex, what's he using you for?*

Sex. The answer came easily and obviously to her. A man such as Dorian liked sex, even needed sex. But what if sex *wasn't* the end for him, but the means? The means to what? There was nothing she had that he could possibly want. He technically outranked her if he cared to claim it. His family was richer than hers, again if he wished to claim the connection, while her shipyard teetered on bankruptcy. He wasn't looking to marry. There was absolutely nothing she had that he didn't also have. She was overthinking it. Perhaps sex was all it was for him, too. But she couldn't get one thought out of her head—*what if it's not?* What if last night had been calculated for something more than a romp in her sheets?

Which was why, in spite of her favourable thoughts about what had transpired the previous night, the first words out of her mouth when he came up to the office were, 'Did you get me drunk on purpose, knowing full well it would make me late to work?'

Dorian stopped in the doorway, his customary grin on his lips. 'Feeling a little tap hackled, are we?' Damn him for not showing a single side effect and he'd drunk twice as much as she. With a tan like his, he wasn't even pale. It wasn't fair.

'Well, did you?'

Dorian took off his tool belt and hung it on the coat rack. 'No. I'm sorry you're feeling poorly, though. Get some coffee in you and the worst will pass. I can send a runner over to a nearby tavern and get something if you like.'

Elise shook her head. She hated coffee. 'No. My headache's nearly gone. I had hot chocolate this morning.'

'Good, then we can proceed with business. I came up because we need to talk about…'

Elise drew a breath. *Last night.* Of course he'd want to talk about it. They would need ground rules. They would need to be clear on expectations or the lack of them before this could happen again.

'The rigging.'

Elise blinked twice. *The rigging?* He wasn't going to talk about last night? She couldn't decide what was worse. Actually talking about last night or not talking about it at all.

Not talking about it treated the incident as if it hadn't happened.

'Yes, the rigging,' Dorian repeated. 'I need to get the mast cut. Have you decided to go with cutter or ketch?'

'I think cutter.' Elise quickly redirected her thoughts from pleasure to business. 'I've been thinking since our earlier discussion...' *since the night you came to my house and we drank tea by the fire* '...that cutter rigging gives us the option for installing an inner forestay, which would be useful if someone was looking to sail the boat in both river currents or in the heavier weather of open water.'

'But ketch rigging is more minimalist. If there was an accident, the ketch rigging can go forwards with only the mizzen and headsail functional,' Dorian argued.

'My ships don't have accidents,' Elise countered. 'I don't build ships assuming they'll be destroyed. I build ships designed to win races first, limp home under their own power second. If you build for defeat, that's exactly what you'll get.'

Dorian smiled at her. 'Bravo, well said. Then the cutter rigging it is.' The compliment warmed her inexplicably. 'Now, is there something else you wanted to discuss?' His blue eyes were dancing and she had the distinct impression she was being teased.

'No. What gave you that idea?' Elise leaned back in the desk chair, steepling her hands and deciding to play along.

'You seemed startled that I'd come up to discuss rigging. Perhaps you anticipated us talking about something else?' Dorian crossed the room, skirting the desk and circling her chair.

'Such as?'

'Such as last night or tonight or tomorrow night?' Dorian's voice was low and private, caressing her as assuredly as a touch.

'I thought you might want to discuss the rules of our association since they seem to have changed overnight, literally.' Elise thought her reply was quite sophisticated, worldly even.

Dorian chuckled. '*You* thought *I* might want to discuss such things? Or is it you who needs to discuss it with me? I don't need rules, Elise. They ruin the spontaneity. For instance, if we had rules, I might not be able to do this.' He bent and nipped at her ear lobe, eliciting a gasp of startled delight. 'Or this.' His tongue flicked along the shell of her ear, tickling, teasing in its circuitous path.

It was positively wicked. She needed another word in her vocabulary. With Dorian, wicked was the new normal. He proved it by sliding to his knees in front her.

'Dorian, what are you doing?' Elise gave an undignified yelp at the feel of his hands running up her legs. 'Someone could walk in.'

'And see you sitting behind the desk? Fancy that. I'm sure no one *sits* behind their desk at work.' His thumbs were at the apex of her thighs, one on each side of her mound, stroking, teasing. 'They won't see me. The desk blocks all view of anyone who might be underneath it. Of course, they might think it odd you find ledgers so very exciting.' His head had joined his hands beneath her skirts, up her legs. He blew against her. 'It's up to you, Elise. What will an intruder see? A woman engrossed in her work or her pleasure?'

She'd always thought of herself as a person of good self-discipline, but the moment Dorian's tongue flicked along the furrow of her mons, she was lost. There was no doubt anyone who happened into the office would see a woman claiming her pleasure. Dorian's tongue moved up to lick across her pearl, teasing every last sensation from the little nub until Elise was entirely lost, her hands gripping the arms of the chair, her bottom sliding down ever further in the seat as Dorian conjured up a pleasure so intense she was helpless against it. Perhaps it was the risk of discovery; perhaps it was the host of physical sensations assailing her all at once. The arms of the chair were no help.

Her hands slid into Dorian's hair, anchoring and urging, her hands saying what she could not, words having escaped her abilities. *Hurry, hurry, take me there to the place where I will shatter.* There was fierceness now in his seduction. Dorian's breath came rapid between her legs, his own body trembling. His hands cupped her buttocks, sandwiching her between his hands and his mouth most intimately, and then it came, wresting from her a cry of elation while Dorian's head slumped against her thigh in satisfaction.

'Pleasure,' Elise breathed. 'They would see pleasure, but not much else considering how far I've slid in the chair.' Dorian chuckled contentedly, the rumble of his laughter muffled against her leg.

'Why are you doing this, Dorian?' She idly combed through his hair with her fingers, savouring the quietness of the moments that followed such an intense climax.

'Doing what?' Dorian murmured.

'Seducing me. Don't deny it.' She wished there was a cot in the office. She was feeling rather drowsy.

'I wasn't aware you were opposed to it.'

'I'm not. I just want to know why.'

Dorian lifted his head. 'I slept with you, Elise, because you're a desirable woman and, if my actions haven't made it clear, I'd like to do so again in the very near future.' A grin took his face. 'And you? Why are you seducing me?'

Elise smiled and gave him a taste of his own. 'If my actions haven't made it clear, I am using you for sex.'

Chapter Sixteen

What was he doing? Dorian checked his cravat one last time in the little cracked mirror he'd hung over his improvised washstand of two stacked crates. A white ewer and tin basin stood atop the structure, the ewer sporting a hairline fracture of its own running down the side. It wasn't enough to make the pitcher leak, but it was enough to claim a matched set—cracked ewer, cracked mirror, he liked to joke.

He could add himself to the set these days. He was cracked in the head the way he was mooning after Elise Sutton. He was Dorian Rowland, he didn't chase after any skirt. *They* chased after him. But here he was, digging out one of his three good outfits from his trunk, tying a cravat and haring off for supper with Elise.

Dissatisfied with his knot, Dorian yanked on his cravat and tried again. He never should have started calling her that. He should have stuck to Princess. He could hardly fault himself for pushing for first names. Any master of seduction knew using a first name early and often was a key component in convincing a woman of his genuine interest. Well, he'd certainly succeeded there. He'd seduced her and himself in the process.

What had started out as a game to position himself for the boat was rapidly turning into something more. He liked the haughty princess. He liked teasing her with his outrageous comments; liked coaxing her ever so subtly to push the boundaries of convention, and goodness knew he liked what they'd done today in the office. Her pleasure had been contagious and he'd been caught up in it as well.

Dorian grimaced at the reflection of his cravat. It wasn't perfect, but it would have to do. It had been a long time since he'd cared about the state of his cravat and even longer since he'd had a valet to tie it for him. While he'd been in the Mediterranean, he'd lived aboard his ship and done for himself, careful not to put himself above his men. This was just one more reminder that he had to caution himself when it came to Elise Sutton.

She had him caring about things that hadn't mattered, *wanting* things that hadn't mattered for quite a while. Three outfits were plenty. He'd gone months at a time without even needing *one* of them. But this evening when he'd gone to dress, part of him wished there was at least a different waistcoat to put on, one she hadn't seen before. He'd worn each of his outfits already: the one to call at her house that evening they'd drunk tea, the other when he'd called the afternoon he'd sent Charles Bradford on his way and the last to dinner at Giovanni's. Going to Giovanni's had been risky. Giovanni knew about him, could have spilled the entire sordid truth to Elise. Giovanni wouldn't have meant any harm. To Giovanni, he was a hero. But Elise would not see the heroics in the things he'd done. Why should she when his own father certainly did not?

Remember the plan, Dorian told himself, shutting the door to the shed behind him and whistling for Drago, who was turning out to be quite the guard dog. He was to convince Elise not to sell the boat. Then he was to convince Elise to sell or give the boat to him on generous terms. He'd pay her for it, he just didn't have the money upfront, something she could relate to.

Dorian stopped in the yard to rub Drago's head and stare up at the boat. It was really coming along. It would be every bit as magnificent as he'd imagined, perfect for running cargos in the Mediterranean, legal or otherwise. Of course, there was more money in 'otherwise'.

'Stay, guard the boat,' he told Drago. The yacht had to be completed for his plans to move forwards. If the boat were destroyed, his seduction would have been for naught. Well, not for naught, he'd rather enjoyed it. It wasn't as if it had been unpleasant work, or work at all, which was the problem. Genuinely liking Elise hadn't been part of the plan, but it was now. Although, she might not like him if he kept her waiting. She'd invited him to dinner and he was running late. The carriage had probably been outside already for a good ten minutes.

Dorian secured the gate and settled into the

carriage. He felt in his coat pocket to assure himself it was still there, a small gift for Elise. He might be the Scourge of Gibraltar, but he had enough breeding to know a man didn't show up for dinner empty-handed. Manners seduced just as surely as kisses.

His previous visits had been different. He'd been strictly an employee then, reporting on business. The gift was small, something from his travels, but it was all he had to offer. He was currently not a rich man, although once he could have dazzled her with silks and spices and jewels beyond compare. *And arms. Don't forget the arms.* A gun wasn't exactly an appropriate hostess gift. Then he remembered the pistol she'd wielded the first day they met. It had been bulky and unwieldy in her hands, too heavy for her. Maybe Elise *would* like a gun, a lady's pistol perhaps with a pearled handle, one that could fit in a reticule.

A lamp glowing through the lace curtains welcomed him when he alighted. Everything was as it should be, a quiet town house preparing for a quiet evening. No one could argue anything improper, Dorian thought as he climbed the stairs. There were other carriages in the street, taking people to evening entertainments. Not nearly as many carriages as there would be in a few weeks when the Season started. Then, this quiet square would be thronged. A man sat across the street, reading a newspaper on a bench near the key park.

If he hadn't been so absorbed in the mental exercise of picking out a gun for Elise, he might have noted how odd it was to be reading the newspaper on a park bench this time of night when the light was fading. As it was, Dorian didn't think much of it, his thoughts occupied with other things.

Elise was waiting for him in the drawing room, looking particularly lovely in a gown of deep turquoise, her hair drawn up high on her head with a few tendrils left to curl temptingly at her neck.

'Dorian, welcome.' She came to him with outstretched hands, the greeting warm and yet formal, just the right tone to strike in front of the servants, he thought, taking those hands and bending in to kiss her cheek, the kind of greeting close friends or family relations might exchange. What a hostess she would make, sitting at the head of some nobleman's table—or his table in the Gibraltar villa. What was he thinking? He couldn't ask her to sit at his table. He'd seduced her, but he couldn't keep her. It wasn't in the plan. This sudden change of feeling wasn't in the plan, either, and he didn't quite understand where it had come from, only that it was here. Elise Sutton had definitely become more than a physical interest.

Her eyes were alight with excitement. He knew instantly she had news, *good* news. 'Something has happened since I saw you this afternoon,' Dorian remarked. It must have been good because she was definitely recovered from any lingering effects of her hangover.

'Yes, and there's just enough time to tell you before dinner.' Elise went over to the console table against the wall and opened a drawer, taking out a paper. 'No machetes. My drawers aren't nearly as exciting as yours.'

Dorian grinned. 'Your drawers were plenty exciting this afternoon, as I recall.'

'And here I thought you were going to be on your best behaviour.' Elise handed him the paper, but not before the slightest hint of a blush stained her cheeks.

'What's the fun in that?' Dorian took the paper and scanned it, noting the seal of the Royal Thames Yacht Club at the top and the signature of the club president, Commodore William Harrison. 'You have membership? *You?*' He hadn't wanted to bring the subject up with her before, but if she meant to keep racing with them, she'd need membership with her father gone.

'I do.' She looked so pleased with herself, so lovely and smug he didn't want to bring her down. Yet it was so extraordinary and unlikely that they'd award membership to a female.

'How did you do it, Elise?'

'I simply signed my brother's name to the application and wrote a letter asking that the membership which my father had held be continued.'

Dorian smiled. His princess was inventive. 'Was there a reason William couldn't do it himself?'

'He's away at Oxford, it would take too much time to bother him.' She turned away to put the letter back in the drawer, but he sensed she was far more uncomfortable with that answer than she had been sharing her deception.

Dorian went to her, his hands at her arms. 'Tell me, Elise, will William be surprised to hear he's now a member of the Royal Yacht Club?'

'It hardly matters. The membership is paid and the deed is done. There's nothing William can do except cause unnecessary awkwardness.' She turned to face him, her arms twining about his neck, lips parted in invitation. 'I have champagne chilling with dinner to celebrate.'

'Then we shall celebrate.' But Dorian recognised her efforts for what they were—a distraction, a very lovely one, a very inviting one. She could not have made it plainer that she didn't want to talk about her brother. Interesting. He'd been under the impression they were close. But in his experience, one did not look gift horses in the mouth, one kissed them, except when stiff butlers might walk in at any moment to announce dinner. He'd wait and hope for better things when those butlers weren't around.

Fortunately, the butler and footmen made themselves scarce after laying the meal. Elise had arranged for the meal to be served *en famille* and had kept the fare simple: a roast, baby potatoes and carrots and fresh bread along with the promised champagne and a tray of cheeses and fruit at the ready, waiting on the sideboard for dessert.

The table had been thoughtfully prepared, too: two chairs situated close to one another, two single candles in silver holders instead of a massive, imposing candelabra. It was a daringly intimate setting. It made Dorian wonder if perhaps tonight she meant to seduce him. A most arousing thought indeed.

'I told the servants we didn't need to stand on ceremony tonight,' Elise explained, delightfully flustered for a moment.

'That's all right,' Dorian whispered huskily at her ear, his hand light but proprietary at her back as he ushered her to her seat. 'It's much more fun to sit on it.'

What a terribly bold comment. Elise wished she had some witty comeback but she came up with nothing but a pointed look that said she understood the naughty nuances. As far as she was concerned, he could sit on it, lay on it, jump on it, she didn't care which as long as they didn't talk about William.

Evans poured champagne before retreating

with the rest of the staff. Elise took a sip to cover her nerves. Ice-cold champagne was her absolute favourite, one of the few things she'd enjoyed about her Seasons in London. Dorian had guessed correctly that William would not approve. Her brother wasn't opposed to the yacht club, he just wouldn't see the need for it, not when he felt they should be closing the shipyard and moving on.

But Dorian wasn't as compelled to leave the subject alone. 'How is William doing with his studies?'

'He's doing fine. He loves it.' There'd only been the two letters since he'd left, but she justified their scarcity knowing he was busy. 'He doesn't have much time to write once he's immersed in his studies.'

Dorian laughed. 'Oxford must have changed since my time. Are you sure it's his studies he's "immersed" in and not some pretty tavern wench?'

Elise fixed him with a disapproving stare. She might be at odds with William over the shipyard, but he was her brother. 'I am sure. Not everyone goes to Oxford to carouse.' Still, she was a little surprised he'd gone to Oxford at all. He didn't seem the university type. Libraries and lecture halls seemed far too confining for the likes of Dorian Rowland.

'Everyone gets the education they need at Oxford, books or otherwise,' Dorian put in. 'There's no question of that.'

Elise leaned forwards. 'What kind of education did you get, Dorian?'

'Otherwise.' Dorian winked and she laughed. 'And it's served me well in my line of work.'

'Which is?'

'Building ships, sailing ships,' Dorian answered easily between bites of the meat.

'That's all? Just building and sailing ships? That's hardly scandalous.' It wasn't nearly scandalous enough to be so completely cast out of society. The candlelight was doing fabulous things to his hair, burnishing and shadowing all those golden hues.

'It is if you're the son of the Duke of Ashdon. Dukes' sons don't deal in trade or carpentry,' Dorian answered calmly.

'But you were a captain of your own ship. Surely that's enough to garner respectability and it's not as if you are the heir. Your father should have been glad you had turned your hand to something.' Elise wasn't going to let go of this chance to learn more about the socially exiled Dorian Rowland.

'Is reconciliation really so out of the question?' she asked softly. Her family had been everything to her and she missed it dreadfully now that it had fallen apart, everyone scattered to their own corners, living their own lives.

Dorian drained his glass. 'Yes. And we'll leave it at that. This is supposed to be a celebration.' He refilled their glasses. 'To the Royal Thames Yacht Club and the hopes of next season.'

And to the hopes they wouldn't mind too terribly much once they realised William had no intention of showing up at any of the races, Elise added silently. She was through the first hurdle. She had the membership. It was time for the second. She drew a deep breath. 'There's something else I hope we can celebrate tonight as well.'

Dorian's eyes glittered wickedly with indecent thoughts that made her shiver with anticipation. 'I am sure there is.'

Best to come straight out with it. 'I want you to captain the yacht on the opening trip.'

She'd made her decision once word had come of her membership application.

'Elise, do you know what you're asking?' Something clouded the glitter of his gaze.

'Yes, I am asking you to stay beyond your contract. We'd agreed you could go once the boat was done, but now I need you to stay. It's not for much longer than originally planned,' Elise argued gently. She really did need him to stay. It made sense. He knew the boat, every last timber of it. He'd be the only one to have taken it for a trial. He had no pending engagements to be elsewhere that she knew of. He'd mentioned nothing other than the need to pay back Halsey for the confiscated cargo.

'Elise, it's more than that.' Dorian shook his head, looking distinctly uncomfortable for the first time in their acquaintance. 'You're asking me to enter into society. Society and I parted ways a long time ago.'

'Perhaps it's time to re-enter,' she answered staunchly. 'What do you have to lose? If they've already rejected you for good, then nothing changes. But if they were willing to give you another chance, opportunities might open up.' She felt a bit dishonest here. She was hoping those opportunities might be with her shipyard. Perhaps he could be persuaded to stay on as master builder.

He reached for her hands, covering them with his grip, warm and firm. 'Elise, I'm not worried for me. I don't care what they think of me now or ever. I've made my choices. I am worried for you. Don't you see what association with me could do to you? All your plans will be for naught.'

'People know you're here already.' Something tugged at her heart to hear him speak so disparagingly of himself. 'Charles knows, and who knows who else knows by now that you're working at the shipyard?'

'A select group of yachters probably do know,' Dorian agreed. 'That's not the same as the whole of society knowing. It's also not the same as flaunting it in their faces. The yachting community might tolerate me being around behind the scenes, but to put me up on your deck in the role of captain would be to rub their noses in it. You need someone who will be good for business.'

Elise cocked her head to one side, considering. '*You* will be good for business. I am banking on you and all your notoriety,

Dorian, and of course a fast ship pays for all. No one will care if you'd stolen the Crown Jewels when the boat is as fine as ours.' She'd known it would be a hard sell. She shouldn't be surprised that he was proving so resistant. She *was* surprised she felt so very desperate inside when she'd had his measure all along.

Elise eyed the remaining champagne, just a bit in the bottle, but enough for what she intended. 'It seems like you could do with a little more persuading. Let's see what we can do about that.'

She knelt before him, hands at the fastenings of his trousers, pleased to note that he was rising for her already, his manhood roused at her first touch. Pleased, too, that he understood this was a game of sorts. She wanted to do this for him. It was as arousing to her to touch him, to take him like this, as it was for him to be taken. This was no literal act of whoring herself to get what she wanted.

Elise opened his trousers and took him in her hand, feeling the pulsing heat of him. 'You are so big.'

Dorian chuckled, sliding down in his chair to better position himself for her. 'That's what every man wants to hear, Princess.'

'I doubt every man is as well endowed,' Elise said coyly, starting to move her hand up and down his shaft, smoothing the bead of moisture from his tip over the entirety of his length. She reached for the bottle of champagne and glanced up naughtily at him while she poured the remnants over his length.

'That's a bit cold.' Dorian jumped a bit at the contact. She felt a moment's guilt.

'I know, but my mouth isn't.' She closed her lips over the head of his shaft, taking in the salt of him and the dry sweetness of the champagne all at once. It was a heady ambrosia made all the more delicious when mixed with Dorian's moans of approval. She worked him with her mouth, sucking and licking until she was sure all his reservations had deserted him.

He was pulsing and tense, she could feel the muscles of his thighs quivering with the effort to hold back, his hands clenching the sides of his chair, his back arching his body up to her. That's when everything shattered.

Literally shattered.

Her head flew up from between Dorian's legs and Dorian exploded from the chair with lightning speed. He raced towards the drawing room. She was steps behind, skittering to a stop at the sight of broken glass on the floor and flames from the destroyed lamp racing up the heavy curtains.

Oh, lord, her house was on fire.

Chapter Seventeen

Elise grabbed a vase, the first item she laid eyes on with any water in it, and doused the curtains with a splash, petals and all, to little effect. Dorian seized a section of the curtains that hadn't caught fire and yanked hard, bringing down the *portières* with a crash. 'Watch your skirts!'

Elise backed away just in time to avoid catching fire herself while Dorian smothered the flames with great stomps from his boots. The room filled with her staff, alerted to trouble by the commotion and already carrying buckets. Dorian shouted orders and the flames began to diminish. They were gaining on it. Five minutes later, they conquered it. She wasn't going to lose the house, but what a mess!

There was a jagged hole in the broken window, glass shards scattered on the floor and the curtains obviously beyond repair. Smoke and flames had damaged the hard woods where the curtains had landed. Dorian's decision had likely saved the house. If the flames had gone up the curtains to the ceiling, nothing could have stopped the fire from spreading. Smoke and water stained the furniture.

Elise began to make mental notes. Furniture could be cleaned and repaired, she'd need new curtains, and a carpenter to repair the floor and she'd need a new window. That would be the first priority. She could imagine what the house looked like from the street.

The neighbours! An involuntary gasp escaped her and she covered her mouth with her hand as if to try to hold it in. What must they think? With a shattered front window, there was no disguising the disaster. 'There will be no hiding this,' Elise mused out loud. Her eyes met Dorian's across the room where he stood by the broken window. 'Is there a crowd? Is it very bad?' she asked, hoping for the best.

Dorian's response confirmed the worst. 'Shall I get rid of them for you?' He didn't wait for an answer. He strode to the door and stepped outside. She could hear his commanding tones carrying down to the street. 'We're all fine here, just a rock that was kicked up by a passing carriage. You can go about your evenings. Thank you for your concern.'

'They're gone.' Dorian smiled when he returned inside, looking all the more handsome for the mess he sported. His hair was loose, his shirt mostly untucked from the waistband of his trousers—that was her fault, not the fire's.

Elise couldn't decide what would cause the worst scandal tomorrow: the fire or the fact that her neighbours would know without equivocation a man had been with her in the town house when it had occurred. Sensible neighbours would be thankful she hadn't been alone. Without Dorian, the house and perhaps theirs would have been lost. But Mayfair neighbours weren't sensible. They'd see only the breach of protocol in Dorian's presence instead of the luck.

'Elise, you're pale. Come with me. Evans can handle things from here for tonight. Mary will send a tea tray.' Dorian took her arm and she let him lead her away to a small sitting room at the back of the house. Now that the crisis had passed, she was starting to shake. A mixture of fear and anger swept through her. She was more than glad to turn the situation over to Dorian for the moment. She let him take the tea tray from Mary. She let him put a warm tea cup in her hands while she tried to formulate a coherent thought.

'Why would someone do this?' she said at last, the heat of the tea cup rallying her senses.

'You know who and you know why,' Dorian chided gently, fixing his own cup. 'What happened tonight is a terrible thing, but you can hardly be surprised. We've been waiting for the other shoe to fall since Tyne's thugs visited the shipyard, since the fuse was lit to ignite the tar barrels. Now it has.'

He paused and Elise waited for him to say the rest. 'I told you the day of the fuse fire we were lucky. The intent had been to scare us, not really to ignite the barrels. Tonight was about more than scaring us. Tyne is getting desperate. He wants this situation resolved soon.'

'I won't give him my boat. It would be fairly hard to anyway since he hasn't made an offer and technically I don't know it's him behind all this madness.'

'He agrees with you,' Dorian said solemnly. 'At this point he knows you won't give over the boat, not as long as you live. If you were dead, it might be an easier matter. There'd be no one left who cared what became of the boat.'

She looked up from her cup. 'No one except you.' It was true. William would gladly be rid of it and her mother had already washed her hands of it.

'There would be me. I'd rather it didn't come down to that, though.' Dorian took her hand. 'I want to go after Tyne. I want to confront him and put an end to this.'

Elise shook her head. She knew what he meant. 'I won't sanction murder over a boat, Dorian.'

'Think of it as self-defence. As long as he lives, you are not safe.'

'As long as I have something he wants, I'm not safe,' Elise amended. 'As soon as I sell the boat, I'm no longer of interest to him.' It would be imperative now to go forwards with plans to sell the yacht. The brief fantasy Dorian had invoked over wine and pasta of keeping the boat would come to an end out of vital necessity. There could no longer be consideration of any other plan.

'Don't be a fool, Elise. Tyne can live on revenge alone. Don't think for a moment he'll forgive you for thwarting him. It may not be as easy as you think to sell the yacht. Yachtsmen and sailors are a superstitious lot. If Tyne were to spread rumours about the boat, buyers would be thin on the ground.'

'Are you saying it's hopeless?' Elise challenged. 'I'm damned if I do and damned if I don't? I didn't take you for a fatalist, Dorian.'

She made to rise, but Dorian pulled her down. 'Not a fatalist, Elise, a realist. You don't know him like I do.'

'I would if you'd just tell me,' Elise snapped. Anger had overcome her fear. How had her life become so complicated that she was in her mother's drawing room, alone with a man and discussing the murder of another man who wanted her boat as if it were a casual item on a meeting agenda? 'You tell me nothing of yourself, nothing of our apparent common enemy and you expect me to take all my direction blindly from you. That has never been my way and it won't ever be my way no matter how good in bed you are.'

A horrid thought struck her. She rose, shaking off Dorian's hand. 'Is that what all this seduction has been about? Gaining my blind compliance? I suppose next you'll be offering to take the boat off my hands as a favour to lead Tyne away from me while satisfying some hidden agenda of yours!'

'You dare to talk about agendas and using people?' Dorian rose, too, eyes flashing. She'd pushed him too far in her own anger. 'I'm not the one who only an hour ago was using all of her seductive prowess to convince me to captain her boat. If anyone has been underhanded, it has been you! You're the one who has applied for yacht club membership by forging your brother's signature on the application. I've never been other than what I seem.' He held his arms wide in a gesture of transparency. 'What you see is what you get with me, Princess.'

'I did what I had to do,' Elise fired back. Dorian's eyes were blue coals of rage. He hadn't missed the implication that perhaps he'd been used along the way. Well, let him infer what he liked.

'Are you always that free with your favours, then?'

But not that. How could Dorian think such a thing? How could he *say* it? Her hand came up of its own volition, slapping him hard across the face, the sound of it a loud and unmistakable clap of skin on skin. 'Get out. I don't want to see you until the yacht is done. For both of our sakes, I hope you can finish ahead of schedule.'

'I can finish, Princess,' Dorian said with nasty innuendo. 'I will expect to be paid for my services.' Looking straight past her, he strode out of the room, shoulders square, head up as if he had nothing to be ashamed of.

And maybe he didn't except for those last words. Elise sank to the sofa, her heart hammering with the emotion of the quarrel. How had things become unravelled so fast? She hadn't meant to pick a fight with him. But the dam had burst and all the doubt had come rushing out, probably because the dam hadn't been well built in the first place. Perhaps this was what happened when one slept with a man one didn't really know and then tried to convince oneself the feelings were genuine. The truth was he'd been very blatant about not wanting to discuss his past. He'd been just as blatant about that as he'd been about not wanting to discuss their one night. What had he said? *No rules?* It couldn't get much clearer than that.

Tears started to burn in her eyes. She covered her face with her hands. She'd been so very foolish! It wasn't just sleeping with Dorian that had been foolish. It was everything else: thinking that what they'd done would mean something; that she could outwit the villainous Damien Tyne; that she could build this boat and salvage the business. All she had to show for her efforts was a broken window, a fire-damaged town house and a madman after her. And what had she done? She'd sent away the one man who could help her find her way out of this mess. Oh, *foolish* didn't begin to cover it.

She needed to apologise. But she'd be damned if she was going to chase after Dorian Rowland in the dark to do it. She didn't have much left after tonight, but she had her pride.

Dorian stopped at the corner. He leaned against the lamp post, catching his breath. He should walk back in there and apologise. He'd said rough words to her, words a decent man didn't say to a decent woman. It was further proof he wasn't a decent man. But dammit, a man had his pride if nothing else. She'd accused him of seducing her for ulterior purposes. *She's not far from the truth and you know it.* But it wasn't like that, not when it had come down to it. He'd slept with her because he'd wanted to, because he'd desired her. He still desired her.

Tonight was supposed to have ended differently. The necklace in his pocket was a sad reminder of those intentions. It still could, if he'd just go back. And what? Beg? Grovel? Elise had been angry. He'd seen her temper on full display, her wit sharp, her tongue cutting. Maybe it was better this way. Yes, it was *definitely* better this way.

Dorian began to walk. First down one street, then another, and another until he was too far away to conveniently turn back, his mind rolling out all the reasons he was right to have left. He would not beg. He could apologise for his words, but not his choices, and that would not be enough for Elise. He could say he was sorry for his secrets, but he would not tell them. She would truly despise him if she knew the things he'd done. The motives behind them would not be enough to clear him in her conscience.

What was the point anyway? Confessing all to Elise wouldn't solve anything. It wouldn't protect her from Tyne, it wouldn't change the nature of their relationship—which was temporary. He couldn't keep a woman like Elise. She'd wanted to talk about their relationship this afternoon. That should have scared him. His gut usually twisted at the mere mention. Talking about relationships meant admitting to having them—the very first step on a slippery slope to commitment. But this afternoon, the familiar twist hadn't been there. Still, he'd diverted the discussion because he could offer her none of the reassurances women looked for.

What he could do, though, was make enquiries about Tyne, help her resolve the doubts about her father's death and he could finish her boat. Then he could give her up. He could walk away as if she were just another woman he'd slept with. Only she wasn't. The realisation was so strong, struck so deeply, Dorian had to stop walking and steady himself. How had that happened? She had him dressing up and climbing unstable trellises. She had him thinking about captaining her yacht and re-entering society, something he'd sworn never to do, and all for a pretty face. Oh, no, she wasn't just a pretty face. That was how it had happened. He'd fallen for her intelligence, her passion, her boldness. The reasons hardly mattered. What did was that he'd *fallen.*

'Get a grip on yourself, Rowland,' he muttered under his breath. *'Build the boat and walk away. She's just a woman you can't have.'* But that didn't solve anything because he never walked away from a challenge.

Heaven help him. He wanted Elise Sutton. He might even love her.

Heaven help her when he was finished with her. He wanted Elise Sutton with a vengeance. Damien Tyne paced the small, crude office he kept on the Wapping docks. It was not nearly as nice as Blackwell and the East India set-up or as well located. He and Maxwell had guessed poorly and invested unwisely, while Richard Sutton had done the opposite. Sutton had leased the more-expensive site at Blackwell while he and Maxwell Hart had bet on the cut-through to be built between Limehouse and Wapping, joining the docks directly to the Pool of London. The cut had never materialised, although it had been talked about a great deal over the last twenty years.

It only fed his vengeance to know Rowland was doing more than building the boat. His man had reported Rowland's presence at the town house after hours on several occasions, the latest being four nights ago. Rowland had come for dinner, all dressed up and riding in the Sutton carriage.

Rowland's ability to land in the most lucrative of beds never ceased to amaze him. He'd taken Rowland's ship, effectively running Rowland out of business for the nasty turn of events over the incident with the pasha. It should have broken Rowland. Without a ship, Rowland couldn't run his cargos and he'd be too dangerous to be hired by another. No decent businessman would risk his ship being hunted down simply because Rowland was at the helm. Even with all that against him, Rowland had thrived. The lucky bastard was now privy to the elite innovations of Richard Sutton's last yacht, bedding the lovely Elise and living the good life without expending a pound of his own money.

Tyne pulled out his pocket watch and flipped it open. It was nearly eleven in the morning. Miss Sutton should be receiving Maxwell's offer right about now. Perhaps after the fire four nights ago, the tide would begin to turn in his favour. Elise should be frightened. This game was serious and, without meaning to, Dorian would have helped it along. If he cared a whit for Elise Sutton, he would have cautioned her that this was for real. That he, Tyne, would stop at nothing. What would she think about Maxwell's offer? Would she look at it with relief or with suspicion?

He could picture her slitting open the envelope, her green eyes scanning the letter, the pulse at the base of her neck leaping in surprise, shock or excitement. He could picture her doing other things, too. Unfortunately, she'd been doing those things with Dorian Rowland. But very soon, she would be doing those things with him, for him and he would have his revenge on them both at last.

Chapter Eighteen

Elise studied the sheaf of documents in her hand, unsure what to make of them. They contained an offer for the shipyard, now of all times. Charles stood at the French doors leading out to the rose garden, patiently letting her peruse the paperwork. He'd been the harbinger of this latest development, arriving with the papers shortly after eleven that morning and turned out in his daytime best.

She had not seen him since the day Dorian had all but driven him out, but Charles didn't seem to hold that against her. He was the epitome of concern, exclaiming over the fire damage and worried for her safety. He said he'd been away on some business for his father in Southampton. She hoped that was the truth. She didn't want Dorian to have alienated him. She might not be head-over-heels in love with Charles Bradford, but her friends were few and far between these days. It made her question the offer all the more. Should she view it with suspicion or serendipity? Beyond the sitting room she'd taken over as her office at the back of the house, repairs continued on the town house—repairs that strained her budget. This offer would solve that financial need and more.

Elise's eyes returned to the final number at the bottom of the last page. With that kind of money, she could easily pay Dorian and his crew for their work on the yacht and walk away with a sum that would keep her and her family comfortably. For her part, she would not need to worry about relying on her mother or brother for funds. She could continue to live in the style to which she'd been raised and maintain her independence.

To do what? What would she use that independence for? Without a shipyard, there'd be no point in designing yachts that would never be built. She knew what her brother would say and her mother, too.

'It's a good deal, Elise. It's more money

than the investors offered to pay.' Charles turned from the doors, ready to engage in persuasive conversation.

'Is that what you are to convince me of?' Elise gave him a thin smile. She understood the role Charles was sent to play. He was the messenger, chosen carefully to use his leverage as her friend to bring back an affirmative decision to this business man, Maxwell Hart.

'Anyone would tell you the same,' Charles replied. 'I'm not here to mislead you, but to help you if you have questions and to offer my opinion if you ask for it.'

That was a more pliable, gentler side of Charles, Elise noted. Usually, he was very rigid with his black-and-white views on life. Her own smile softened in answer. 'I appreciate that, Charles. I do have questions. Who is Maxwell Hart and how do you know him? I don't recall him from my father's associations.'

'My father knows him through some shipping arrangements. He's wealthy. As an importer, Hart knows the value in the shipyard's position. He has a warehouse and a boat works over in Wapping, but he's looking to move to a better location and your location is the best there is, as you well know.'

Charles fiddled with a porcelain figurine on the fireplace mantel. 'Personally, I think he's given up hope that a cut-through will ever be built at Wapping.'

Elise could understand that. The cut-through had never materialised and the difference between the more tedious waterways at Wapping and the efficiencies of the East and West India docks with their modern developments was quite marked. 'The offer seems straightforward,' Elise began, unwilling to share everything that had occurred lately, 'but it comes at a most interesting time.'

Interesting was a delicate way of putting things. It came at a time when a dangerous man was attempting to damage the yard and steal her boat. It would be all too easy to sell out and pass Damien Tyne on to the new owner. But selling out came with a price, too. She suspected the offer was so high because of the yacht. The documents clearly stated the yacht was to remain with the yard.

'It seems to me that it comes at a most opportune time,' Charles corrected. He made a gesture towards the door. It stood half-open, not entirely blocking out the sounds of repairs being done in the front room. 'You've had a run of bad luck these last months, Elise. The tide could be starting to turn in your favour.'

'That's just it, Charles. Perhaps this seems too perfect, too suspicious.'

Charles looked affronted. 'Are you implying Maxwell Hart is attempting to force you out through coercion? Do you really think a man willing to pay such a sum would resort to throwing rocks through your windows or lighting the very shipyard he wants on fire?' He shook his head. 'I don't see the logic.'

Put that way, she didn't see the logic, either. Charles was right. It made no sense to think this man would ruin the property he wanted to acquire. It made even less sense when she knew, as Charles did not, that Damien Tyne was behind the attacks. Unless Dorian had been wrong all along about Tyne and about Tyne's motives.

It had occurred to her in the days since her quarrel with Dorian that she'd accepted his explanations at face value. Perhaps he'd lied about the thugs' reasons for breaking into the shipyard. Perhaps they hadn't been there looking at her yacht, but had come for him. She'd mentioned as much the night he'd first told her of the break-in.

'It's a difficult decision to walk away from all I know and everything my father worked for,' Elise said slowly, trying to articulate the hollowness that filled her at the thought. She didn't expect Charles to understand.

Charles took the seat across from her, an earnest look on his face. 'Think of it this way, Elise. You can walk away now and make a *lot* of money, or you can wait until the last moment and be politely forced out when the shipyard can no longer sustain itself. If so, you'll end up with nothing except for the yacht and that's *if* you can find a buyer in time. Hart is willing to pay you for the shipyard, the boat and the contents of the shipyard if you walk away now.' Charles loved numbers. His whole face lit up when he talked about projected profits.

There was sense in that. The offer was tempting. She saw the profit in it. It was why she hadn't immediately discarded the option. Her dream of building her father's last boat and selling it had been financially motivated. She'd hoped to use the money to keep the boat works open for herself. If she sold to Hart, she wouldn't *need* the company to support herself.

Then Dorian had come along and filled her head with the idea of keeping the boat at a time when she'd been susceptible to such a concept. After seeing the hull completed, it was harder to imagine letting someone else take the boat. But Dorian had filled her head with a lot of other unworthy notions, too, and in the end it hadn't got her anything but heart-ache and disappointment. Charles had real numbers and results to support his position.

'You may tell Mr Hart that I will think about it.' Elise clenched her hands in her lap, willing herself to speak the words before she could change her mind. 'I will let him know in a couple of days.'

Charles nodded neutrally. 'He will be pleased to know you are considering it. May I give you something else to consider? Perhaps something of a more personal nature? It cannot have escaped your notice, my dear Elise, that I have held you in great esteem for some time now and that esteem has grown into affection.'

Oh, lord, he was going to propose. Elise felt her stomach tighten into a ball. He was outlining his prospects which, she thought cynically, would look a lot better once he calculated in her profit from the shipyard. 'I had wanted to wait a decent interval, Elise, but I think now is the better time,' Charles went on. 'After all this to-do with Rowland and the shipyard, I think the sooner we can marry the better.'

In other words, she needed a husband to bring her into line. Elise bristled at the very idea she couldn't manage her own life, not that she'd done a great job of it to date. But she could hear the lifeline Charles was throwing her in the proposal. She knew she had to consider this offer as carefully as the one that had come from Maxwell Hart. Marriage to Charles was her last chance to claim respectability. This was society's way of letting her know they would not hesitate setting her aside if she continued down this current path of independence and the flaunting of convention.

Elise looked down at her hands, clenched to whiteness in her lap. 'I am honoured, Charles, and yet surprised by the suddenness of your offer. It bears thinking about and I must ask you to give me some time to do that thinking. It would not be fair to you otherwise.'

He looked more disappointed over this pronouncement than the one she'd given him over Hart's offer. 'What would not be fair, Elise, is to leave you at the mercy of that bounder, Rowland. He is a bad influence.' A bit of anger fired in Charles's eyes. 'In the absence of any female companionship at the moment, or any family members to guide you, I fear he's convinced you to court scandal by leaving off your mourning and by continuing your efforts at the shipyard. He has clouded your good judgement; perhaps he has even turned your head. But you are smarter than that.'

Was she? Elise thought Charles might be wrong there. She saw him to the door personally, effusing her thanks for his visit and going through the motions of farewell, but most of her mind was focused on Dorian. It had been difficult to sit through the interview with Charles and not wonder what Dorian would have made of it all. What would Dorian think of Hart's offer? What would Dorian think of Charles's proposal and the exigencies behind it?

Elise shut the door behind Charles and pressed her forehead to the cool wood. She hadn't seen Dorian since the night of the fire.

Good lord, it had been only four days! She was acting as if it were months. She'd not meant for even four days to pass, but the hiring of workmen and overseeing repairs had kept her here when she'd wanted to be at the shipyard. There'd been no chance to apologise and she hadn't wanted to do it in a note. She doubted what she needed to say could be said accurately in writing anyway.

Elise drew a breath. There was no time like the present. She would take Dorian's lunch down personally and then they would talk.

Elise came to an abrupt halt inside the shipyard. She shielded her eyes against the bright sky and looked up. It was amazing what four days could do. The mast, the rigging, was all complete. Men climbed the boat, hanging sails, and at the top of it all was Dorian, in culottes, sans shirt and shoes, swinging from the lines with the ease of a trapeze artist. She'd only seen circus performers with that kind of grace. Watching him now, seeing her yacht so near completion, was enough to make her want to forgive him on the spot. Really, it was enough to make her want to beg his forgiveness.

She had to be cautious with such emotions. He'd built her boat, that was all. She had to be careful the accomplishment didn't unduly outshine their differences. She'd had doubts about him once again just this morning and those doubts were justified. And there were harsh accusations between them, proof they didn't know each other as well as they should. Just because he'd finished her yacht, didn't mean he was off the hook.

She caught his eye and waved up at him, pointing to the hamper at her side, and then enjoyed the sight of him shimmying down a rope to the boat deck. He sauntered towards her, his culottes low on his hips, his hair loose. She should be used to the sight of him by now. She'd seen him naked, for heaven's sake. But her heart did a somersault anyway at the blatant sensuality on display.

'I brought lunch. I hoped we could talk. There are things that need to be said.' They weren't the most elegant words. She hoped they'd be enough. She bit her lip, waiting for his response. Was he still angry? She'd accused him of trying to steal her boat. Would his answer be something flippant and crude?

She'd not realised until now how much she wanted, needed, to talk with him.

She knew a moment's relief when Dorian nodded and called over to a tall young man working at the helm, 'Johnny, I've got business to take care of, you're in charge.' He looked at her. 'Will I need my shirt for this?'

'Unless you want to talk in the office? I have the carriage. I thought we might drive out towards Greenwich.'

'Give me a moment to change.'

Dorian returned quickly, dressed in trousers, boots, shirt, the appropriate coats and an expression far too serious for her liking. He picked up the hamper. 'Shall we?'

The formality of his tone hurt. It made it difficult to find her tongue, to start the conversation she'd come to have. But she didn't want to start it in the carriage. She wanted to start it at lunch, on the grass on the bluff overlooking the river with the whole afternoon spread out before them. For now, she opted for small talk. 'The yacht's nearly done.' She started with something positive.

Dorian gave a thin smile so different from

his usual grin. 'It is done. We just need to name it and take it for a trial.'

A month ago those words would have filled her with elation. Today, her first reaction was sadness. Dorian's job was complete. He would be free to leave.

'It's a good thing. The yacht club's trip is next week.' Elise offered a smile. Good lord, this conversation was stilted. She wanted their former easiness back, she wanted his shocking bluntness back. She wanted it all back. Had their quarrel really ruined everything? How could she not have realised what was at stake? If she had, Elise doubted she'd have chosen to rip it apart with callous words.

Dorian stretched his long legs, his gaze lingering on her face. 'Is this how you want our discussion to go? Short factual sentences or are you hoping for something more?'

There was a hint of his old seduction in those words and her hopes rose. She was tempted to play with those words and come up with a witty response, but it was too soon. She had made her move by coming down here. He needed to make the next one.

He did. 'As for me, I am hoping for something more.' He paused and she held her breath. 'It does me good to see you, Elise. I regretted our parting the moment I left.'

'I should not have let you go like that.' Elise felt relief course through her. They were dancing towards reconciliation with their careful words.

'I should have come back. I thought about it. I stood at the lamplight on the corner for a long time, thinking about just that.'

'I meant to come sooner, but I couldn't get away.'

'How are repairs going?'

'Good—noisy, but good. They'll be done soon.' She waved the subject away. She didn't want to talk about repairs. 'This...' she made a gesture between them with her hand '...doesn't mean we don't have to talk about what happened.' She didn't want him to think an implied apology on both their parts was enough. Rapprochement was only one of the reasons she'd come down here.

Dorian's answer was quiet and sincere. 'I know.'

By the saints, it was good to see her! He wasn't relishing the upcoming conversation, but he was relishing this moment. She'd come.

He'd begun to fear she wouldn't. He'd thrown himself and his men into work on the yacht, keeping long hours to get it done. It had become a personal labour for him. This would be his gift to her. He would make her the most beautiful of racing boats, the fastest and the sleekest. Whatever he couldn't say to her, couldn't give to her, he could pour into the boat.

By tacit agreement, they waited until they were settled on the bluff, the picnic spread out before them while they watched the boat traffic on the water. He waited for Elise to start. He would let her lead the conversation. Would she start with business or pleasure?

'I received an offer for the yacht and the shipyard today. Charles brought it just this morning. It was not from Damien Tyne.' Business and pleasure mixed, then. He knew what she implied.

She was watching him for signs of surprise or something else. He kept his features neutral. 'You think I lied about Tyne.' It was not a question.

Her answer was just as careful. 'I think I was surprised the offer wasn't from him after all the trouble he's put us through.' *Hypo-*

thetically. The word hung unspoken between them. She wasn't sure any more that he'd told her the truth. The doubt stung.

'Who did the offer come from?' Dorian ventured. Damien Tyne didn't necessarily have to offer directly, all the better to protect his involvement.

'Maxwell Hart. I'm not familiar with him, but Charles's father knows of him. He has a boat works in Wapping.'

Dorian felt as if he'd been punched in the gut: clarity at last. 'That gives Charles and me something in common,' he said drily. 'It just so happens that I know Maxwell Hart, too.' Hart. Of course. Tyne had worked with Hart before. *Boat works* was a rather liberal term for what Hart had in Wapping. He had a warehouse that stored goods of a questionable nature. The boat-works portion was where he outfitted ships for dangerous adventures before sending them south with Tyne.

Dorian watched Elise swallow, disappointment shadowing her face. 'You *were* thinking of selling,' Dorian said in soft amazement.

'Thinking only,' Elise said quickly. 'Nothing has been decided.' She plucked at a grass stem. 'It was just an idea. I wanted to talk to you first.' It was an implicit statement of trust and absolutely the best thing she could have said to him. She didn't completely doubt him. Normally, he wouldn't care what anyone thought, but when it came to Elise, everything was different. He cared very much. She was looking at him, those green eyes demanding an answer when all he wanted to do was roll her under him and bury himself in her until they both forgot all the difficulties and impossibilities that lay between them.

'Is it really a bad idea? Hart wants the yacht, too, that's why the price is so high.'

Dorian set aside his baser urges. 'Yes, it's a bad idea.'

'Are you going to tell me why?' She threw down the ultimate gauntlet. This had always been the sticking point between them. It was what she'd wanted from the start—to know him, to know what he knew. She still wanted it. It had been at the heart of their recent quarrel.

Dorian lay back on the grass, his head propped against a boulder. 'I'll tell you, Elise, although you might regret it. You'd better open that bottle of wine in the hamper. It's a long story.' When it was over, she might not be the only one regretting it. Yet this was the only way forwards, painful as it might be. What better way to prove to her he was sorry for the other night than to tell her about Hart and Tyne? Of course, the opposite was also true. What better way to lose her for good? He couldn't tell her about Hart and Tyne without telling her about himself.

Chapter Nineteen

'Tyne and Hart were the ones who took the *Queen Maeve* and scuttled her before my eyes. I watched her burn.' He'd watched more than a ship burn that night. He'd watched his livelihood, his dreams, everything go up in smoke, down with the ship. It didn't matter which cliché one used, in the end there still was nothing left.

'Why?' Elise was looking at him with something akin to pity in her eyes. He didn't want her sympathy. She'd lose it soon enough when she heard the rest. There were plenty of people who thought he'd got what he'd deserved and it wasn't as if he hadn't known the risks.

'I crossed them.' Just as Elise was crossing

them now with her refusal to sell the yacht. 'I've told you before that Tyne was an arms dealer. He did the dirty work, the meetings with the pashas and chieftains, he made the actual deliveries. But Hart was the supplier. Hart never leaves England. He sets up the shipments, finds the arms—good solid British arms or sometimes French—and he sends them to Tyne. That's what he's got up at his warehouse in Wapping.'

'Then what's Tyne doing here? Shouldn't he be sailing his ship somewhere?' Elise's mind was running ahead of the story.

Dorian drew a breath. 'He doesn't have one at present because I sunk it in revenge for the *Queen*.' If there was a touch of manly pride in his tone, so be it. He might have been bound and helpless the night the *Queen* burnt, but he did not let anyone harm what was his without retribution.

Elise's expression grew masked. 'What happened? We seem to have skipped over the part about why you crossed them.'

This was the harder part to tell, the part where he wouldn't seem so heroic. Perhaps he'd look no better to her than Tyne and Hart. 'Arms are a lucrative and arguably legal market in the Mediterranean. I saw a chance to make money and I took it. It's not just Turkey where there's military unrest. There's Egypt, too, and Greece and amongst the desert chieftains along the north of Africa in Algiers and Morocco—parts of Spain, too.' He gave a grimace. 'Not everyone is happy with the return of the Spanish monarch, and for whatever else the French liked or didn't like about Napoleon, he's made them greedy. They see the profit of colonies close to home. Algiers and Morocco are just across the sea and the French are drooling already at the thought. The British will never tolerate simply handing those ports to the French so we've moved inland, thinking to rally the sheikhs to our cause, convincing them the French will take their independence.'

Dorian shrugged. 'It's a lie, of course. It will be some time before anyone actually threatens the independence of the nomad sheikhs.'

'You've seen them?'

'Yes, I had to journey inland quite a way to make my deliveries. But that's not the point. The point is, I sold arms, too. Mostly, I operated out of Gibraltar and made small runs to

Algiers. But as time went on and my reputation for quality arms grew, I began to see the allure of moving further east.'

Elise nodded, the pieces coming together. 'That's how you crossed them. You became too big, too successful, and then you infringed on their territory.'

Dorian pushed a hand through his hair. 'Exactly. There were warnings—a little accident here and there meant to encourage my leaving. I retaliated by being bigger and bolder.' He told her of the pasha's daughter and stealing the arsenal in order to sell it to his rival. 'Of course, the best part to me was that the arsenal had been supplied by Tyne.' It had seemed symbolic at the time. Tyne had been furious.

'Tyne offered to buy the *Queen*, several times. But I was too proud. I couldn't sell her. I had built her. I'd paid for her with my own money saved from my runs. She was the one thing I had that truly belonged to me.' His eyes were on the sky, but his thoughts were much further away.

'One night, Tyne came after me. He seized or killed most of my crew. We did try to resist, but we were outnumbered. I suffered a blow to the head and when I recovered consciousness, I found myself bound to a tree on a bluff overlooking the harbour. I had a perfect view to watch my ship burn.'

Elise fiddled with the grass, twisting the blades into little wreaths. 'Why didn't Tyne kill you? That would have solved his problems.'

'Dead men can't be broken and Tyne does like to break a man. Besides, I think he worried about repercussions in England. My father likes to pretend I don't exist, but if anything did happen to me my father might suddenly get paternal again. Tyne didn't want to risk it.' Dorian sighed. There was more to tell, but perhaps this was enough for now. Perhaps she'd spare him and puzzle the rest out.

'You do see why I've told you all this?' Dorian rolled to his side and propped himself up on one elbow. 'You are crossing him now. He's issued his warnings and yet you do not relent. He's behind Hart's offer. The offer is your last chance. Tyne will come for your boat, and maybe even for you.' There was no maybe about it; he just couldn't bring himself to say the words.

The thought was enough to make him

shiver. For all her boldness, Elise was no match for Tyne. 'He most certainly will come for me, though.' On his own, Dorian could handle Tyne. But Elise complicated things. She could be used against him, making her doubly valuable to Tyne.

'Then it's good I'm alone.' Elise looked up at him with a forced smile. 'With my mother and William away from London it will be harder for him to reach them.'

She was starting to understand. Dorian reached up his free hand to push a strand of hair out of her face. 'You're not alone, Elise.' She had him for whatever that was worth. He definitely came with disadvantages. He was a magnet for Tyne. He'd cost Tyne his ship and an expensive cargo of Russian guns for the Turks, a deal that had taken over a year to put together. But he could defend her. 'I'm here.'

'For how long?' The question was ruthless. In one simple question she'd united the business and pleasure sides of their relationship, linking them irrevocably together once more.

'For as long as it takes, Elise.' It was the best answer, the most honest answer he could give. He would not leave her open to Tyne's treachery, but neither could he articulate anything permanent about their relationship. Nor could he articulate anything temporary. He wondered if she'd thought of that.

'And then?' Elise pushed on, seeing only the temporary nature of his answer. 'Where will you go after this?'

'It will depend.' Dorian shrugged. 'It's not a priority right now and it won't be a priority until Tyne is dealt with and you're safe.' He wanted to kiss her, wanted her to stop thinking about the future and start thinking about right now.

A coy smile hinted at her lips. 'What is a priority, Dorian Rowland?'

'You.' He was hungry for her. He had to know she'd let him protect her, that his disclosures hadn't driven her off.

'Right here? Out in the open?' The prospect of something so risky spoke to her. Her pupils widened, her pulse quickened.

'Yes.' Dorian kissed her neck, his free hand in her hair, drawing her, urging her close to him. They had all afternoon. He would take this nice and slow.

'No.' He felt her body tense in resistance, a mirror to her words.

'No?'

She gave a rueful smile. 'Apparently there's one woman in the world who can resist Dorian Rowland.' She looked down, away from his face. 'I'm sorry, I can't.'

Dorian blew out a breath. 'Is it because of the things I said that night? I had no right. They were unconscionable and they were untrue.' He'd regretted those harsh words the moment he'd spoke them.

'No. We were both angry.'

'Then what? Don't you trust me, Elise?' The words sounded ridiculous coming from him after all he'd told her. He'd run arms, he'd stolen arms, he'd destroyed another man's ship in retribution. Why *should* she trust him?

Elise scooted away from him and stood, surely a bad sign. Most of what he wanted to do on a picnic blanket required sitting down at least.

'I trust you to protect me against Tyne.' But not from himself. He thought he understood. He rose, too, prepared to persuade her otherwise. Her next words stalled him full force. 'Dorian, there's something else. Charles came with two offers today. The other was a proposal. Charles has asked me to marry him.'

And she was considering it. He wanted

to shout, 'No, you're mine!' but he had no idea what that meant—did it mean *he* wanted to marry her, or merely that he wanted to sail away with her and make love on sandy beaches until they tired of one another? How could he promise anything to her?

Dorian schooled his features into bland neutrality and cocked an eyebrow. 'Are congratulations in order? Have you accepted him?' Surely his instincts weren't wrong. She couldn't have, not when she'd been his not so very long ago.

Her own features mimicked his in their neutrality, some of the earlier stiffness returning to their conversation. 'No, I have not. I just thought you should know.' *I will not be sleeping with you or kissing you, putting my mouth on you, or anything else until the situation with Charles is resolved.*

Dorian studied her face, watching for some telltale give-away. '*Will* you accept?'

'I don't know,' Elise answered slowly. 'It will depend on what happens with the shipyard, I suppose.' There was a flicker of hope in her eyes that suggested it depended on more than the shipyard, that it might depend on him.

'We haven't done very well today.' Elise gave a little laugh. 'I still don't know whether or not to take the offer. Either of them.'

Dorian laughed. At least she wasn't going to run home and accept Charles's proposal. He still had a chance if he wanted to take it. 'We might be doing better than you think.'

She shot him a dubious look. 'I would hardly call inviting all-out war with an arms dealer doing "better than we think".'

'If you sell, it's more than understandable.' He would hate that decision, though, and she would come to hate it, too. It would haunt him all his days to see that yacht in Tyne's filthy hands, but if it kept Elise safe, he would live with it. 'If you choose to resist, I'll protect you to the best of my abilities. Either way, I can't make that decision for you, Elise…' he gave a wicked smile and leaned in close to her '…but I can do this.' His hand cupped the sweep of her jaw, just before he kissed her.

He tasted the sweetness of her, the strawberries and wine mingled on her lips, he felt the small straight ridges of her teeth where his tongue ran over them. Most of all, he felt compliance, ever so briefly, before she remembered her resolve, but it was there. And that meant there was hope indeed.

'I told you, I can't,' Elise protested softly.

'But I can. Charles didn't propose to me.' Dorian kissed her again just to prove his point.

Elise stood at the launch gate of the shipyard. In her hand was the rope cord that would send the bottle of champagne sailing into the side of the yacht. Excitement and trepidation coursed through her in equal parts. The breeze off the water toyed with her hat and she reached a hand up to steady it. The wind was good. In spite of overcast skies, conditions for the test sail couldn't be better.

The momentous day was finally here. She was well past the point of no return and had been for much longer than she'd realised. Since the beginning there had been no question of selling the yard, or even of selling the boat, even if she was only now coming to realise it. She understood it now, though, standing on the launch site while the sun rose with Dorian beside her. This boat *belonged* to her, it was a product of her plans, her designs, her efforts.

Yet for all the pride she felt in the moment, there was a loneliness, too. Past launch days had been huge festive events, her father a great showman. The launch gate had been crowded with invited guests. Other yachts of invited celebrants had been moored in the river to join the sailing, and a select few would be aboard the prized vessel. There'd been food and champagne and a rousing speech from her father. Even the members of the royal family were present on occasion.

Today there was no such pomp. Today there were only a handful of people: herself and Dorian and enough crew to get the boat launched. She'd named the yacht *Sutton's Hope* and Dorian had made her hold up a lantern last night so he could see well enough to paint the name along the prow. The paint had dried just in time.

'This is it, Elise, give the rope a good yank.' Dorian came to stand beside her, the last of the preparations done. Dorian, *not* Charles, was here with her, came the reminder. Dorian had helped her realise this moment, a moment Charles had not been in favour of from the start. Charles had scoffed at her ambitions.

Dorian had embraced them. That should count for something.

Dorian was dressed in buff breeches and a thick sweater against the early morning chill. He looked well rested in spite of the late night. Elise knew she did not. She'd hardly slept with her mind so occupied with the yacht launch, the contretemps of Damien Tyne and Charles's proposal. She'd spent most of the night weighing Charles against Dorian, although her practical side didn't know why. It wasn't as if she had to choose. Charles had asked for her hand, Dorian had asked for nothing.

'Elise, the rope,' Dorian prompted again with a smile.

She let go and watched the bottle give a satisfying smash against the side. Her father would have loved to have been here. She'd not dared to write to William or her mother with an update. William didn't know yet that he'd signed on for a membership with the yacht club.

Elise helped Dorian and the other two crew members get the yacht under way in the river, but she was eager to stand at the railing and feel the wind in her face and feel the roll of the boat beneath her. She was nervous, too. Would the great experiment with the buoyancy bags compensate for the narrowness through the centre of the boat? It would be absolutely tragic if, after all this, the design simply didn't work.

For the trial, they'd planned to sail down the Thames to Gravesend. The route was the standard below-the-bridge racing course used by the yacht club. It would be a good chance to see how the sails tacked in the wind. Already she could feel the cutter rigging picking up the breeze. The boat *felt* fast. She could hear Dorian calling out instructions. She didn't remember the point at which everything fell silent on board, only that Dorian had come up behind her and boldly wrapped his arms about her, his body warm and comforting.

'She's doing magnificently,' Dorian reported. 'The cutter rigging was exactly the right way to go. The new cut on the sails has made an enormous difference with the windage.'

Elise smiled. 'That's precisely what I wanted to hear.'

'The *Hope* is fast, Elise.' Dorian's voice

was at her ear, low and intimate. She should dissuade him from such liberties. It wasn't fair to Charles or to Dorian or to her. If she meant to accept Charles, it was the height of cruelty to tempt herself like this. She didn't need to compare kisses to know Charles did not rouse her, *could not* rouse her, like Dorian did. There would be none of the pleasure, none of the fire she felt with Dorian. But there would be honour and Charles would respect her. No, that would be misleading to think so. What kind of respect? Respect only if she acceded to his wishes. He would never countenance something like today.

'How fast?' She was fishing for compliments now.

'Fast enough to outrun them all.' Dorian blew in her ear. 'Don't tell me you haven't thought about it.' She'd thought about it all last night in the long dark hours: about keeping the yacht, about rejecting Charles, about sailing away from London. Let Tyne and Hart have the shipyard if she could have Dorian. Fanciful notions all. If Dorian was right about Tyne and Hart, her ethical conscience wouldn't allow conceding to such blackguards.

'Thought about what?' She breathed in the wind-tinged scent of him, a man out of doors and in his element.

'About keeping the yacht and racing it on your own.'

'Oh, that.' So not about keeping him, then. What would he say if she said she'd thought of sailing away with him?

'You could pay the workers from prize money.'

'That's a big risk. What if we didn't win?' She had no cash reserves to pay those wages. She was worried enough about paying them in the very near future. She had no buyer. She'd have to sell off furnishings if one didn't materialise soon.

'We'd win, Elise. She's a champion in the water.' Dorian sounded confident. It made her want to believe in so many impossible things.

'There's a regatta right after the opening trip, with a four-hundred-pound purse and a silver cup, sponsored by the royal family. They're calling it the Saxe-Coburg Cup in Albert's honour.'

'You are surprisingly well informed for someone who shuns polite society.' Elise gave him a suspicious smile. This was the perfect opportunity to bind him to her just a little longer if she dared. 'To do such a thing, I'd need you at the helm. Would you do it?' They'd not finished that discussion the night of the fire and he'd been reticent. She turned in his embrace, her arms about his neck, Charles forgotten for the moment. It was hard to remember much of anything when she was with Dorian.

Dorian swallowed hard, his jaw clenching. 'If it's what you want, I'll do it.' She didn't pretend to understand all the reasons why he was so reticent to associate with society, but she knew the decision cost him mightily.

Elise beamed and rose up on her tiptoes to kiss him full on the mouth. 'Can we sail the yacht ourselves?' she asked softly, her mouth inches from his.

'We could manage.' He gave her a teasing wink. 'You're not the only one who can innovate. I borrowed some mechanics from ketch rigging and adapted them to your cutter rigging to make the yacht more efficient for a small crew.'

'I am suitably impressed. Put the crew aside at Gravesend with fare to get home and I'll give you a proper thank you.'

Dorian grinned. 'And Charles? Does this mean you've refused his offer?'

Elise nodded, more solemn now. 'I don't think I ever could have accepted him, not when I really thought about it.' There was more to it than that, but for now she was interested in kissing Dorian with the wind in her hair and her decisions made. There would still be a fight ahead of her. She didn't believe for a moment simply making decisions solved her problems. She would continue to persevere. Maybe there was a miracle out there for her where she could keep the shipyard, keep the boat and maybe, just maybe, she'd find a way to keep Dorian without needing him too much.

'She's a beauty.' Damien Tyne handed off the binoculars to Maxwell Hart. 'Just look at her.'

'That's my fiancée you're talking about,' Charles said tersely, raising his own binoculars to his eyes, his horse shifting under him on the bluff as they watched *Sutton's Hope* pass in the sunrise.

'I meant the boat, but the comment suits either way,' Tyne teased meanly. 'I don't know if I'd use the binoculars if I were you. You might not like what you see. It appears Rowland shares our assessment of the latter.' He elbowed Hart and the two of them laughed.

Charles grimaced, his anger rising as he stared through the eye piece, watching Dorian come up behind Elise and wrap her in his arms. 'How dare he!' Charles spluttered. No gentleman behaved so boldly with a woman.

'How dare *she*?' Tyne inserted with a sideways glance in his direction. 'It doesn't look to me like she's overly upset. In fact, they look quite cosy, quite comfortable with one another as if…'

'Don't even say it,' Charles ground out. He'd thought the same thing. They looked much too easy together for this to have been the first time. The way Rowland was whispering in her ear, the way she turned in his arms, laughing up at him, confirmed those jealous suspicions. Rage boiled through Charles. 'I'd like to see him dead.'

Tyne laughed. 'That can be arranged, my young friend. That most *definitely* can be arranged.'

'Not yet,' Hart cut in sharply in a tone that made Charles think Tyne wasn't truly joking.

'There's still a chance she might accept the offer and then any nasty conclusions to our business with her can be avoided.'

'Always the optimist, aren't you, Maxwell?' Tyne shook his head. Charles looked between the two. When he was with them, he always felt as if there was another game going on between them that he and the others weren't privy to; that somehow this was about more than a simple business venture to build fast boats.

'I can't afford not to be. I have to live here after you leave to soak up the rays of the Mediterranean,' Hart reminded Tyne. 'Raising the ire of the Duke of Ashdon might not bother you, but it will make business on this end deuced difficult for the rest of us. It won't matter if we have the yard and a fast boat once Ashdon gets done.' That was more like it. Charles understood that sort of rationale. Hart knew what was good for business.

Tyne groused and scuffed the toe of his boot through the dirt. 'When's the opening trip?'

'Five days, why?' Hart asked.

'Let's give her until then. If she's not responded to the offer affirmatively by the opening trip, I get to work my magic.'

Charles felt a shiver. He didn't mind Tyne and Hart carving up Rowland between them, but now they were dragging Elise in, too. 'Now see here, Tyne, my father and I won't stand for seeing Elise hurt.'

Tyne gave a cold smile, his gaze fixed on the boat growing smaller in the distance. 'She'll come out of it all right if she's smart. So will you, Bradford.' Tyne turned and fixed him with a stare. 'Don't get any ideas about betraying us at this late date. She's not the only one who needs to play this smart.' He paused for a moment. 'Are we agreed then, Maxwell? Opening trip?'

Maxwell Hart gave a nearly imperceptible nod, the line of his jaw set grim and tense. 'Opening trip it is.'

Chapter Twenty

'I've put the crew off. I gave them money for fare back and a pint or two.' Dorian came up behind Elise and wrapped her in his arms, enjoying the feel of her as she sank into his body. This was one of his favourite positions with her—his arms about her, the two of them at the rail of a boat. They had stood this way, too, the night they'd gone to Vauxhall.

'We have the boat to ourselves,' he murmured in her ear. She turned and put her arms about his neck, her eyes dancing with life, her cheeks flushed from the wind. She looked utterly alive in his arms. There would be seduction today. Their bodies were primed for it with the thrill of the morning sail. The privacy of the cove he had anchored them in ensured it. But he was going to have to decide very soon what to do about her. Their time together *would* end. After the opening trip there was nothing to hold him here except the personal. Would she ask him to stay? Would he be willing to pay the price staying demanded? Or would she come with him if he asked? Could he make her happy in Gibraltar? That was a fantasy that had taken up far too much of his nights lately—sailing away with Elise and finding the happy ever after.

'I do not like the look in your eyes one bit.' Elise laughed up at him, but he feared she'd seen too much. Perhaps she understood, too, that this affair could not go on indefinitely without reaching a resolution. It was time to redirect. 'Come eat, Elise. I've got our picnic laid out.'

She'd been lost in thought when he'd returned. He'd left her at the rail with those thoughts and taken time to spread the blanket on the deck and lay out the picnic: cheese and bread, apples and, best of all, champagne. Elise loved champagne, loved to do wicked things with it.

'You've been busy.' Elise sat and tucked her skirts around her. He joined her, pulling off his boots. The sun had broken through the clouds and the blanket was warm. The boat bobbed gently beneath them. For the moment, everything was perfect.

'My father would have loved today,' Elise said softly, as unwilling as he to disrupt the peace around them. He'd guessed she'd been thinking of her father. How could she not on such an important day? Whether she knew it or not, Elise Sutton had an enormous capacity for love. He suspected, however, it was a capacity she guarded carefully.

'*Sutton's Hope* would have made him proud.' Dorian popped the cork on the bottle and poured out two glasses. 'You would have made him proud.' He handed her a glass. 'Shall we have a toast? To Richard Sutton, to his vision and to his daughter.'

Elise blushed, her eyes watering a little at the tribute. He was glad she understood he was sincere. 'Thank you.' She touched her glass to his. 'How about a toast to the builder? To Dorian Rowland, a most extraordinary man.' Her eyes met his, and he let their gaze hold, a feat more difficult than he would have thought. Of all the things they'd said to one another over the past weeks, these toasts might have been the boldest.

These words were the closest they'd come to any verbal expression of their feelings. They'd done things together: rash things, intimate things, dangerous things. But never once had they spoken of how each made the other feel, as if saying the words signified a commitment neither were prepared to make.

'People say things like this when they believe someone is leaving, perhaps never to be seen again. It's one of the reasons I hate farewells.' Dorian set down his glass and reached for the wheel of cheese. 'Do you think I am leaving, Elise?' He passed her a chunk of cheese and slice of bread. He'd not planned to address their future today, but perhaps now was the right time after all.

Elise took the slice of cheese and bread from him, gathering her thoughts. Her answer, when she made it, would be careful. 'I think your business obligations to me are nearly over. If you stay, it will be out of something more. Staying will require some decisions.'

'We are dancing around it again.' Dorian gave a wry smile. 'It was one thing to use me for sex before the Season, but once everyone comes to town you'll need something more substantial. Is that it?'

He watched her swallow the champagne hastily to keep from choking on it. The bolder turn of the conversation had caught her off guard. 'Yes, something like that. Sex is fine for now, but eventually it has to mean something.' She stared into her glass, watching the bubbles disappearing. 'I'm afraid that's my fatal flaw, Dorian. You should know it before it's too late. Sex has to mean something to me. It can't just be for fun, not always. If we were to continue, eventually, I fear I would expect from you more than you might be prepared to give.'

How could he answer that for her when he wasn't sure he could answer it for himself? What was he willing to give? It was easier to know that answer if she'd come away with him. But what if the only way to have her was to stay? Her shipyard was here, everything she wanted was here. Would she leave it all for him? Would it be fair to expect that from her when he wasn't sure he could give it in return? But that wasn't all she was asking him with the revelation.

She was telling him something else, too—that *this* had happened before. He'd known, of course, he wasn't her first lover. There'd been someone else who'd tempted her and failed her. She'd expected love where there'd been none. A spurt of anger went through him, anger directed at the nameless man who'd teased her so carelessly. Dorian's thumb was under her chin, tipping her face up, forcing their gazes to meet when she would have preferred to have avoided it. 'Is that what happened the last time?'

'Yes.' She met his gaze evenly. There was defiance in her tone. 'I was more emotionally invested. He was more physically invested. At the time, I didn't understand the difference until it was too late.'

'Do you think that will happen here? That you are invested, but I am not?'

She gave him a wry smile. 'It would be too easy to love you, Dorian, even though I know what kind of man you are. On occasion, I suspect I'm already halfway there. After all, I've turned down a perfectly good suitor for you on my own volition.' Then she shook her head, 'But, no, Dorian. I don't think it could happen here. I'm smarter and wiser and you've made no secret about your intentions and that makes all the difference.'

Leave it to Elise to mingle compliments with a scold, but he was moved all the same. What would he do with that affection should she let it loose? Could he be trusted with it? Dorian rocked back on his heels and cut more bread while his mind reeled. She loved him. He wanted to celebrate that, wanted to jump up and down with the thrill of that knowledge. But the last part held him back, the part about intentions. He sensed the crux of the story lay there. 'Why don't you tell me about secret intentions? We're well fortified if this is a long story.'

'There's not much to tell. I was eighteen. I was in the throes of my first Season. My father's social circle extended to the lower rungs of the peerage and we had the royal patronage by then. It enabled me to garner the attention of a different kind of gentleman, the sons of barons, which meant there were titles to go with the estates. Before, the most I could have expected were the attentions of nice gentry farmers with lands and a comfortable income. I became infatuated with a Mr Robert Graves, heir to a baronetcy in Devonshire.

He was dashing, a little wild, but it appeared he liked me, too. Before I knew it, we were dancing together every night, he was driving me in the park and we were sneaking out to the gardens for kisses.'

'Kisses?' Dorian waggled his eyebrows, pretending shock. A little levity was not amiss. She was starting to relax.

'Well, considerably more than kisses. We became intimately involved. I had no qualms over it. I was certain he had marriage in mind and we wouldn't have been the first couple to anticipate matrimony. He talked about plans and I assumed those plans were for us.'

Dorian's anger flared. 'Who were they for?' He'd like to wring the bounder's neck.

'For his fourth cousin, Miss Mary Southmore,' Elise said quietly. 'What hurt most was the way he broke it to me. He said he had never harboured any intentions of marrying me. I was a craftsman's daughter when all was said and done. My family built boats. I never should have believed anything more could come of it.'

'I'm truly sorry.' It explained much about Elise, about the guard she kept on her feelings, not willing to reveal too much.

'Fortunately, what I felt for him wasn't real love and I learned from that mistake.' Elise gave a sad smile.

'Not every man sees the world as Robert Graves does,' Dorian put in softly. He stretched out on his side, drawing her to him, wanting to show her there was honour in him yet, that he could be trusted to deal honestly with her.

'No, but a good lesson all the same.' She snuggled down beside him, their faces close.

He pushed a strand of hair back out of her face. 'We both know I'm not Robert Graves, Elise, not in temperament or in practice.'

'I know,' she whispered, her breath catching as he moved against her ever so slightly, enough to close the gap between their bodies and to make his arousal known. Her hand slipped between them, finding the length of him. Lord, he loved the feel of her hand on him.

'Now there's something else we both know, Elise. I'm dying to make love to you.'

She smiled. 'I thought you'd never ask.'

He leaned over, raising himself above her, hands braced on either side. She was beautiful beneath him, her hair falling down about her shoulders, her green eyes looking up at him full of desire, a desire for *him* that was nearly overwhelming. Her hands were at the waistband of his trousers, unfastening, freeing. He managed her skirts and undergarments with a hand, his mouth trailing kisses down her throat, need rising with each touch. The wanting of her consumed him.

'God, how I want you, Elise. You don't know, you just don't know.' He was mumbling incoherent phrases against her throat, his breathing ragged. He moved, positioning himself. He was sliding home into the depths of her and nothing had ever felt this right. She was locked about him, holding him, rocking with him in his rhythm as he slid and thrust, pushing them towards the release he desperately wanted and never wanted; how he'd love to stay like this with her forever! In these moments there was no threat from Tyne, no social dilemmas to unravel regarding their future. There was only the knowledge that he was made for this moment and she was made for him and that was all that mattered, until it shattered into a million shards of pleasure, peace and perfection.

In the aftermath of that release, one question intruded: what would he be willing to do to have such a moment again? Could he stay for her? For this?

He'd stayed for her! Today, Dorian would be at the helm of the boat and at her side. He would stand with her on one of the most important days of her life: the day she showed the world Elise Sutton could build a yacht.

That one thought raced through Elise as she made her way through the streets leading to the docks. It was the opening trip and the streets were crowded with people anticipating the start of the yacht season. Spectators gathered along the waterfront to see the boats, sails hoisted, preparing to set out. Elise understood their excitement. She felt it, too. After a long bleak winter, there was an undeniable thrill at seeing the Commodore's pennant flying from his yacht at Blackwell as it had in seasons past, a sign that while some things change, not all things change.

She let the excitement of the opening trip fill the pit in her stomach. Even if there was just the opening trip to worry about, she'd still have had butterflies. It was her first official outing since her father's death. There would be those who would look askance at such behaviour.

But there was so much more. There'd been an ugly scene with Charles the day before. She had officially rejected his suit and he'd shown himself to be a poor loser. There was Tyne and Hart to worry about. She couldn't keep them dangling much longer, but to refuse them outright put her in harm's way. Then there was Dorian and the host of feelings and dilemmas he raised.

He was here for now, but for how much longer? Had they really reached any sort of consensus on the boat in spite of their disclosures and torrid lovemaking? Charles had not been wrong when he'd accused her of being infatuated with Dorian. She was and quite possibly more. Charles had insinuated Dorian had put her up to this nonsense with the yacht, but Elise knew better. She'd have ended up here, flaunting convention, with or without Dorian. Dorian simply made it easier. With Dorian, she had an ally.

Dorian was waiting for her beside the yacht, a welcome sight in the press of people. He was dressed in the new outfit she'd had sent over: spotless white trousers and a navy-blue jacket. He looked like the other captains, only *more*—more alive, more vibrant.

'Miss Sutton, your yacht awaits.' Dorian handed her up with grave formality that she might have believed if it hadn't been for the familiar twinkle of mischief in his eye. 'Several people have been eyeing the boat.'

'Jealous, were they?' Elise laughed, forcing herself to relax. She'd worked hard for this day. She *wanted* to enjoy it. Ladies passed by on the arms of gentlemen, many of them casting coy glances in Dorian's direction. 'I wonder if it was the yacht everyone was looking at?' she teased Dorian.

'Probably not,' he admitted honestly, taking his place at the helm. 'You'd better be prepared for scandal by dinner.'

Scandal would be better than some of the other options she'd mentally braced for. Elise went to stand at the railing and looked out over the river at all the boats assembled. She recognised several of them; the *Lady Louisa*, the *Brilliant*, the *Phantom*. All of them had been her father's competitors and friends over the years. She waved to a few acquaintances on boats nearby. Some of them waved back.

Well, Charles had warned her. Dorian had

warned her. She'd built a boat, she'd forgone mourning and she'd hired a scandalous captain. What should she have expected? Still, it was one thing to anticipate being snubbed—it was another to actually have it happen. It was rather eye-opening to realise that she would be the larger source of scandal than Dorian.

A fast boat will pay for all. Elise repeated her sustaining mantra. They would see what *Sutton's Hope* could do and they'd cease to care about anything else. She'd come to the conclusion that she could build other boats like the *Hope* without selling it. In theory, it was a conclusion that gave her the best of both worlds. Of course, she had to impress them today and then she'd have to impress them on the race course. Rather, Dorian would have to impress them.

She needn't have worried on that account. Dorian knew exactly what to do. The opening trip was technically non-competitive, but that didn't stop people from jockeying for position behind the Commodore's yacht or from showing off. Dorian made the most of the *Hope*'s sleek manoeuvrability, deftly coming up on the Commodore's starboard side for prime positioning. A few captains, less concerned about issues of social status and more concerned with appreciating good sailing, shouted back good-natured comments.

Most of the captains had been hired for the event as they would be for the races. Few owners captained their own yachts any more, having learned from experience that a well-built yacht wasn't always enough to win. One needed a talented captain, too.

The Commodore came to the railing of his yacht and called over, 'That's a fine-looking yacht, Miss Sutton. Is that one of your father's?'

'The last one, sir, and the only one of its kind!' Elise called back proudly over the wind.

'She's a gem. I look forward to seeing her race.'

One down. Elise hid a triumphant smile. At least they weren't going to kick her out of the yacht club. Without membership, she wasn't eligible for the regattas.

The opening sail took them past Erith and Rosherville, all the way to Gravesend where rooms had been spoken for at Wates Hotel. There would be dinner and dancing to celebrate the opening of the season. Some people would drive home in prearranged carriages. A few, like Dorian and Elise, would sail back although it would be dark.

Dorian was dazzling at dinner, all manners and polish. He charmed the ladies with flirtatious banter and compliments. He impressed the men with his knowledge of ships and the state of English presence in the Mediterranean. Surely, *this* Dorian Rowland could be received back into society.

Chapter Twenty-One

The thought hit her hard. Was that what she wanted? Dorian to stay in London and take up his mantle as a duke's son? She supposed so. She'd certainly thought of Dorian staying. She'd not spent much time dwelling on the details of it. Surely, the latter would be part of it. Elise wasn't the only one who thought so, either. The ladies' retiring room was full of the same conversation. There wasn't a woman there who didn't want to talk about Dorian.

'I thought I'd faint when he sat down beside me at dinner.'

'He's so handsome!'

'Oohh, those blue eyes seemed to look right through me.'

'What I wouldn't give for my husband to

look at me like he did.' That was just the matrons. The daughters were equally as giddy.

'Mama says he's not received!' one girl whispered behind her painted fan.

'I think that makes him even more delicious,' another said, trying to be wicked.

'He's still a lord. He's the Duke of Ashdon's son,' another added practically. 'His wife would still be a lady.'

On it went. Elise would have laughed at their nonsense if it hadn't so closely mirrored her own thoughts. Part of her wished Dorian was always like this, the perfect fairytale rogue who turned out to be a gentleman in the end. The other part of her knew better than to want that or to believe it. Dorian wasn't going to magically become a prince. He wasn't exactly a pirate, either, but somewhere in between, and that would not be good enough for London society.

Elise wondered what the ladies would think if they could see him in his culottes, his chest bare, a knife between his teeth or up against the throat of an unruly worker. The silly girls in the retiring room had no idea what Dorian could do to them, their minds limited to a chaste kiss stolen in a dimly lit garden. But she knew and it was beyond any of their imaginings. Worse, she didn't want to think of anyone else being the recipient of such decadent efforts.

Elise left the retiring room as soon as she could, unable to stand any more talk of Dorian. A few women cast unfavourable looks her way as she passed. She didn't need to hear what they said to know the content of the conversation that would take place shortly. She'd heard similar snatches throughout the evening. The gentlemen had been polite at dinner, asking her questions about *Sutton's Hope*, but the women had been less so.

'It's shameful how soon she left off mourning.'

'I hear she's attempting to run her father's business.'

'To show up here with Lord Rowland, of all people! Doesn't she know better?'

To which one catty woman responded, *'She knows better, I'd wager my pin money on it.'* The woman might as well have called her a blatant hussy. It was patently unfair that Dorian, who was a real scoundrel, had shown up after years of absenteeism and been an object of acceptable curiosity while she hadn't done more than try to make her own way in the world and was shunned for it.

'Smile, Elise. People are watching. You look as if you want to flay someone alive.' Dorian materialised at her side the moment the orchestra struck up. 'The retiring room all you'd hoped it would be?'

'Stop it. It was awful. Everyone in there was talking about you,' Elise groused. Smiling was the last thing she felt like doing.

'If you don't like the conversation, my advice is don't spend so much time in the ladies' room.' Dorian laughed. 'Now, come and dance with me and let's give them something to really talk about.'

'You were waiting for me?' Elise felt her spirits lift as she took his hand and let him lead her out to the dance floor for the opening waltz.

He gave her a naughty half-grin. 'There's no one else here worth waiting for.'

'That will come as a disappointment to many of the ladies present.' Elise put her hand on his shoulder, wanting to read more into his words than she safely should. He'd made her no promises save to defend her against Tyne should it be necessary. 'Don't you want to know what the ladies were saying?'

Dorian shook his head. 'Not really. I can guess and it won't happen. I'll never turn decent. They can all let go of that fantasy right now.'

Elise smiled, but she understood the warning was there for her, too, just in case she needed the reminder—and she did. She'd been toying with the premise of a decent Lord Dorian Rowland off and on all day. 'I like you just the way you are.' Although the liking made things more complicated. 'I wish society would say the same thing about me.' She gave a little pout as they turned at the top of the ballroom. Dorian was a masterful dancer. 'Today hasn't gone well in that regard.'

Dorian smiled, but didn't deny it. 'You knew there was a chance of that. Still, today was not an entire loss. People are impressed with the boat, as we'd hoped.' Dorian swung her in a tight turn to avoid the other dancers, his grip firm on her waist, possessive.

We. How she loved the sound of that! Elise smiled up at him. 'Impressed enough to order from me?' If she meant to avoid selling the shipyard, she had to have orders and soon.

There'd been no sign of Tyne and her boat had shown well, but Tyne and Hart couldn't be fobbed off forever. 'A decision must still be made about Hart's offer.' After her reception today, her earlier resolve was wavering. Maybe she should take the money and ethics be damned.

'Really? I thought you'd made your mind up.' Dorian raised an eyebrow in disapproving challenge.

'I keep prevaricating. The day of the trial run, I was certain I could keep the yard and the boat. But I don't know if I'm willing to risk so much. If I turn them down, I am engaging in war.'

'And your principles? You know what those men are, Elise. You would take their money and give them a prime location from which to carry out their activities?'

She gave him a sharp, serious look. 'I've never heard you talk like that. You've run arms, too. You can't turn hypocrite.'

'Not like them.' Dorian's tone was equally harsh. 'Those men are nefarious. I don't care if Charles Bradford and his father have decided to consort with them. The Bradfords and their ilk can't make men like Tyne decent. I'd rather you didn't do any amount of business with them.'

'Then you'd better hope I find buyers for the boat design because it's all I've got left to support myself with.'

'You can't build boats without a shipyard,' Dorian shot back. 'I guess that settles it. You couldn't possibly sell right now. Where would you build your boats if you did?' He was right. She hated when he was right.

'This is hardly the place to talk about business,' Elise snapped. He was dancing her breathless with his grace and speed. She could barely think, let alone contemplate the options laid before her.

'Or the night,' Dorian whispered seductively at her ear. 'We had a beautiful day on the water, a delicious dinner, and I have a fascinating woman in my arms.' She felt his hand at her back pull her closer to him. 'Why don't we go back to the yacht, drink champagne and make love? I've wanted to get you out of this dress since I saw you in it. Come with me, Elise.' His eyes were hot as he said the words. She'd follow him anywhere in that moment, so potent was his gaze, the touch of his hand at her back. If only he'd ask her to go somewhere else besides the boat and bed.

It was cold on the river when they returned. Elise shivered as she lit the lanterns. A fog had formed in their absence and the sail home would be slow.

'Elise,' Dorian called out, working the sails. 'Go below to the cabin and stay warm. Open some champagne and I'll be down shortly. But don't, under any circumstances, take off that dress. I want to do that.'

Elise climbed down the ladder to the cabin, her mind on the lovemaking to come. Maybe tonight, she'd finish what she'd started with the champagne the night of the fire. Between her distraction and the darkness, it didn't register until too late that she wasn't alone. Someone was in the cabin! She could make out the vague form of a man.

She summoned a scream, but it never came. A rough arm seized her from behind, dragging her against a barrel-chested form, a hand clamped across her mouth. A match flared to life across the cabin, illuminating the form of a man, this one with dark satanic eyebrows and black eyes. He calmly lit the lamp and crossed his legs, sliding a sharp-looking knife out of a sheath.

'Please, Miss Sutton, have a seat. I don't believe we've been formally introduced. I'm Damien Tyne.' He fingered the knife. 'I believe we have unfinished business.'

Real fear came to Elise for the first time since the whole duel for the shipyard had begun. The man before her was evil personified, from the devilish wing of his dark brow to his sinister eyes. She knew instinctively he was a man who gave no quarter. She had not truly guessed the depths of such malevolence.

The fear fuelled her. She fought her captor, kicking and twisting in his grip, but she was no match for the burly giant. He wrested her into a chair and shoved a gag in her mouth in spite of her best efforts to stop him. Tyne tossed him a length of rope and fright coiled in her belly at the thought of being entirely helpless against the knife, at being unable to warn Dorian.

Tyne gave her an oily smile. 'We can't have you running off until our business is concluded. How long do you think it will be before Rowland joins us? I do so look forward to meeting him again.'

Elise strained her ears. She could hear Dorian's footsteps overhead. She could hear him call out her name, wondering what was taking her so long to retrieve the champagne. She struggled against her bonds, desperate to warn him, to tell him not to come down.

'Elise! Whatever are you doing?' His voice was closer now, his feet nearing the ladder. She willed him to stop, to use some sixth sense to know danger waited below.

'Ah, good,' Tyne muttered. 'It won't be long. Your lover and I go back quite a ways, Miss Sutton. Perhaps he's told you?' His eyes slid in Bart's direction. 'Get ready.'

Elise watched in horror as Bart positioned himself behind the doorway with a club. Dorian's boots appeared first. He had a fraction of a second to take in Tyne's appearance, his hand reached instinctively for the knife in his boot but he couldn't retrieve it before Bart's club met with his skull. The thud of wood on a skull sickened her. Elise felt her stomach churn. She watched Dorian collapse unconscious. She was on her own. It would be up to her to save them both.

Chapter Twenty-Two

Why in blazes did his head hurt? Dorian groaned against the pain. There was bound to be a lump. He attempted to raise an arm to test the side of his forehead and found he couldn't. In his befuddled state it took a moment to realise why. He was bound at the wrists and ankles. What was going on? This was not Elise's doing.

He pushed his fuzzy mind past the throbbing to gather his thoughts. Elise had gone down for champagne. He'd come to check on her and then? Tyne! He remembered that awful last moment of consciousness. Tyne sitting on the cabin bench, looking smug, fingering his bloody, ever-present knife, and Elise bound to the chair, eyes wide with terror. He'd bent for his own knife, but too late. He'd been set upon from behind.

The reality of the situation hit him with full force. Tyne had Elise. Dorian had no idea how long he'd been out. How much time had Tyne had? What had he done to her? Dorian willed himself not to panic. He was alive and for the moment that was all that mattered. He couldn't save Elise if he was dead. Tyne must have crept on board the yacht while they'd been at dinner. Dorian sorely wished he'd hunted the man down in spite of Elise's objections.

He forced his eyes shut against the great temptation to take in his circumstances. To open them too early would be careless and dangerous. Once he indicated he was conscious, the next level of the game would be engaged. He needed to be ready. There was light, he could feel it on his face. He could also feel hardness beneath him. The bastard had left him on the floor, probably right where he'd fallen. He could also feel stillness. The boat wasn't moving. Had Tyne pulled into shore somewhere? That seemed unlikely and it would indicate he'd been unconscious for some time. Tyne wouldn't risk pulling to shore so close to Gravesend where another of the yachting party might notice them. Dorian thought it was more likely they'd dropped anchor. Tyne would want the isolation of the water for whatever he had planned.

Dorian opened his eyes, his vision focusing on the bench. Tyne was there, all right, one leg negligently crossed over the other and drinking champagne. *His* champagne. Dorian knew a surge of anger, but none so great as the surge that took him at the sight of Elise, still bound to the chair. Her gag had been removed. There was no reason for it, Dorian supposed, now that he could no longer be warned.

'Ah, you're awake,' Tyne said in tones of false conviviality. 'We were wondering when you were going to join us.' He held up his glass of champagne. 'I am anticipating a celebration. Miss Sutton and I are about to reach a business agreement, aren't we, my dear?'

'Don't sign anything, Elise,' Dorian ground out, levering himself up into a sitting position against the wall.

'Not even to save you, Rowland? I think you might change your mind on that,' Tyne said silkily. He nodded to someone on the periphery of Dorian's vision. 'Bart, you know what to do.'

A hulk of a man approached, armed with Dorian's own blade. Dorian recognised him as one of the men from the break-in. 'Time for a little revenge, Rowland. Shall I start with your face or your hands, or maybe with something a little more dear? I seem to recall I owe you for a kick in the groin.' He jerked the knife in the direction of Dorian's testicles. Dorian drew up his legs. If the man got any closer, he could get one good kick in and it would hurt. Bart seemed to understand it wasn't going to be easy. Across the cabin, Elise choked on a scream.

'So you do care for him a bit. I was beginning to wonder, although you two looked cosy a few days ago during the trial run.' Dorian felt Tyne's gaze on him. 'I like to watch, you see.' A cold finger of anger ran down Dorian's spine. Tyne had spied on them. How much had the man seen? Tyne's gaze returned to Elise. 'Do you know why I like to watch, Miss Sutton?' He trailed a finger down Elise's jaw. Dorian's insides clenched.

'I like to watch because it's all I can do any more, thanks to Rowland. He gave me an injury that has subdued my abilities to perform as a man should.'

'Was that before or after you burnt his ship?' Elise retorted. Dorian mentally applauded her bravado, but she had no true idea what she was up against. Tyne's evil knew no limits.

Tyne laughed. 'It was after, my little spitfire. As I said, it has *subdued* my abilities, it hasn't rendered them entirely useless and you seem to have a salubrious effect on them, my dear. Perhaps in a while we'll see just how salubrious.'

Elise did pale at that. 'I'll sign the deal if you let us go.'

'No!' Dorian yelled, keeping an eye on Bart. Bart's next move would bring a fight. He might be bound, but he was not helpless.

'Can I do him now, Boss?' Bart called out.

'No, I've changed my mind. It might be more fun to watch these two argue since they're at cross purposes. She wants to ink the deal and he doesn't.' Tyne finished his champagne and poured another glass. 'Bart, go up on deck and see how we're doing. The three of us are going to talk for a while.'

Dorian knew what was coming next. Tyne's

favourite weapon aside from his knife was mind games. 'Don't believe anything he says, Elise.'

'Don't believe anything *he* says, Elise,' Tyne interjected. 'You're a pretty girl and a smart one to run your father's business. Have you thought about why Rowland doesn't want you to sign the deal? It's very simple. You're worth more to him with the shipyard. What are you without that? What could you possibly have that would appeal to a man like Rowland?' Tyne picked his nails with the knife. 'He's nothing more than a pirate. Has he told you? He ran arms.'

'Yes, I know all about it, Mr Tyne,' Elise snapped with impressive fortitude. Some of her colour was returning now that there was just the one knife between them.

'And you hold with that occupation? He encourages warfare, Miss Sutton. If there's no war, there's no business. He doesn't care for national loyalties. He'll sell guns to the French to use against the English if there's enough money in it.'

That wasn't how it had happened. Dorian gritted his teeth, struggling with his bonds. He was almost there. He could feel the ropes starting to slip. If he could just get his hands free, the playing field would be a bit more equal.

'I understand you do the same,' Elise replied coolly.

'I might. What do you care about what I do? You're not in love with me.' Tyne grinned cruelly. 'He would drag you down with him, turn your shipyard into a clearing house for weapons. He's seduced you into ignoring reason.' Tyne chuckled. 'What else has he told you? Has he filled your head with visions of sandy beaches and the Mediterranean? Has he convinced you to keep the yacht, spinning tales of racing it for prize money maybe?'

Good lord, Dorian groaned. The man had eyes everywhere. But what came out of his mouth next was by far the most damning. 'Make no mistake, Rowland wants this yacht. This boat is fast. He'd be unstoppable in it and he's willing to make love to you to get it.' He paused. 'I see the thought has crossed your mind, Miss Sutton. Why is Rowland so willing to invest his time in this project? You've wondered.'

'These are *his* plans, Elise,' Dorian argued, horrified to watch her eyes dart to him with the old doubts rising in their depths. Hot words from their old quarrel flooded back to him. She'd accused him of what Tyne accused him of now. But there was clarity, too. Tyne and Hart's plans were clear now. They wanted the better location to expand their own arms business. Tyne wanted to take the yacht back to the Mediterranean where he could continue to sell weapons to those who would fight the Empire while Hart arranged suppliers from here.

Dorian gave a final tug, his hands slipping free. He would wait for his moment. Tyne rose and leaned over Elise, his blade slipping through the ropes. 'Miss Sutton, if you'd come up on deck with me? You have five minutes to make your decision. If you choose not to sell, we'll have no choice but to fire the yard. If you choose not to relinquish this yacht to me, we'll have no choice but to fire the yacht as well. A pity, really, since you'll be on board. It's an incredible craft. Your father knew it. But like him, you'll be able to go down with the ship.' Tyne winked to Dorian as he shoved Elise up the ladder. 'You can go down with the ship, too, Rowland.'

You first, you conniving bastard, Dorian

thought, reaching to undo the ropes at his ankles the moment he was alone. *You first.*

Elise stood at the railing, shivering from cold, from fear, her thoughts racing in a thousand directions. Tyne and Bart flanked her on either side. She knew where they were. They were across from the shipyard. She could see the pier dimly. She'd been foolish to think any decision she could make would matter. She could no more save herself than Dorian could. She was just tied with a different type of cord. Tyne would not hesitate to kill her or Dorian. Tyne had killed her father, demonstrating he'd go to any length. Dorian had been right in that regard and therein lay her one last hope.

'I think you're bluffing,' she said with quiet authority.

'I beg your pardon?' Her words caught Tyne off guard as she'd meant them to.

'You're bluffing,' Elise repeated. 'You won't fire the yard. You've worked too hard for it.' Even as she said the words, she knew he wasn't. In the distance, she could hear Dorian's dog barking. Someone was there, waiting for the signal.

'I won't let Rowland have it. If I can't have it, neither of us will have it,' Tyne answered with an unconcerned shrug. 'You should believe me. The same goes for you and the yacht, in case you're wondering.'

'What guarantees do I have you'll let us both go if I sign?' Elise replied smoothly. Dorian's cynicism had rubbed off on her. For the moment she was glad of it. She stared across the dark water, gauging the distance. Could she swim for it? The distance was not great, but the waters were choppy and cold. Her skirts would be heavy within moments and it would mean leaving Dorian to his own luck. Even if she made it, there'd be an enemy to deal with once she came ashore. Whoever waited in the yard was not her friend.

'Two minutes, Miss Sutton. Bart, prepare the signal.'

'Is this the deal you made my father?' Elise asked as Bart moved away. If she meant to jump, she'd need to do it now while there was just one of them.

'No, he never saw me coming. It was easy enough to fix the steam valves. I didn't trust him. If he suspected anything, he might have left a letter or a clue behind and alerted you.'

Tyne chuckled. 'I've been most generous with you. It was Hart's idea. He thought two deaths in the family would be suspect. *He* felt things would follow a natural course of events without violent intervention, but you exceeded our expectations and our time limit. You've had all the time in the world, Miss Sutton, and now your time is up.'

'You're wrong, Tyne. Your time is up,' came the unmistakable rough tones of an angry Dorian Rowland.

Elise turned, instinctively moving away from Tyne, but not fast enough. Tyne grabbed her about the waist and hauled her to him, blade pressed to her throat. She stifled a gasp, not wanting to distract Dorian with her fear.

'I see we're of a like mind.' Tyne sneered at Dorian. 'You've got my Bart and I've got your girl.'

Dorian shoved Bart aside, his corpse already limp. She hadn't realised. 'Bart's dead and you'll be joining him shortly.' There would be no signal to the shipyard. The boat works was safe, that was something at least. 'Put her aside, Tyne. It's always been about you and me. Let us settle this once and for all.' Dorian held his arms open in a 'come-on' gesture, tempting Tyne to battle.

'Better yet, fight me for her,' Tyne growled. 'Maybe you'll live long enough with my knife in your gut to watch me have her. It will be the last thing you see before you die.' He released her then, shoving her into Dorian, hard. Dorian stumbled from the sudden impact, caught off balance. Tyne took advantage, leaping towards Dorian as Dorian pushed her aside to safety. The gesture cost him. Tyne's blade sliced into Dorian's arm. Even in the dark she could see the blood seeping from the gash.

Dorian switched the blade to his other hand. 'Come on, are cheap tricks all you have?'

'Better than you, Rowland, you've only got one good arm now.' Tyne laughed.

'It's all I'll need.' Dorian advanced, creating a graceful, lethal dance about Tyne in a tight circle that left little margin for error.

Determined to make herself useful, Elise crawled to Bart's form, frantically searching in the dark for what she wanted. Her hand closed over the metal of a pistol butt and she knew a moment's relief, then a moment's terror. She had a weapon and the weapon was empty. Still, there might be a chance to use it. She willed herself to watch and to wait.

But watching was hard. Dorian struggled. Blood flowed from his arm. He couldn't toy with Tyne for long and Tyne knew it, too. Elise saw Tyne's plan instantly. All he had to do was wait Dorian out. Dorian's strength would fail unless he struck soon. And he did. Dorian made a swift lunge, catching Tyne in the shoulder. Blood spurted. She covered her mouth with a hand to keep in a scream, the only thought she had was *good, the playing field is equal now.* Dorian staggered, his back to the rail, clutching his shoulder. The effort had cost him.

Tyne advanced clumsily, giving no quarter. This was her chance if she meant to take it. She couldn't stand there and watch Dorian die. What had Dorian told her once about his death? Ah, she had it. Elise stepped forwards, pistol raised as she called out, 'Do you think the murder of a duke's son will go unpunished, Tyne? Kill Rowland and the Duke of Ashdon will bring down a retribution so swift and sinister you'll wish you'd died.' Out of the corner of her eye, she saw Dorian edge towards her, leaving Tyne alone at the railing.

The words had the desired effect. But she didn't want Tyne to have too long to think about them, lest he decide she was bluffing. She held the gun steady. 'This has to end, Tyne. Neither of you is in any shape to fight.'

Tyne's breathing was ragged. Even in the dark, he was pale. 'What do you propose?' His eyes slid to the waters. She knew what he was thinking: did he have the strength for a getaway? Could he reach the water before she fired?

'A race. My yacht against a yacht of your choosing. Winner takes all. A duel on the Thames. My second will call on Maxwell Hart tomorrow.'

'Done,' Tyne growled and then he was gone in a surprisingly fluid moment over the rail. She heard the splash of him hitting the water and she lowered the gun to her side, weary. She slid to the deck, her legs turning to jelly now that it was over.

'What have you done?' Dorian half-staggered, half-crawled to her side.

'Saved your life.' She thought he'd be a

bit more relieved. Frankly, he sounded ungrateful.

'You've risked the boat, Elise.' Dorian lay on his back, catching his breath.

'I had to do something. You weren't having much luck,' she said briskly. She fumbled with his shirt, dragging it off him. Her first thought was to stop the bleeding.

'How does it look?' Dorian tried to peer down at the gash.

'It could be worse.' Elise fought back bile to look at the damage. It was bloody, but the gash was not as deep as it might have been. 'It hasn't hit bone,' she assured him.

'It hurts like hell,' Dorian groaned.

'I'm sure it does, but you'll live.' It wasn't said glibly. A few minutes ago she hadn't been so sure either of them would.

'You could have shot him.' Dorian groaned as she wiped at the blood.

'I could have, but that requires bullets. I only had a boat.'

Dorian tried to sit up. 'God, Elise. You faced him with an unloaded gun? What were you thinking?' Dorian bent his head to hers. He was warm and sweaty and he smelled of life.

She put her hand against his cheek. 'I was thinking I loved you, silly man.' She didn't give him a chance to respond. 'Let's get you on your feet and down below where I can take care of you properly.'

It was cumbersome work getting him below, but she managed. The yacht was stocked with staples for the day voyage. There was alcohol for cleaning the wound and fresh bandages for any incidental injuries. Once below, Elise made quick work of bandaging.

'How's your head?' Elise said, tying off the bandage.

'Still reeling.' Colour had returned to Dorian's face. That had to be a good sign.

Elise reach up, fingers in his hair to search out the damage from Bart's club. Bart had certainly got the worse end of that deal. But Dorian's hands closed over hers and drew them away. 'I'm not reeling from the bump. Sit down, Elise.'

'What is it? Are you sick? Feeling nauseous?' Elise asked anxiously, searching his face for a sign.

Dorian shook his head. 'It's not from any injury. It's from you.' His hands tightened over hers. 'It's not every day a man hears "I love you". It's not every day a woman risks the thing she holds most dear for him, either.'

Elise flushed. 'Well, it's done. Now we have a race to win.' She paused, the enormity of what she'd done sinking in. 'We will win, won't we? You said the yacht was fast, that it was unstoppable. Is it true?'

Dorian gave a half-smile. 'I guess we're going to find out.'

Elise nodded. There was going to be a lot of 'finding out' in the next few days. She loved Dorian Rowland. She'd confessed as much tonight. But how far would she go for that love? How much of what Tyne had said tonight was true? Could she live with a man who had no national loyalties? Most of all, would that man even ask her to? Had she risked it all for a man who couldn't love her back once again?

Chapter Twenty-Three

'You've been up a while, Dorian. I missed you.' Elise joined him at the rail where he stood watching the morning come alive. Sunrise was his favourite time of day, a luxury he'd seldom been able to afford himself. They'd stayed on board last night, trying out the new bed. There'd been no question of trying to dock the boat in the dark with the fog and him sporting only one good arm, even though they were just across the water from the shipyard.

Elise had wrapped a blanket about her shift and her hair hung loose and dark about her. His groin tightened. Sunrise was his favourite time of day for other reasons, too. There wasn't anything quite like making love in the morning. It got the day off to the right start. She stood beside him in silence, taking in the quiet of early morning with him. If only life were this simple, waking aboard a boat each day with her. Neither of them spoke. He knew both their minds were full, although he doubted her mind contained the erotic thoughts plaguing his.

He passed her the cup of coffee he held in his good hand. She smiled as she took it. Perhaps that was a good sign she wasn't angry. She'd told him she loved him and he'd not given the requisite response last night. Or maybe it was a bad sign? Maybe she'd rethought that confession and no longer cared? 'What happens now, Dorian?' she asked in the stillness.

He looked at her, taking in her chemise and the blanket. He let a wicked grin play across his mouth. 'I take you back to bed and make good on my promises from last night before we were so rudely interrupted.' A man had to try, after all.

She smiled in spite of the shake of her head. 'We can't keep going to bed instead of resolving our issues, as delightful as the option is.'

Dorian leaned on the railing, looking out

over the water. 'What's on your mind, Elise?' It would be one of two things: him or Damien Tyne.

'There are some things Tyne said last night,' Elise began hesitantly. 'He sells arms to anyone who will buy, even the French. He sells them good English guns to shoot English soldiers. Do you?' she asked in a tight whisper. 'Are you of the same mind? Was he right about that?' She was watching him, holding her breath. That had to bode well. She hadn't given up on him. She wasn't regretting her efforts last night, but she was deciding. He knew that much. Elise was a businesswoman. She would be weighing what she could live with and what she could live without.

'I've run arms in the past. I've told you as much. There's good money in it and in my youth the thrill was quite extraordinary,' Dorian admitted. 'But never, Elise, never did I sell to the French or to anyone knowing beforehand that those arms would be used against England.' The discrepancy hadn't been enough for his family. Would it be enough for her?

'What do you run these days?' She still hadn't looked away.

'Expensive items others aren't willing to risk. It's hard to explain, Elise. These days it's about speed. Britain might have tamed the Mediterranean, but people will pay well to get their items to market faster than anyone else. There's still danger. There are those who will pay to stop goods from reaching markets in order to enhance their own profits. It's simple supply-and-demand economics.' Dorian shrugged. 'We have an expression in the Mediterranean. If the sea belongs to no one, it belongs to everyone.'

Elise nodded. 'That phrase has been bandied about Britain quite regularly in the last decade. My father even used it in his own conversations with investors.' She gave a little laugh. 'I think it might be the Navy's secret motto.' Elise paused. 'I'm starting to see why Giovanni was so grateful to you; why it was so important you took his wine to market.'

Now it was his turn for questions. 'Why do you care, Elise, if I ran arms to enemies or not?'

'Because I have to know how much loving you will cost me and whether or not I can pay that price, just in case you might love me, too,' she said softly.

He should have said the words last night. But even now with a second chance before him, he couldn't say them. 'Don't you know the answer to that already?' He'd like to take her below and show her.

'I'm not sure I do.'

'I can't change for you, Elise, if that's what you're thinking.' He might as well get it out in the open. If she thought he'd reconcile with his family and stay living in London, she'd be severely disappointed. She had to know that already. 'My family believes I am a traitor. As for myself, I have no wish to rejoin society's fold. I have no desire to stay in London *ever.* I was only here because I had a cargo to deliver and I'll be leaving as soon as I can arrange a ship back.'

'I wouldn't dream of asking you to change. I thought I'd made that clear.' Elise looked away, but not before he sighted tears in her eyes. She'd known his answer and had still been disappointed by it. Had he somehow misread what she was fishing for? Was there something else she wanted from him?

Elise straightened her shoulders. 'Well, we have a race to win. I imagine we both have business to take care of before then. How's your arm?'

'It will be fine.' Dorian threw out the rest of his coffee into the river. 'I'll get us ashore.' So much for a morning tumble. So much for a second chance. Maybe it was better this way. What good could saying 'I love you' do if he couldn't be there for her? An impossible relationship would hurt all the more when he sailed away after the race. He really couldn't stay any longer.

'I'll see that you have your money, Dorian. Will you be able to pay the workers for me? I will need a day or two to get the funds.' She halted. 'Seeing as how the boat isn't going to sell, I'll need to speak to someone about our art collection. It should bring enough to cover expenses.'

'I can make those arrangements.' If they were in Gibraltar he could have given her the money. But he had no funds here. Here, he was a veritable pauper. It was better this way, he repeated to himself. Gibraltar beckoned. In Gibraltar, he was a king and he was free. He turned from the rail to watch Elise walk back to the cabin, her hips swaying beneath the blanket, her hair gently buffeted by the breeze. Something new inside him, something that had just begun to live since he'd met her, was starting to die. And he knew, *just knew*, it would never be resurrected if he didn't save it now. It couldn't end like this.

There was only one thing he could think of to say. 'Come with me, Elise. Come to Gibraltar.' The words were out of his mouth before he could think. She turned. His world stopped. *Let her answer be yes.* He closed his eyes and waited for Elise Sutton to seal his fate.

Say yes. Her fate hung in the balance. Conventional wisdom would have her reject the proposal out of hand, but the realities of the past months suggested otherwise. She didn't belong here. Yesterday had made that clear. She could build the fastest ship the world had seen and it wouldn't be enough. At the beginning of this adventure it had seemed straightforward: build a ship and everyone would respect her. She would pick up where her father had left off.

But yesterday's outing had proved otherwise. She would not be allowed to. There was no place for her here. Society had spoken.

Richard Sutton's daughter would not be permitted to build her boats here. The race with Tyne would be the final scandal. After that, any bid for respectability would be over. Still, she wouldn't go with Dorian simply because there was no place here for her. There was her heart to consider as well.

'Say yes, Elise.' Dorian held her gaze intently. She could not be swayed by that gaze.

'Say yes to what, Dorian?' She took a step towards him. Women couldn't go haring off to foreign ports with men without certain guarantees, guarantees she didn't think he could give.

'Say yes to building your yachts in Gibraltar. We can sail them up to England for those who want them and there's a market down there from the Spanish, the French—everyone, really. People need boats for business, for pleasure. And no one would care about the silly things. Think how grand it would be, Elise—you and me, bashing about the Mediterranean, building yachts, racing yachts, the sandy beaches, even the dolphins. I have the most beautiful house in the hills.'

She gave a little laugh. He could make her laugh at the most inopportune times. 'I'd been warned you might try that line of reasoning.' She'd moved within arm's reach of him, her body unable to resist what her mind felt compelled to argue against.

'It's a good line. Is it enough, Elise, to convince you to be my wife and live in Paradise forever? I love you. I should have told you last night.'

In that moment, she knew what she wanted and it stood before her, even though accepting it broke every rule left to her. Elise Sutton threw caution to the winds. 'Yes, it's enough.' She twined her arms about his neck and kissed him hard on the mouth. Why not? What had the rules ever got her?

'Does everyone understand the rules?' Commodore Harrison stood on a bunting-draped dais above the crowd assembled for the race. In the days before the race, rumour of the event had spread throughout fashionable London. Elise shaded her eyes against the sun and looked up at the dais. 'The race shall begin here at Blackwell and shall end at the Thames Tavern. The course shall pass Erith, Rosherville, Gravesend and Lower Hope Point. There shall be no foul play, no cutting across the other's bow or the like. This is to be a fair match, gentlemen.'

Across from *Sutton's Hope*, *Phantasm*, Tyne's personal yacht, bobbed black and sleek on the water. The breeze was good today, and both boats' sails billowed eagerly. Elise looked away, trying not to concentrate on the fine lines of Tyne's boat. Dorian stood at the helm of *Sutton's Hope* with Drago beside him. He radiated confidence and her own confidence soared. Dorian would not fail them.

Them! Her heart beat a little faster at the prospect. They'd win this race and then they'd go to Gibraltar and start their life. The future lay just past today. Dorian's eyes met hers. His hair was down, his eyes glowing with fierce competitiveness. He was dressed for the sea today in his culottes and bare feet, his shirt open at the chest, his shoulders bare of any coat. He'd not wanted to be confined by any concession to fashion today. He'd need all his strength at the wheel. For a moment he looked past her and mouthed the words 'My father.'

Elise turned to catch sight of the Duke of Ashdon's coach along the side of the river, in line with so many other carriages ready to follow the progress of the twenty-mile race. She smiled at Dorian. 'Better not let him down then.'

'Gentlemen, at the ready!' the Commodore shouted out and the crowd stilled. The flag was dropped and they were under way.

The water was smooth in the early going and the *Hope* made the most of the wind. The *Phantasm* sailed beside them, easily keeping pace, the crowd on the river banks cheering them on. Plenty of money would pass hands today. But by Gravesend the weather began to change. The sun of the morning gave way to clouds. The cheering crowds thinned out, daunted by the mounting winds and greying skies. By Lower Hope Point, a full storm was engaged.

Sutton's Hope began to rock. Elise prayed the narrow frame and the buoyancy bags would hold. The last portion of the race was upon them. *Phantasm* began to make its move, slicing closer to the *Hope* in the water. Now that witnesses had thinned to almost nil, Tyne was taking more chances.

'Take the wheel, Elise!' Dorian yelled over the wind. 'We need to reef the mainsail, we need a flatter entry point for the wind or we'll flip.'

Elise took the wheel, feeling the yacht buck beneath her, the wheel fighting her to stay on course. The last thing they needed was to drift too close to shore and chance the rocks. She shot a quick glance at the *Phantasm*. It was pulling ahead and Tyne was refusing to reef his sail, taking a gamble with the wind. Above her, Dorian was in the rigging, working the sails—first the Cunningham to move the draught point. He managed with confidence, unfazed by the height and the wind, but she'd relax when he was safely back on deck.

She felt the results of reefing immediately. The wheel stabilised, the boat no longer pulling against her, but the *Phantasm* was moving ahead. 'Reefing has cost us some speed,' she said over the wind when Dorian claimed the wheel.

'Not for long. The wind will start to work against him,' Dorian said confidently. 'By the time he is forced to reef, it will be too late. It's always easier to bring in the sail before the storm hits in full than during.

'It's time to make our move, Elise.' They'd charted this course in the days before the race. The race would be won in the last miles.

They'd take advantage of the *Hope*'s low hull and the *Phantasm*'s confidence.

Dorian drew up slightly behind the *Phantasm*, using the other boat as a shield against the wind to regain speed. Tyne waved an angry fist their direction. 'Stop draughting, Rowland!'

Dorian shouted back, 'You should have reefed your sails when you had the chance!' When the yachts were even, Dorian swung back out into the centre of the river, using every trick he knew to harness the wind and gain an edge. He needed a slight edge to dominate the river. The plan was to block out the river through serpentines and swerves so the *Phantasm* could not pass them in the curves at the end of the course.

'Go, Dorian! Now,' Elise shouted, surveying the course from her post at the prow of the ship. This was critical. If they could manage this manoeuvre, they'd have the race.

Tyne realised his mistake too late. In an effort to hold position, Tyne swerved into the *Hope*. If Dorian veered, he would give up his position on the river. If he didn't, they would likely collide unless they simply weren't there when Tyne's boat arrived. They needed more speed.

'Elise! The wheel!' Dorian was at the ropes, adjusting the sails with swift, sure movements, the wind in his wet hair, his shirt plastered to his chest. He looked primal in those moments, a man against all. He looked triumphant in the next as the *Hope* shot past the *Phantasm*'s intended strike point.

The Thames Tavern point came into view through the rain, the last spot before the Thames gave out into the open ocean. A few carriages waited on shore. Elise thought she could see the Commodore and the flag. The *Phantasm* was close, though. She could see the crew. She imagined she could hear Tyne cursing over the wind. But it didn't matter, they were almost there. Then they were, sailing past the flag, victorious and whole. They had won!

She turned to throw her arms about Dorian in celebration and screamed. She couldn't believe it. Tyne was breaking the rules! The *Phantasm* had turned too sharply and was aimed at the stern of the *Hope*. At these close quarters there would be no escaping. 'Dorian, no! Don't slow the boat! Full speed!'

Dorian let the sail fill, they shot past the Commodore, the *Phantasm* close behind. A new race was engaged, a race with no rules and the open sea ahead of them. Dorian was grim at the wheel, the sails were open in spite of the dangers. There was no margin for caution now. He was desperate for speed, calling on all his expertise to marshal the wind to his advantage.

'Grab hold of something, Elise, we're going to tack hard to starboard!' It was all the warning she had before the boat lurched, waves rising grey and menacing as the yacht took to its side.

Dorian tacked again and again, creating a zig-zag pattern through the water, each pass drawing them closer to land. 'Isn't it dangerous to get so near shore?' she shouted.

'That's the plan! We want to lure them in and turn sharp enough to avoid the rocks while they get stuck on them.'

In a flash of insight, Elise understood. 'But we could wreck!'

'Not if your design holds. She's tacking beautifully, Elise.'

But the rocks neared and Elise paled. Dorian had nerves of steel, but she did not.

'Does Tyne guess?' It looked like the *Phantasm* was keeping up fine.

'Oh, he guesses.' Dorian smiled. 'But he thinks he's smart enough to avoid it.'

Dorian tacked, once more, twice more. The *Phantasm* neared. She could see Tyne's dark eyes, they were that close. Tyne drew a gun. At this angle, with their side exposed, Tyne would not miss. 'Dorian!' she cried out. Dorian turned, but not fast enough. The shot fired. She threw herself at Dorian, knocking him aside. They went down, sliding across the tilting deck. The bullet whistled overhead, the boat was listing, waves rose, slopping the deck. Dorian scrambled to the wheel, struggling to right the yacht. Balance was slowly restored.

Elise scrambled upright, sopping and wet. 'Look!' Behind them the *Phantasm* had run aground, the yacht caught up on the rocks. 'He'll be arrested.'

'I don't know about that.' Dorian breathed heavily, his clothes dripping.

'I do. Your father's there. That's his carriage, isn't it?' Elise pointed in the distance at the entourage on the coastal road converging on the grounded yacht. 'He followed us the whole time.'

Dorian laughed. 'Well, I'll be.' Then he sobered. 'We're well past the finish line. Shall we go back and claim your prize?'

Elise wrapped her arms about his waist. 'Why go back? The ocean is right there. Seems like we should just keep going. We meant to anyway in a few days.'

Dorian's blue eyes looked down at her. 'Do you mean it? What about all your things?'

Elise smiled up at him. 'Everything I need is right here.' And it was. She reached up and kissed him. Her practical side couldn't resist asking, 'You do have the five hundred pounds from your last job though, right?'

Dorian laughed. 'Tucked away in my wife's reticule.'

His wife. She liked the sound of that. It was almost true. She'd be his wife in truth just as soon as they reached Gibraltar. 'Good, it's right where it belongs then.'

'And you are right where you belong, in my arms.'

Two weeks later, Elise stood on the beach in Gibraltar, her hands clasped firmly in

Dorian's grip, the gauzy white fabric of her dress fluttering against her legs. Her feet were bare, her toes curled into the warm sand while she listened to the vows that would bind her to Dorian Rowland for life. They were pronounced man and wife as the sun sank over the sea as if on cue. There could be no more perfect wedding in the history of the world, even if this one was attended by more waves than witnesses. Her heart was full.

Dorian bent to kiss her. 'You have succeeded in living most scandalously, Mrs Rowland.'

'I have succeeded in living well,' she replied. Life had become infinitely simpler the moment she'd stepped on to *Sutton's Hope* with nothing more than Dorian's trunk and the money in her reticule. 'Thanks to you.' She meant it. With Dorian, because of Dorian, she was who she was meant to be.

Dorian drew her away from the priest, taking her to the water's edge and letting it lap their toes. 'Is it all you'd hoped?'

'You're all I hoped,' Elise answered honestly. Dorian was something of a modern pirate, racing the tides and merchants to market for the best prices. There were definitely those who were jealous of his success. But he was also something of a king here in this part of the world, she'd discovered. People came to him, asking for favours, asking for help. And he gave it. Some of those people were farmers like Giovanni's relatives; some were diplomats looking for ways to broker alliances through goods and trade. Wherever Dorian went, life would always be exciting and it would always be fast—she'd see to the last part.

'I think this turned out pretty well, Mrs Rowland,' Dorian said as the last rays of light disappeared on the horizon. 'You needed to be lost and I needed to be found.' It was true. She'd had to lose everything to find the one thing that mattered. Now that she'd found him, she'd never let him go.

'Our wedding night awaits,' Dorian whispered naughtily. 'Shall we?' He gestured towards the stairs leading up the cliff to the Spanish-style villa.

Elise smiled. She was about to be royally screwed. Funny how her adventures kept coming back to that same point. This time quite literally and with the emphasis on the screwed.

* * * * *

Special Offers

Every month we put together collections and longer reads written by your favourite authors.

Here are some of next month's highlights—and don't miss our fabulous discount online!

On sale 6th September

On sale 6th September

On sale 16th August

Find out more at
www.millsandboon.co.uk/specialreleases

Visit us Online

0913/ST/MB43